FLIRTING WITH DISASTER

Mollie was determined that her insufferably arrogant husband realize that he was not the only handsome and charming man in the world.

To prove her point, there could be no better person than Prince Nicolai Stefanovich, visiting England from distant Russia and bringing with him a combination of flawless good looks and beautiful manners that made him the magnet for every London lady's longing eyes.

But now, as Mollie stood with the prince in a moonlit garden and saw his gaze moving approvingly over her lovely body, she began to wonder if she had not gone too far in playing with this particular form of fire.

Then, as the prince's burning lips crushed down on hers, she knew she had. . . .

LADY HAWK'S FOLLY

SIGNET Regency Romances You'll Enjoy

LADY HAWK'S FOLLY

by
Amanda Scott

A SIGNET BOOK

NEW AMERICAN LIBRARY

NAL BOOKS ARE AVAILABLE AT QUANTITY DISCOUNTS WHEN USED
TO PROMOTE PRODUCTS OR SERVICES. FOR INFORMATION PLEASE
WRITE TO PREMIUM MARKETING DIVISION, NEW AMERICAN LIBRARY,
1633 BROADWAY, NEW YORK, NEW YORK 10019.

Copyright © 1984 by Lynne Scott-Drennan

 SIGNET TRADEMARK REG. U.S. PAT. OFF. AND FOREIGN COUNTRIES
REGISTERED TRADEMARK—MARCA REGISTRADA
HECHO EN CHICAGO, U.S.A.

SIGNET, SIGNET CLASSIC, MENTOR, PLUME, MERIDIAN AND NAL BOOKS
are published by
New American Library,
1633 Broadway,
New York, New York 10019

First Printing, January, 1985

1 2 3 4 5 6 7 8 9

PRINTED IN THE UNITED STATES OF AMERICA

For Gordon, Kevin, and Russell
characters all

1

After two days of torrential rains, the clouds had parted at last, allowing sunshine to splash the Weald of Kent with color once again. The spectators crowding around and upon the numerous carriages that surrounded the twenty-four-foot, roped ring at the foot of a low hill near the village of Gill's Green might have appreciated the sun's warmth had they chanced to give it a thought. However, their attention being firmly riveted upon the action within the ring, it is doubtful whether many of them noticed the sun's appearance at all.

The odds were four to one on Alf Porter's Black, a bruising pugilist with a reputation sound enough to bring the commander-in-chief, Gentleman Jackson himself, all the way from London to referee his match against a promising comer known to all and sundry as the Irish Dancer. By the tenth round, despite the odds, the mill had arrived at that doubtful state where things seemed not to be going so easily as anticipated, and many of those among the teeming crowd were nervously expressing uncertainty as to how they ought best to proceed with their wagers. The Black's opponent had shown himself off in fine style. After having been knocked down in the third, fifth, and eighth rounds, the Irishman had rallied in prime twig, and notwithstanding many severe hits in the ninth and the terrible punishment he had received throughout, still he stood up for the tenth undismayed, proving either that he was a glutton or that he possessed courage and skill of no ordinary nature.

The Black stood game, and midway through the round, he sliced in a severe body blow; but the Irishman treated it with indifference, and in return not only milled the Black's head but, in closing, threw him. Many of those who had not seen Alf Porter's Black fight before groaned loudly and began to hedge their bets. As the round ended, the Black fell again, heavily.

"Two to one in cartwheels Alf Porter throws in the towel before the end of the fifteenth!" shouted an enthusiastic young spectator to two sprigs of fashion mounted on prime cattle beside his green-and-yellow high-perch phaeton.

"Done!" responded the larger of the two with commendable promptitude.

In tones not meant to carry beyond his ears, his companion tersely demanded to know where his wits had gone begging. "Anyone can see the Black is as sick as a horse now, Ramsay. He'll never fib his way through four more rounds."

"Merely feeble, Mo . . . my friend," retorted Lord Ramsay Colporter, correcting his slip smoothly. "And for the love of heaven, keep silent. I'd no notion we'd see so many of the Fancy here today. 'Tis on account of Jackson condescending to judge the match, of course, but all the same, after all this rain, the road from London must be knee-deep in places."

"Much that would signify," his companion observed, chuckling. "I'll warrant they made their way as cheerfully as if they'd been trotting along a bowling green."

"Well, there are too dashed many of 'em," Lord Ramsay muttered, eyeing the crowd warily. "Tilt your hat lower."

"I can scarcely see as it is." But the curly beaver hat was tipped obediently to a more concealing, not to mention more rakish, angle.

"All we need is for someone to recognize me and come trotting over, demanding to know when Hawk means to come home. Not that I can tell them," Lord Ramsay added with a sigh. "Do you see anyone you know?"

Under the brim of the beaver hat, crystal-clear green eyes, rimmed by thick, dark lashes, scanned the crowd with good-humored intent. "A few. I know old Queensbury, of course, and Lord Yarmouth. And I have met Mr. Craven and Major Mellish. There are some others, too, but no one who will pay the slightest heed to a couple of lads down from Oxford to watch a mill."

Lord Ramsay appeared to be unconvinced, but at that moment a tumultuous cheer erupting from the crowd drew his attention once more to the ring, where the Black, sweat streaming in rivers down his sleekly muscled body, seemed to be in trouble. Defending, and retreating from his opponent's blows, though still valiantly attempting to put in a flush hit, the Black was now against the ropes. Quickly the Irishman caught hold of the upper of the three of them in such a singular way that his opponent could neither get in a hit nor fall down.

The crowd was in an uproar, and the seconds began shouting to separate the two fighters. Their calls were soon taken up by the spectators, but Jackson, shaking his head, insisted that by rule he could not separate them until one of the men had fallen. Word of the decision spread rapidly through the crowd, whereupon some two hundred persons surged forward to achieve the separation themselves. Despite the jostling, the two young fashionables kept their seats and seemed only to enjoy the ensuing melee. It took some time to sort things out, but the interval seemed to have done the two combatants good, for when the twelfth round began, both rallied forth with excellent spirit.

It was now that the Black began to justify his reputation. The Irishman fought furiously, but his blows appeared to have less effect than before, while the Black showed up in fine style, flooring him twice before the end of the round. In the thirteenth the Irishman rallied desperately, but his blows now fell short more often than not, and midway through the fourteenth round a tremendous left-hand blow from the Black felled him like a stone to the ground, where he lay motionless.

"By Jove!" Lord Ramsay exclaimed. "I do believe the Irishman's done for."

"He looks well nigh dead to me," replied his companion, the green eyes narrowing slightly. "Do you truly enjoy this sport, Ramsay?"

"Oh, aye, 'tis beyond anything great! Why, men will be talking about this match for months. Look there, the Irishman's seconds are just now throwing in the towel. They cannot bring him up to scratch. He showed game, right enough, though."

The applause and shouting made further conversation impossible for some moments, and when it began to fade, Lord Ramsay realized he was being hailed by the young man in the yellow-and-green phaeton.

"You stay here," he ordered, "so that fella don't expect a proper introduction. And mind you don't fall into conversation with anyone." A grin being the only response he received, he turned his attention to his horse, doing his best to angle near enough to the phaeton to exchange calling cards with the young gentleman. A few moments later he was back.

"I daresay we'd best get out of this before someone does collar me," he said then. "I don't know many of the members of the *beau monde* as yet, but that's not to say there aren't one or two of Hawk's friends here who would recognize me."

Obediently, the other horse was turned to follow in his wake, and they made their way carefully through the excited crowd to the roadway. Once there, Lord Ramsay gave spur to his mount, leaving his companion little choice other than to follow suit. The road heading north along the Kent-East Sussex border toward Hurst Green was well-drained, so they were able to maintain a brisk canter, slowing only while they passed through Hurst Green itself and briefly into East Sussex to follow the London-Hastings highroad. But silence reigned between them until they had passed back into Kent over the stone, arched bridge spanning the River Bourne some miles above the point where she raced into the Rother. The Bourne's waters were running higher and more swiftly than was their wont, because of the recent rains, and the noise of the rushing water made conversation impossible. But then, as they turned up the Bourne Valley road, instead of breaking once more into a canter, Lord Ramsay seemed content to keep to a slower pace. His companion put a hand up to straighten the beaver.

"Don't you dare to take off that hat," Lord Ramsay warned.

"Some of my hair got twisted. It is hurting me."

"You have my sympathy," he replied, grinning, "but if you take that hat off, we shall both end in the briars. I shudder to think what Hawk would have to say to me, should wind of this newest escapade reach his ears."

"It would take a stiff wind, would it not, to carry the word all the way to Spain?"

"He's bound to return one day, however, and if it is all the same to you, I'd as lief my first interview with him be a pleasant one."

"Mine will not be, I daresay. Your busier relatives will have informed him of the many lapses in my good behavior over the past four years."

Lord Ramsay chuckled. "I wonder if he's heard about Margate or your visit to the Bartholomew Fair. You have not precisely exerted yourself to play the dutiful wife, Mollie."

She glanced at him saucily. "And I suppose you think your brother has been an *excellent* husband to me?"

Colporter laughed. "I think he has never even known you. How could he when he left to join Wellington not two weeks after your wedding?"

"Well, he had been courting me for two years, after all," Mollie replied. "Not that that counts for much, I suppose. He never had time to visit Rutledge Park. There's not much by way of sport there, of course, and in winter we were nearly always cut off by the weather. He and I saw each other only at very proper affairs during the Season, where I behaved myself like a very proper little lady."

"And where you were constantly surrounded by other contenders for your lovely hand, if the tales I've heard are true."

"They are." She gave a little toss of her head. "I was enormously successful, you know. All the crack, in fact. I had my choice of them all."

"Yet you chose Hawk." Lord Ramsay's gray eyes narrowed under the thick, straight brows that reminded Mollie so forcibly of her husband's. Ramsay was younger than Hawk, of course, nearly ten years younger. And his features were softer than she remembered Hawk's being. She wondered now how well she actually remembered Hawk. Four years was a long time.

"I chose Hawk because I thought he seemed the most likely of the lot to add some adventure to my life," she said now. She didn't choose to describe the way a mere look from that tall, tawny-haired man or the mere sound of his low-pitched voice, for that matter, had sent the blood racing hotly through her body. "He was forever talking about hunting and cockfighting and curricle-racing."

"He was a noted Corinthian, was he not?" Ramsay put in with unmistakable brotherly pride. "They still speak of the time he raced against Sir James Smithers from Westminster to York in October. What an event that must have been!" He glanced more sharply at Mollie. "Surely you didn't expect him to take you along on such expeditions!"

She shrugged, and the green eyes glinted beneath the dark

lashes. "I should have known he'd be like any other man, thinking only of his own pleasures, expecting his wife to remain complacently at home while he goes off adventuring. Life is most unfair to females, Ramsay."

He appeared to give the matter some thought. It was one of the things she liked best about her young brother-in-law. He never gave one an automatic, learned response. Her opinions carried weight with him.

The road had begun to narrow now, and the lush green forest seemed to creep right to its very edges, but neither Lord Ramsay nor his companion felt the slightest tremor of unease. Times had been peaceful lately, hereabouts, and they were now on Colporter land. Nearly the entire Bourne Valley belonged to the Marquess of Hawkstone.

Finally, clearing his throat and choosing his words carefully, Lord Ramsay said, "You could scarcely expect Hawk to take you with him to the Peninsula, Moll."

"Well, no, but he needn't have dumped me at Hawkstone Towers with your charming parent, either!" Mollie snapped.

Lord Ramsay chuckled. "That *was* a rum go, and no mistake. Papa was a cursed old marplot, to wrap the matter in as clean linen as possible. Lucky for all of us that Aunt Biddy was here as well."

"Indeed." Mollie's expression softened at the thought of Lady Bridget Colporter, who had shown her nothing but kindness over the past four, sometimes unutterably difficult years. "I think it is a great pity she was never allowed to marry."

"What? And leave poor Papa to fend for himself! Lord knows Mama, what with one miscarriage after another, was unsuited to the task. I daresay she went to her reward with nothing but relief after Harry was born. Aunt Biddy had all the care of Papa, the four of us, and Hawkstone Towers in her dish. How can you be so unfeeling as to think Papa ought to have shared some of that burden?" The gray eyes twinkled merrily, but Mollie glared at him.

"That was so like him. First to send your mother to an early grave with all his demands upon her for sons and more sons, and then to make poor Biddy into a near prisoner to cater to his needs. Your father, Ramsay, was naught but a selfish, contumacious old bastard!"

"Tut, tut," scolded his lordship. "Such language from a gently nurtured female."

Mollie chuckled, the grim lines in her face smoothing at once. "As if you've never heard me call him a bastard before."

"Not bastard. Contumacious. Where do you come by such delightful words, m'dear?"

Laughter gurgled up. "And you with an Oxford education!"

"A near education. Not done yet, remember? One more term. But now that we're done mourning dearest Papa, I mean to enjoy the Season and then follow Prinny to Brighton with the rest of the swells before I bury myself in books again. A man about town, that's me, as of next week."

Mollie became serious again. "Do you think Hawk will approve of your remaining out of school till Michaelmas term, Ramsay?"

"Much good it will do him to disapprove," responded that young gentleman recklessly. "He can scarcely stop me."

They rode in silence for some moments. Despite the sun's rays filtering through the thick, overhanging trees, little warmth penetrated to the roadway, and Mollie began to feel chilled. Reaching back to unknot the leather thongs that held her heavy duffle coat in a roll tied to her saddle, she deftly shook out the coat and began to slip her arms into the sleeves. Her horse was well-trained, but it was an awkward business nonetheless, so she smiled gratefully when Lord Ramsay reached out to assist her.

"What did you think of your first mill?" he asked.

"I enjoyed the crowd's enthusiasm," Mollie replied frankly as she shrugged into the coat, "but the action itself was too brutal for my taste. Why, if the two men had not been of different colors, there would have been no way to determine one from the other by the tenth round, so bloodied were their features."

"But consider the skill, Mollie! The sheer manliness of the sport! To see two pugilists, full of gaiety and confidence, nobly opposing one another, to prove which is the better man. Why, 'tis a sport enjoyed as much by the ragtag and bobtail as by the flowers of society, something all men can enjoy together without thought for class or standing. 'Tis a most democratic entertainment, m'dear."

Mollie grinned at his enthusiasm. "If it is merely an entertainment, Ramsay, then why do they not take steps to protect the combatants? Their skill, gaiety, and confidence could be as easily displayed if their knuckles were padded, and their heads and bodies protected from serious injury. A fencing match, after all, may be just as thoroughly enjoyed by the spectators when the foils are buttoned as when they are not. More so, in fact, for one may concentrate the more fully upon the skill of the fencers when one need not fear to see one or the other spitted before one's very eyes. Why, until the Irishman began to sit up and rub his head, I feared the Black had truly killed him. And in another match, someone may well do so.''

Lord Ramsay was staring at her in astonishment. ''You would put padded gloves on such men and rig them out in armor? For the love of heaven, show some sense. Where would the sport be in that? How could the Black win any sort of decisive victory if he could not even knock his opponent down? Cover his hands! My God, Mollie, do not let any other fancier of the sport hear you suggest such a ridiculous course.''

Abashed, Mollie begged his pardon for her foolishness, and they rode on together in perfect harmony. But it was not long before she found her thoughts returning to her husband. She wondered, as she often did, just when he would see his way clear to coming home again to take his rightful place as master of Hawkstone Towers.

Four years before, not two weeks after their wedding, the news had reached London that General Arthur Wellesley, who had already begun to acquire the charisma that attends extraordinary leadership, had replaced Sir John Moore as Commander of the British Army in Portugal. Men insisted it was the beginning of what would undoubtedly be one of the most brilliant campaigns in military history, and Hawk had immediately announced his intention to be part of it.

Mollie had been merely nineteen at the time, and as the former Lady Margaret Hazeldell, daughter of the powerful Earl of Rutledge, she had been accustomed to having her own wishes put foremost by a host of besotted admirers. Even Hawk, though he had never pandered to her wishes quite so blatantly as her other beaux, had still done all in his power to win her. It had therefore come as a shock to her to discover that he could leave her flat, just to follow some whim of his own. She was certain now, with the gift of hindsight, that she had merely been another challenge to a man who reveled in challenges. He had won her in the face of major opposition, but once she was safely his, he had rallied immediately to pick up the next gauntlet.

Hawk had promised, when he had left her with his awful father, that he would not be gone long. He was as certain as could be, he said, that Bonaparte would be routed in a trice and that, in the meantime, Mollie would enjoy reigning over Hawkstone Towers, exchanging confidences with gentle Lady Bridget, and helping to mind the then five-year-old Lord Henry Colporter.

Mollie shuddered now as she recalled those first dreadful weeks in Kent after Hawk had gone. The old Marquess of Hawkstone had been a demanding, temperamental tyrant who wanted all about him to run smoothly without so much as having to lift a finger to assist in the running. Mollie had not found it difficult to understand why Hawk had previously spent as little time as possible at his family home, where his every move and opinion were belligerently questioned and cross-questioned by so harsh a parent. But understanding his wish to leave and forgiving him for leaving her had been two entirely different things.

At first there had been occasional letters from him, and she knew he had reached the Peninsula in time to take part in General Wellesley's famous victory at Talavera. Then the army had moved into Spain, and there were fewer letters. Then none at all. When the dispatches arrived in London after the battle of Salamanca, his name had been listed among those wounded, and Mollie had been frantic for nearly a week. But then a letter arrived from Hawk, informing her that he was not seriously injured and had chosen to recuperate in a village near the Portuguese border. Thus, he wrote, he would be able to return more quickly to action when his wounds healed.

There was nothing but a brief note or two after that until several months after the old marquess relieved them of his presence by choking to death on a fishbone one night. He had expired in the midst of berating Lady Bridget for failing to note that several stones in the postern-gate causeway had been loosened by a recent storm, and it had been Lady Bridget's fluttery protest that she never had reason to travel upon that causeway which had so incensed him. Consequently, Mollie had had her hands full for some time after the tragic event, trying to convince poor Lady Bridget that she had not murdered the marquess. When Mollie finally had a moment to consider the matter, she had assumed that Hawk would return as soon as word of his father's death reached him. However, from some cause or other, it had been nearly a month before he learned of the situation, and when he did, he had simply scrawled a note informing her that he was too much occupied to return at once and advising her to rely upon his uncle, Lord Andrew Colporter, to attend to any matters of business that his bailiff could not cope with.

Having kept a close watch over the dispatches as they appeared in the London papers, Mollie had no doubt that Wellesley, now Viscount Wellington, might well have failed at Madrid without Hawk's invaluable assistance, so she was able to swallow the fact that her husband was too busy to come home immediately, but she could not so easily accept his advice with regard to Lord Andrew.

Since by that time she knew as much as anyone and more than most about the running of the Colporter estates, and since she quite heartily despised both the sanctimonious Lord Andrew and his Polly-pry wife, she ignored Hawk's suggestion with a nearly clear conscience. Because her conscience was not quite so clear with regard to certain other matters, she also breathed a sigh of relief at the delay, and went about her business as usual. Two months later, concerned by the fact that Lady Bridget still wore an expression of constant anxiety on her plump, normally pleasant countenance, Mollie had ruthlessly dragged the poor, feebly-protesting woman off to Margate, hoping the crisp sea breezes would restore the roses to her cheeks. That she had also taken the opportunity to liven up her own dull situation was a matter that she knew might well cause her an uncomfortable moment or two at some vague point in the future.

A little smile tugged at her lips now as she remembered Lord Ramsay's earlier teasing reference to the episode. He had never blamed her for her behavior then. He had, in fact, asserted that he couldn't imagine why anyone should expect for a moment that she ought to mourn his father's passing. Anyone in his right mind, he had said, would expect the entire family to rejoice. But Mollie knew she had behaved badly. Others knew it, too. And if Lady Andrew Colporter had not immediately sent Hawk a full, undoubtedly exaggerated report of Mollie's activities, then some other of his busybody relations must have done so. She sighed deeply, then glanced over to find Lord Ramsay regarding her quizzically.

"Tired, Moll?"

"A little," she admitted, "but I was just thinking of Lady Andrew and the things she has no doubt amused herself by writing to your brother."

"A pox on the woman. Has Hawk . . . Never mind. None of my affair," he said hastily.

Molly smiled at him. "I have no secrets, Ramsay. Has he ever mentioned hearing anything? Isn't that what you were about to ask?" He nodded. "Never," Mollie said. "Of course, he has written so infrequently and never very much to the purpose."

"Do you write to him?"

Color crept into her cheeks as she remembered the long, rather childish letters she had written after his departure, but she answered steadily enough, "Not for a long time. Or at least not the way you mean. I wrote to inform him when Haycock caught those poachers on the north ridge and when we had the causeway repaired, and last year when Mr. Brewer questioned my authority to draw funds for the refurbishing of Lady Bridget's rooms when we returned from Margate. He replied to Mr. Brewer very quickly on that occasion, I'm glad to say."

"I detect my uncle's fine hand there," Lord Ramsay murmured. "Punishing you for your raking, no doubt."

"Punishing Lady Bridget, you mean," Mollie returned angrily. "He read her the most dreadful scold. As if she could order my coming and going or would try to do so. I am certain I told you all about it when you were down for the long vacation."

"You did, and I thought then as I think now that we'd all of us do better without Uncle Andrew's interference. Why, even Gwen was saying, only last week when I passed through Pillings on my way here, that—"

But what his older sister had had to say was destined to go, for the moment at any rate, unrepeated, for Lord Ramsay broke off suddenly and gave his full attention to the roadway in front of them.

"I say, Mollie," he said after a moment or so, while she

watched him curiously, "I think we've got company up yonder."

"What makes you think so?" She had noticed a number of tracks in the mud, but had given them little thought. The road was fairly well-traveled by the men from Hawkstone.

Lord Ramsay's brow was furrowed as he concentrated his attention downward. "There shouldn't be so many tracks as these. You forget the rain washed the road clear. There were a few ruts this morning, but scarcely any tracks beyond the ones we made ourselves."

"Still it would take but one small group of horsemen coming from Hawkstone to make a number of tracks," she pointed out. But then, even before he could speak, she realized a fact that contradicted her suggestion. "All the tracks are heading toward the castle, aren't they, Ramsay?"

"They are." There was a slightly grimmer note in his voice. "And they are fresh, too, Moll. Only observe that pile of dung yonder and the scrape there on that stone. A horseshoe made that recently enough that it's still white, and you can see tiny bits of metal glinting. There's another. If we'd been riding at a normal pace, I daresay we'd have overtaken them by now." He reined in, cocking his head. "Listen."

Mollie obeyed. In the distance, through the trees, she could hear the faint jingle of spurs and harness. There were riders ahead. "What shall we do, Ramsay?"

"Well, we can't risk your being seen, that's flat," he replied. "And the only place they can be going from here is Hawkstone. We'll have to cut through the woods and across the ridge to the postern causeway. Even if we hurry, we'll be only a hop and a skip ahead of them."

He wheeled his horse into the woods and gave a nudge of his spurs to urge it to greater speed. With a grin, Mollie followed, keeping her head lowered and attempting at the same time to keep the curly-brimmed beaver from flying off her head. They seemed to fly under rain-soaked, low-hanging branches, over fallen logs, through nearly marshy meadows, and across the gurgling, storm-swollen brook that fed into the river below, but both riders knew every grass and stone in these woods, and they suffered no mishap, though the horses' flanks were heaving and well-splattered with mud by the time they emerged into the clearing by the lakeshore and saw the postern causeway straight ahead of them.

The sight of the huge gray-stone fortress filling the island in the center of the sparkling blue lake sent a glow of pride racing through Mollie just as it always did. Fascinated from the first moment she had laid eyes upon it, she had come to know the castle's history as well as anyone.

She knew that as a result of the number of successful French raids across the English Channel in the late fourteenth century and the great fear that the raiders might well begin to plunge farther inland, Sir Ninian Colporter, a well-known knight at court and a veteran of Edward III's wars abroad, had applied for a license to crenellate Hawkstone House, a mansion he had built on a hillside overlooking the Bourne some years before. Permission was granted on the understanding that the castle would protect the immediate countryside from an invading enemy. Interpreting "crenellation" in a very broad sense, Sir Ninian had abandoned the existing house altogether and chosen a new site on the island in the middle of a small lake, the waters of which drained into the Bourne, thence to the Rother and on to the sea at Rye.

Though externally Hawkstone Towers displayed a symmetry of walls and towers common to the period in which it was built, the inside was much more sophisticated, a properly designed fortified courtyard house with splendid private suites, separate servants' quarters, chapel, and other amenities remarkable for their number and extent. Therefore, its residents were quite comfortable, and despite the difficulties of those first weeks so long ago, Mollie had come to love this magnificent, ancient home of the Colporters.

The horses' hooves clattered now on the cobblestones of the causeway, one of two leading to the castle gates from the lakeshore. Only the main causeway was part of the original castle, and it had been designed at a right angle to the entrance, so that an advancing enemy would be exposed on his unshielded right flank all the way to the little island, where he had to turn in order to proceed across the drawbridge to the barbican, a tall central tower that had originally been heavily fortified. From the barbican one still had to pass through a multiplicity of defenses to reach the central courtyard.

The second causeway was of a much later date and led through the postern gate to the stableyard. There were various trails leading away from it on the lakeshore, but there was no proper road such as that which led to the main causeway.

Though the second causeway was less elaborate, there was still plenty of room to ride abreast and they did not slow their pace below a canter, but suddenly Mollie heard an exclamation from her companion that caused her to glance at him sharply.

Lord Ramsay's attention was riveted upon the entrance to the main causeway some hundred yards or so across the gleaming water to their left. Following his gaze, Mollie caught her breath in dismay. They had beaten the party of riders by only moments, but it was not sight of the horsemen themselves that stopped the breath in her throat. It was the banner flying proudly above them, a hawk displayed, beaked, armed, and crowned. Though the distance was too great to allow her to make out such details as the sword, *argent*, carried in the hawk's left talons or the lily, *or*, in its right, she had no difficulty recognizing the crest of the most noble Gavin Remington Colporter, Marquess and Earl of Hawkstone, Viscount Corbin, Baron Colporter of Chilham and Bourne, Baron Colporter of Falmouth, and le Baron Faucon de Lys, Corbeil, et Grailion. Hawk had come home.

2

With a little cry deep in her throat, Mollie clamped the beaver to her head and dug her spurs into the big bay's flanks. Lord Ramsay was close behind her as she clattered through the postern gate into the stableyard and slid quickly from the saddle.

"Hand me your reins, Moll," he ordered crisply as he dismounted. "Hawk will be detained in the main courtyard, but the sooner you play least in sight, the better. He will ask for you at once."

She glanced quickly around the yard. Teddy, her groom, and Bill, who looked after Lord Ramsay's mounts, were the only ones paying them any heed. She did not think any of the stable lads would cry rope on her, in any event. She was a prime favorite with most of them. Nevertheless, it would not do to be careless. She handed the reins to Lord Ramsay.

"You'd best hurry, too," she said over her shoulder. "If they saw us, they can't have recognized us, but if Hawk comes bang upon you here with a pair of muddy horses, he'll want to know who your companion was."

He nodded. "I'll be along directly. But go, Mollie. I can hear them."

She could, too. The noise from the main courtyard carried easily through the arched tunnel into the stableyard. She had no time to dally. On the thought, she ran lightly across the cobblestones and into the castle by way of a side door leading first to an anteroom and beyond to a large hall, where a fire roared in a mammoth fireplace. The well-worn furniture and threadbare wall hangings proclaimed it to be a family gathering place rather than a room for more formal entertainment, and despite its size, it was a comfortable room. A small, shaggy dog looked up at her sleepily from the hearth rug.

"All alone, Mandy?" The bitch's ears twitched and her

tail thumped in welcome. Slowing her pace, Mollie pulled the beaver hat from her head, freeing her long blond tresses to fall in a tangle of sun-streaked curls down her back. Just then there was a light clatter of footsteps on the simple, two-run wooden stairway at the left rear of the hall. Mollie waited, recognizing the quick, running steps and knowing who would appear on the landing. Seconds later a nine-year-old boy with light brown hair came into sight, his shirt tucked haphazardly into nankeen breeches, which were in turn tucked into black-topped boots. As he hit the turn of the stair, seeming to bounce off the stone wall in his headlong rush, he caught sight of Mollie and came to a precarious halt on the second step below the landing. Excitement lit his face.

"I say, Mollie, Hawk's here! I saw him from the school-room window and old Bates said I could— By the Lord Harry, what have you been up to?"

Mollie chuckled. "Never mind that, rascal. I believe I've mentioned before," she added more sternly, "that it does not become you to swear that particular oath. It was not, as you seem to think, devised out of respect for yourself." The boy merely grinned at her and she shook her head fondly. "You run along and welcome Hawk. But mind, Harry, not a word about this. If he asks you, you may tell him I shall be along directly."

Mischief gleamed in Lord Harry Colporter's eyes as he let his gaze drift meaningfully from her tousled hair to her mud-spattered breeches and boots. "Where *have* you been, Mollie?" Just then Lord Ramsay entered the hall, and catching sight of him, Harry drew his own rapid conclusions. "You took her with you," he accused, his gray eyes flashing. "You wouldn't take me, but you took Mollie! You took a lady to see a mill! Only wait till—"

"Enough, Harry!" Lord Ramsay's tone was sharp. "Go on, Moll. You've no time to waste. I'll deal with this."

"I'll warrant Hawk wouldn't care to hear about such goings-on," Harry said musingly, watching his brother with wary eyes. Mollie, hearing Lord Ramsay's indrawn breath behind her, held up a hand to silence them both.

"Harry," she said calmly, moving up the steps toward the boy, "you are perfectly right when you say your brother wouldn't like to hear that his wife has been to watch a mill. That is one reason we took pains to conceal my identity. But

I know, if Ramsay does not, that I've nothing to fear from you."

Harry's eyes were dancing with mischief now. "What'll you give me to keep mum, Mollie?"

"It's what I shall give you if you don't that should concern you," Lord Ramsay said dangerously.

"Oh, pooh," retorted Harry, unabashed. "Hawk won't let you thrash me for such a thing."

"But Hawk won't know about it till after the fact, brat, which will do nothing to save your hide."

Harry, bristling, looked only too ready, as always, to debate the issue, and Mollie, knowing she had delayed too long already, pushed unceremoniously past him. "This is scarcely the moment for you two to engage in one of your tiffs," she told them roundly. "Ramsay, you must get out of those clothes before Hawk sees you in them. And, Harry, I depend upon you to keep him talking with Lady Bridget so he does not notice how long it takes me to make my appearance. Hurry now, the both of you!"

Harry grinned at her and scooted down the stairs, but Mollie heard him say scornfully as he neatly eluded a smack from his brother, "As if I'd ever split on Mollie!"

Lord Ramsay was shaking his head in exasperation as he followed her up the stairway, but Mollie did not pause to exchange further conversation with him. Instead, she hurried along the stone gallery to another staircase and upward again until she came to her own sitting room and bedchamber.

"Oh, m'lady, I feared ye'd never get here," exclaimed the buxom young woman awaiting her there. "I've a bath ready, but 'tis nearly chilled already! Here now, off wi' yer coat and them dreadful breeches."

"Bless you, Cathe," Mollie said sincerely, "but how were you warned to expect the master?"

"His man come on ahead, m'lady. Lady Bridget sent fer ye straightaway, 'n I just said ye was out riding the day wi' 'is lordship. She be in a dreadful fret by now, I'm thinkin'."

"Indeed, she will," Mollie agreed. "Wondering what the pair of us are up to this time and hoping, whatever it is, it won't come to Hawk's ears." She chuckled, relaxing as she shed her disreputable clothing and sank gratefully into the tub near the crackling fire while Cathe caught her hair up in a knot at the top of her head.

"We've no time t' wash yer hair, m'lady."

"No matter. 'Tis clean enough, though it most likely smells of beaver hat. Fetch some oatmeal, Cathe. That will turn the trick. And send a housemaid to inform her ladyship that I'll be down directly. Lord Harry was to tell her, but in the excitement of greeting his brother, he may have forgotten to do so."

Cathe disappeared to do her bidding, and Mollie sank lower in the big tub. There was no time to luxuriate, however, nor was the temperature of the water likely to remain even lukewarm much longer. So, with a small sigh, she began to lather her body with the delightful jasmine-scented soap smuggled in only the week before from France. The scent was heady, and she remembered that she had also acquired a small bottle of jasmine oil as well. She would use a drop or two to scent the oatmeal before Cathe brushed it through her hair.

Rinsing the soap away, Mollie stood up, letting the water run off her slim, white, delicately shaped body as she reached for the towel Cathe had left draped over the back of a chair, near the fire. She was still drying herself when Cathe returned, carrying a bowl of dry oatmeal flakes. It took very little time to add the oil and rub the oatmeal into Mollie's hair but longer to brush it out again, and Cathe insisted upon doing the job properly.

" 'Twould not do t' go scattering flakes as ye walk, m'lady."

"No, but do hurry, Cathe. I don't wish to greet his lordship in my shift."

"I doubt 'e'd object, m'lady," Cathe responded with a grin. "Not after bein' away four long years, 'e won't."

The girl's words stopped the breath in Mollie's throat. Until that moment, she had been concerned only with righting her appearance before he saw her. Now she began to consider what, exactly, his homecoming might mean to her.

She gazed at her reflection in the glass above the dressing table, realizing she was not the same naïve young girl he had left behind four years before. Oh, her face was much the same: still the same oval shape, with the same pointed, stubborn little chin, the same wide, generous mouth, the same dusting of freckles across the dainty, tip-tilted nose, and the same arched, expressive brows above the same dark-lashed, crystal-clear green eyes. Her hair was perhaps a few shades lighter, thanks to her habit of letting it flow free and hatless while she rode at breakneck pace over the wealds in any kind of weather. That habit was responsible, too, for the light tanning of her face and hands, for as often as not she forgot her gloves as well. She looked at her hands and shook her head.

"My nails are a disgrace, Cathe."

"Aye, m'lady, and 'aven't I told ye time and again ye must 'ave a care. Miss du Bois would 'ave seven kinds of fits an she could see 'em now."

"Well, she wouldn't, because she would never have allowed them to come to such a state." Then, when Cathe's face fell ludicrously, Mollie added with a laugh, "Don't fall into the dismals, goose. I'm not blaming you. 'Tis my own fault that I've allowed myself to reach such a pass that I'm dependent on my dresser to trim and polish my nails for me. I'm capable enough to run the estates without so much as a word of advice from my—or rather, his lordship's—bailiff, yet I cannot attend to the simplest matters for myself. 'Tis a ridiculous state. But I do wish Mathilde had not chosen this moment to visit her family in Christchurch."

" 'Twas to give Miss du Bois a well-deserved rest, m'lady, and well ye know it. She returns the end o' the week to go wi' ye to London. Let 'er enjoy 'er vacation now." As she talked, Cathe had swept Mollie's hair into a pile of curls atop her dainty head. The style gave her slender neck a fragile appearance and emphasized the daintiness of her small, well-shaped ears. It also made her eyes appear larger than ever and gave her an innocent air that Mollie hoped would get her through that first, dreaded interview with her husband. While, behind her, Cathe shook out the folds of a pale-green muslin gown with narrow darker-green ribbons woven through the lace trimming of the bodice and puffed sleeves, Mollie pulled a few tendrils loose from the coif to soften the line around her face and neck. Biting her lips and pinching her cheeks, she wondered if there would be a need to apply a touch of rouge. She often did so in London, but rarely here in Kent, where the practice was more likely to be frowned upon. She decided against it.

As Cathe helped her into the pale-green gown, Mollie was aware of a growing excitement that seemed to begin somewhere deep inside her and spread through her, giving a glow of warmth to her entire body. What would he expect of her? Would he assume that he need only walk through the door to take up all his rights and privileges as master of Hawkstone again? No doubt. Such was the way of men. From Cathe's words, it was clear that everyone else expected him merely to take up where he had left off. A little shiver raced through her at the thought. What would he do if she defied him? If she told him he did *not* have the right merely to move back to his bed and board when the whim struck him to do so? What, then?

Mollie turned obediently when Cathe told her to do so, and held out first one hand, then the other, to have her nails trimmed. Over the maid's shoulder she caught a glimpse of herself in the glass again and licked her lips nervously.

Hawk would no doubt already be annoyed with her if his relatives had informed him about even half the things she feared they might have felt it their duty to tell him. She tried to remember if she had ever seen him angry. All she could call to mind, however, was a lilting laugh and a pair of gray Colporter eyes that crinkled at the corners more often than not. In the face of his father's fury, Hawk had customarily been tight-lipped, and the gray eyes had taken on a chilly glaze, but she couldn't remember him ever losing his temper. And if he hadn't lost it with his father, chances were good that he simply never lost it. Still and all, she decided, straightening her shoulders and lifting her chin, it wouldn't do to cross him straightaway. Not, at any rate, before one had at least an inkling of which way the wind might blow.

Thanking Cathe and taking a last look at her nails, which, though much improved, still were a long way from meeting Mathilde du Bois' high standard of perfection, Mollie scooped up a creamy, light wool shawl to protect herself against the chilly drafts in the great hall, and sallied forth to welcome her lord and master home from the wars, confident that she looked every inch the lady of the castle.

She heard his generous laughter as she approached the landing of the huge double staircase that descended in twin arcs to either side of the great hall below. From the landing itself she could see them all gathered before a huge fire, even larger than the one in the rear hall. There were several men, a beaming Lady Bridget, who was seated in a Sheraton armchair to one side of the hearth, and a dancing Lord Harry, clearly unable to contain his excitement at having his eldest brother home at last. The boyish voice piped above the others'.

"Can I go to Eton sir? Uncle Andrew said 'twas for you to decide, 'cause Aunt Biddy said I wasn't strong enough, which ain't nothing but stuff, 'cause I'm tough as whitleather. Only ask Ramsay. He says—"

"Hush, bantling." Hawk's tone was offhand, for his attention had been claimed, as she had meant it to be, by the sight of his slender, beautiful young wife, gracefully descending the broad, sweeping stairs to meet him. The shawl, draped negligently over one arm, trailed behind her on the steps, beside the short demitrain of her gown. It seemed as if she was unaware of any need to manage either one. Her head was high. The hand not holding the shawl rested lightly on the highly polished handrail. She was looking at him, her gaze seeming to hold his easily. There was a sparkle in her eyes, and although her soft, rosy lips were slightly parted, every poised inch of her bespoke the nobility of her heritage and her rank.

Hawk strode forward to meet her at the bottom of the stairs.

Mollie had heard him hushing the boy, and her first thought was that while she had remembered the lilt in his laughter, she had forgotten that particular caressing timbre of his low-pitched voice. Even the two words, spoken in that offhand manner to Harry, were enough to send tremors of excitement racing through her body. When he looked straight into her eyes, she felt mesmerized, as though she were suddenly walking on air. Though she could not take her eyes from his, she was keenly aware of his size as he strode to meet her. Hawk seemed to have grown both broader and taller in the years they had been apart.

He had not yet taken time to change clothes. He wore a dark jacket, cut loosely to allow room for his massive shoulders to move without binding, but the buckskins encasing his legs did little to conceal the ripple of well-developed thigh muscles. His cordovan riding boots were mud-spattered. He was darkly tanned, and his thick, tawny hair, though darker than hers, was nearly as sun-streaked. He smiled ruefully as he took her small hand in his much larger one.

"Good day, my lady. Forgive me for tarrying here when I

should have been taking the opportunity to rid myself of all this dirt.''

His features were as harsh as she remembered them, but the gray eyes under the straight brows were warm and glowing. Again her body responded of its own accord. Mollie could feel her breasts swelling as the nipples pressed against the fabric of her chemise. Color touched her cheeks when his gaze drifted to her cleavage, but her voice was steady enough when she spoke.

'' 'Tis of no account, sir, if you will but forgive me for taking so long in preparing myself to welcome you home.'' Afraid he would misinterpret matters if she kept staring at him so blatantly, Mollie let her eyelids droop slightly, as if the gesture might somehow prevent him from seeing straight into her mind. But then she discovered she was more aware than ever of the fact that he still held her hand in his.

"You look charmingly, Mollie," he said quietly, "and you smell delightfully of jasmine. Come and meet my travel-worn companions. The thin one there by Aunt Biddy is Jamie Smithers. I believe you've met him before."

"Indeed I have," Mollie answered serenely, smiling at the tall dark-haired man, dressed with the same casual but neat air that his host affected. "How nice to see you again, Sir James." Smithers bowed.

"And the foppish gent with his hands in his pockets, leaning against the mantelpiece, is Lord Breckin. Have you met my lady before, Breck?"

"Not had the honor," the heavyset, dandified gentleman said, straightening and giving a nod in Mollie's direction. "Pleasure, ma'am."

There were several other introductions to be made before the quick tread of boot heels from above heralded the arrival of Lord Ramsay. He hurried down the broad staircase with a grin and a hand outstretched to greet his brother.

"Hawk! Welcome. About time you decided to show your face around here again."

"Thunder and turf!" exclaimed Hawkstone, giving the young man's hand a hearty shake. "Ramsay? I'd never have recognized you, lad. You must have gained a full three stone since I last clapped eyes on you."

"Thereabouts." Ramsay chuckled, looking his brother over from head to toe. "You've changed a good bit, yourself."

"Aye, I've put on a few pounds, but neither of us has changed as much as that young whelp yonder. What on earth have you been feeding him, Mollie?"

Mollie smiled at the glowing Harry. "He has a growing boy's healthy appetite, sir, and will eat well nigh anything." She had been watching her husband closely while he greeted Ramsay, trying to detect any sign of the annoyance she expected him to feel toward her. She was certain he would say nothing to her in front of the others, but she had hoped to be able to judge the extent of his displeasure and thus to be better prepared when the time came to meet it. As she looked up at him now, she saw nothing but warmth in his eyes.

"Mollie's the one who hasn't changed," Ramsay said into the stillness that had followed Mollie's comment. "She never seems to change at all."

Surprisingly, Mollie saw that Hawk seemed shaken by his brother's words. There was the faintest flicker of something that might have been irritation stirring in the gray eyes that looked down into hers, but she couldn't, even with her vivid imagination, think the irritation was directed at herself. Nevertheless, a little shiver nudged at the base of her spine when she realized she was seeing but a trace of what might later be unleashed about her ears. Forcing a smile to her lips, she said, "Nonsense, Ramsay, everyone changes in four years, even the Lady Bridget."

"Oh, dear," said the plump little gray-haired lady seated near the hearth. It was clear to all of them that Mollie's sudden reference to her had cast Lady Bridget into a state of some confusion. Withdrawing her hand from Hawk's, Mollie hastened to her.

"Indeed, ma'am, 'tis true. But how I wish the rest of us could claim to have altered so charmingly. You quite put us in the shade, you know, with your gentle manners and your kindness to everyone."

"How nice of you to say so, my love," responded Lady Bridget with a smile that lit her pale-blue eyes. She patted Mollie's hand. "Is it not pleasant to have dearest Gavin at home again? A man, you know, always seems to make things a deal more comfortable."

"Now, how can you say so, Aunt Biddy," Ramsay teased her, "when you know perfectly well that Papa never made anyone the least bit comfortable?"

Lady Bridget turned to him in flustered protest, but Mollie

cut in swiftly. "Do not roast her, Ramsay. I shan't allow it. You know very well that Aunt Biddy had long depended upon your father and has felt his loss most keenly. She has too much gentleness of spirit to tell you to your head that you've no business to be saying such things to her, but I have not."

Ramsay only grinned at her, but Mollie recollected her manners at once when her husband's voice sounded directly beyond her.

"It seems that even Mollie has changed," he said gently. "Do you often take my unfortunate brothers to task in this manner, my lady?"

She turned to face him, contrite but determined to show him she would not allow anyone to torment Lady Bridget. The laughter in his eyes steadied her. "I do so only when they deserve it, sir, but I should not have spoken as I did in front of Sir James, Lord Breckin, and the others."

"Don't bother your head about them," he said, casting a glance at the gentlemen in question. "Breck's too tired, Jamie's too addlepated, and the others too concerned with their own conversation to pay any heed. You, however," he added, still gently, directing his glance at the elder of his two brothers, "ought to do so."

"Ought I, indeed?" Lord Ramsay's eyes were still twinkling, but both the twinkle and his smile faded when, after a brief silence, he looked questioningly from Hawk to Mollie and back again, the second time encountering a steady gaze with a hint of steel beneath it.

"You owe Aunt Biddy an apology for your hasty words, do you not?" Hawk said quietly.

Resentment flashed briefly in Lord Ramsay's eyes before he turned to do his brother's bidding, and Mollie was surprised to feel a similar resentment of her own at Hawk's interference. It was one thing for her to light into Ramsay, quite another for Hawk to do so. How dared he walk in as if he owned the place, and begin by asserting his authority over them all! Not that it was not all of a piece with what she had expected from him.

It was a moment before she realized how ridiculous her thoughts were. Hawk did own the place. He had every authority. Clearly, Ramsay had realized that fact more quickly than she had, for his apology to Lady Bridget was as graceful as anyone might wish, and there was not the slightest trace of resentment when he turned to warm his back at the fire afterward.

Harry had been regarding them all rather measuringly. Now he stepped forward. "You haven't said yet about Eton," he informed Hawk with studied casualness.

"You've scarcely given me a moment to consider it, bantling," Hawk replied reasonably. " 'Tis not the sort of decision to be made in the twinkling of a bedpost. I shall have to think about it."

"And talk to Uncle Andrew?"

"And talk to Uncle Andrew."

Harry gave a sigh of resignation that brought a smile to Hawk's lips. The boy eyed him speculatively. "Will you have to discuss with Uncle Andrew whether we can still go to London next week, also?"

Hawk lifted an eyebrow and glanced at Mollie. "You were planning to leave for town next week?"

"Yes, we were," she replied. " 'Tis the beginning of the Season, you know."

"Ah, yes, the Season."

Was she imagining it, or was there a flicker of meaning in the gray eyes as he regarded her? "We can postpone our departure if you wish it, sir," she said calmly.

"No, there is no need to do so. It suits my own plans admirably, I assure you."

The gentlemen retired soon after that to prepare for supper, which was served earlier in the country than it would be served once they reached London. Harry followed the others, knowing that his tutor would be awaiting his return to the schoolroom, and Mollie found herself alone with Lady Bridget and Lord Ramsay.

"Oh, my dears," said the elderly lady, "I was frantic when we heard he was coming and no one seemed to know where to find you. Wherever did you go?"

Mollie opened her mouth to speak, but Lord Ramsay beat her to it. "We merely went riding, Aunt Biddy. Nothing for you to be in a fidget about."

"Yes, but do you know, I am nearly always in a fret when you two are out and about together. Only remember how angry Thurston was used to become when you got into scrapes, which you very often did."

"Well, we are older now, and I, for one, am much better behaved," Lord Ramsay pointed out. "I apologized very nicely for joking you, did I not?"

"Indeed you did, though it wasn't necessary. I knew you were only funning. 'Tis simply that I begin to think of Thurston and how tragic and . . ."

Her voice trailed away, and with a speaking look at Ramsay, Mollie reached over to pat the smooth little hands folded neatly in Lady Bridget's lap.

"We know how it is, ma'am. Though I do think," she added a bit tartly, "that it was outside of enough for Hawk to go shoving his oar in when he can know nothing of the situation."

"Well," Ramsay admitted, "I felt that, too, for a moment, you know. Dashed awkward, ticking a fellow off in front of strangers like he did. Still and all—"

"Still and all, nothing," Mollie said. "He had no business to do such a thing to you, and so I shall tell him."

"Oh, no, my dearest one, you mustn't," Lady Bridget protested. "Only think how unbecoming. It will be difficult for all of us at first, you know, growing accustomed to having a master at Hawkstone again, but it is all for the best. Truly it is."

Mollie could not agree with her that their best course was simply to bow beneath Hawk's authority every time he chose to exert it. He had been away for four years, and she knew perfectly well that it would take time before he was ready to take the reins into his own hands entirely. Why, he didn't even know his new bailiff by sight. How could he possibly expect that the man would simply take his orders? But she also knew it would distress Lady Bridget to continue the conversation, so she changed the subject to a more acceptable one. And once they had all adjourned to the dining room for supper, she exerted herself to play the role of the proper lady again. It was not until after supper, when Ramsay had accompanied Sir James and another gentleman to the stables to be sure the horses had all been properly attended to, and several of the others were setting up for a game of whist with Lady Bridget as their fourth, that Mollie found herself having private conversation with her husband.

They were sitting on a little settee in the window embrasure where he had guided her as soon as the others suggested cards. "I feel as if I need to introduce myself to you," Hawk said with a smile.

"Maybe you do need to do something of the sort, sir," she replied. "You are by way of being a newcomer, are you not?"

"Well, hardly a newcomer," he countered, "but perhaps a prodigal son."

"And was the fatted calf to your liking, my lord?"

He grinned at her, and she found herself responding. "Everything has been as I expected it to be, Mollie. I knew I had left Hawkstone Towers in capable hands."

"I expect you are referring to Mr. Brewer, sir. He is no longer with us, however."

"No, Andrew wrote some time ago to inform me that you had hired a new bailiff. Troutbeck, his name is, I believe."

"Indeed, and he is an excellent man," Mollie replied, surprised that he was so casual about it. "Lord Andrew does not approve of him, though."

"No, I collect that he tried to put his nose in where it didn't belong, and your Troutbeck sent him off with a flea in his ear."

Mollie chuckled. "You don't mind?"

"Good Lord, no. The less we see of Andrew, the better I shall like it. Sanctimonious old hyprocrite was used to entertain himself by lecturing me upon the necessity for showing proper respect for one's father. He's one of the reasons I lit out for the Continent. If your Troutbeck has routed him, I have nothing but the greatest admiration for the fellow."

"Well, he hasn't routed him precisely, and he is not *my* Troutbeck, sir. Now that you are returned, at least."

"Ah, yes." He looked down into her eyes, and his own gaze was a searching one. "Perhaps you will tell me why my return has set you in such a tizzy, my lady?"

3

A silence fell between them, and Mollie could feel the warmth flooding her cheeks. She glanced at the cardplayers, all seriously intent upon their game. Still, this was not the place to discuss her peccadilloes. Forcing a smile to lips that were suddenly stiff, she returned Hawk's look as steadily as she could.

"Surely, you exaggerate, sir," she said.

"I don't think so." His gaze did not waver.

She swallowed, careful not to look away. " 'Tis merely that your arrival was unexpected, sir. You caught us unprepared. We are all a little nervous lest you not approve of some trifling thing or other."

"I have seen you watching me much the same way a robin watches a stalking cat, my lady, and over the years I have grown to be a tolerable judge of men. I know the members of the fair sex have certain idiosyncracies, but I am no mean judge of them, either."

"I am sure you are not." She could not help the touch of sarcasm, and the twinkle in his eyes did not surprise her.

"Just so," he said, "so don't try to gammon me, sweetheart."

She was sure the endearment fell cheaply from his lips, but she could not help the little glow of warmth it kindled within her. The feeling steadied her again, and she knew what she could say to him.

" 'Tis as I said before, sir, though it is difficult to make my meaning clear. You are but new to us, a stranger almost, yet a stranger with the power to control our lives. And you appear to be only too ready to exert your authority. Can you blame me for being wary?"

"I've no wish to interfere with your lives."

"But you do so without so much as giving it a thought, sir.

34

Only remember Harry pestering you to let him go to Eton. 'Tis your decision to make, though it should have been mine or Lady Bridget's. We raised him, after all.''

"Andrew should have made the arrangements last year," Hawk said, frowning slightly.

"There, you see, you do not even acknowledge that we might have had a say in the decision. Not that we did," she added. "Lord Andrew would not even consider it. Your father had opposed Harry's going for his own selfish reasons, but your uncle would have it that the boy is sickly and would suffer further ill health at school."

"Good Lord, Harry doesn't look sickly in the least."

"No more he is. Your father merely kept him about for his own entertainment. But he is growing to be too much of a handful for his tutor, so something must be done."

"Well, I can think of no good reason not to send him to Eton at Michaelmas. I'll look into it."

"Oh, thank you, sir." She had forgotten her resentment. "Harry *will* be pleased."

"Well, don't go telling him yet. I still want to speak to Andrew. There may be some other reason you know nothing about. And don't poker up like that," he warned her. "I daresay there are a number of things that neither my father nor my uncle saw fit to confide to you or Aunt Biddy."

"To mere females, you mean." Mollie's lip curled. "I'll have you know, sir, that were it not for Lady Bridget and myself—"

"I'd not have stick or stone to come home to. Is that not what you'd dearly love to say to me?"

It was precisely what she wanted to say to him, but she had recollected herself and knew it would be unwise to speak her mind so freely. She smiled at him.

"I hope I'd not say anything so uncivil. Lady Bridget said we must all allow ourselves time to adjust to your homecoming."

"Aunt Biddy is wise. But you are evading matters, sweetheart, Harry is not the reason you have been watching me so warily."

"No, sir. It . . . it is Ramsay."

"Ramsay!"

"Indeed, sir, you ought not to have ticked him off in front

of those other men," she said, plunging to the heart of the matter.

"Ticked him off, Mollie?"

She bit her lip. "Scolded him, sir. I find I have a habit of using the language I hear most often. Forgive me."

"Willingly. But did you not, ah, tick him off yourself in front of the same two gentlemen?"

"But I apologized for doing so, and it was not by way of being the same thing at all. I have no authority over him, sir."

She had spoken earnestly, and now she watched him, wondering if he had any comprehension of the point she was trying to make. He was silent for a moment, considering her words. Then he looked at her, a question in his eyes.

"There was a moment when I thought he resented what I said to him, but the moment passed so quickly that I decided I was mistaken. And I was scarcely harsh with him, Mollie. Moreover, no one else paid any heed to us, I assure you."

Mollie sighed. "Whether they heeded or not does not signify, my lord. 'Tis enough that they were present. And harsh or not, we are not recently accustomed to bowing before anyone's authority, least of all yours. So, of course Ramsay resented it, but he could scarcely tell you so to your head, especially . . ."

"Yes? Especially, what?" he prompted.

But she had herself in hand again and shook her head firmly. "No, my lord, it is not for me to say more. I should not have said so much."

"Nonsense. You may say what you like to me."

But she shook her head again, knowing she must not. She could not tell tales of Ramsay. He would, in his own good time, tell his brother that he had decided to skip a full term at Oxford in order to be a man about town. No doubt, after this afternoon, he would delay that confession as long as possible.

When she continued in her silence, Hawk gave a little sigh, but he did not press her. Instead, he turned the conversation to the estate, asking first rather general questions and then, as he became aware of the depth of her understanding, more specific ones. In this way the time passed quite amiably until the tea tray was brought in.

The cardplayers had finished their game and Ramsay and the others had long since returned from the stables. No one made much of an effort to stifle yawns, and although Ramsay glanced once or twice at his brother as though wondering if the time were right for private speech with him, he evidently decided against it, for he went upstairs with the other gentlemen as soon as the servants came to clear away the tea service.

Hawk bent to kiss his aunt on the forehead. "Going up, ma'am?"

"Indeed I am," she replied. "What a day this has been. Such a lovely surprise, my dear, having you home again. You have kept us in such a worry, you know, these past years."

"I am persuaded you would like very much to read me a scold for being so long away," he said, "but I hope you will not."

"Oh, no indeed, Gavin. I would not presume to do such a thing. A gentleman always knows his own mind best, after all. Not but what Andrew might not have something to say to you on that head, but you needn't pay him any mind, of course. Not anymore."

Hawk grinned at her. "You cannot know how relieved I am to hear you say so, ma'am, but why not?"

"Why, you are master of Hawkstone now," she replied simply. "What on earth could Andrew have to say to that?"

"Nothing at all, dear ma'am. Shall we go upstairs with you?"

"There is no need to do so, for here is my faithful Prentice, come to see why I am dawdling so. I have been raking, Prentice, but Lord Breckin and I won four guineas at whist, so it has not been for naught. Good night, dear ones. Gavin," she added, placing one plump, smooth hand upon his arm and giving it a squeeze, "I am so glad you have returned safely to us at last."

He kissed her again and then stood with Mollie, watching her go up the sweeping stairway with her dresser.

"Shall we go up, too, my lady?"

"If it please you, sir." Mollie's voice seemed to come from deep in her throat. She hoped he would merely see her to her door, say good night, and be on his way to the master's chamber, which had long since been prepared against his coming. She feared matters would not arrange themselves so comfortably as that, however, and could scarcely claim to a feeling of even the slightest surprise when he stopped her as she turned toward the second flight of stairs at the end of the gallery.

"My things have been put into my father's room."

"I know that, sir," she replied evenly. "My room, however, is still in its same place."

"Not tonight, Mollie."

She let out a small sigh of resignation, but gave it one last effort. "Please, my lord, I need time to accustom myself to your return. You have no right—"

"I have every right, sweetheart. You are my wife."

Her eyes flashed and she controlled her voice only with an effort. "So I am, my lord. Do you expect me to prove my gratitude for the fact by bedding with you once or twice every four years?"

She saw the muscles contract in his jaw and knew she had angered him, but the words had been said. She could not unsay them.

Hawk looked into her eyes, and his voice was tight, so his words surprised her that much more. "I deserved that, Mollie, and I no doubt deserve to hear a good deal more of the same, but I'll be damned if I'll listen to such stuff here in the gallery, where the world can overhear us." He placed a firm hand beneath her elbow. "We have much to discuss, you and I, and it is even possible that we might discuss some of it tonight. But whether we do or not, you are coming with me now. For, like it or not, you *are* my wife and will obey me when I wish to be obeyed."

She glared at him, but she knew she had lost. He was perfectly capable of carrying her if she refused to go with him peacefully. And it occurred to her as well that she ought not to fling her anger at him until she had discovered how much he had learned about her activities. She would not give in meekly, however. Head high, she placed her hand upon his forearm.

"Very well, my lord, if you insist. It is indeed your right. I should prefer time to prepare properly for bed, however."

"Never mind that," he retorted, his voice suddenly gruff. "I'll attend to any preparation you need."

Flushing deeply, Mollie realized her last hope that he might merely be taking her to his bed to sleep had just been swept away. His words made it clear that he meant to claim his full marital rights. Her hand trembled slightly on his arm, and Hawk looked down at her. Her face retained its unnatural color, and her lips were drawn tightly together.

Hawk patted her hand. "Don't be afraid, sweetheart. I'll be gentle."

Her gaze flickered upward. "I am not afraid, sir." She wasn't. He had, four years before, been a patient, considerate lover. So considerate, in fact, that he had scarcely touched her. On their wedding night he had dallied so long with her that she had been nearly ready to scream at him, to beg him to take her. Not that she had not been frightened at first, for she had been. She had known very little about the act of coupling. But with Hawk her fears had soon dissipated, and she had been fascinated by everything he had taught her. But he had been distressed when he had hurt her. It had been he who had insisted upon caution and patience, he who had insisted upon waiting until she had fully healed before indulging himself again in the delights of her body. Those had been his words, but Mollie had doubted him and wondered what she had done to displease him. His insistence upon departing for the Peninsula soon afterward had only reaffirmed her doubts. She wondered why, after so long away from something he had not been enthusiastic about to begin with, he was so anxious to bed her now.

Nevertheless, even before they reached the huge master's suite, her body had begun to respond to him. She could feel her blood stirring, feel the tiny hairs at the back of her neck tingling, the tips of her breasts pressing against the fabric of her gown. Even her toes seemed to want to curl in her satin slippers, and there was a stirring between her legs as well. Before he had shut the door, closing them into the candlelit room with its cheerful fire, its heavy, carved furniture and dark, ornate wall hangings, and the huge, beckoning bed, her knees had weakened and her nose and cheeks felt numb.

Mollie raised a hand to one cheek as Hawk watched her.

"What is it, sweetheart?" She told him, and he chuckled low in his throat. "You are breathing too fast and not deeply enough. Take a slow, deep breath." It was more difficult than it sounded, but she managed to obey him. Then he put his hand upon her shoulder, and she nearly gasped again, stiffening a little when he urged her closer.

"You . . . you said you wished to talk," she reminded him.

"Later."

She looked up then, and there could be no mistaking the desire in his eyes. Whatever he may or may not have felt for her four years before, he wanted her now, and that wanting set vibrations throbbing between them that were nearly tactile. Hawk grasped her other shoulder, and then, roughly, he pulled her to him, his lips crushing hers as he gave full rein to his rapidly increasing passions. Mollie gave a low moan and strained toward him, reaching to entwine her arms around his waist.

At the sound Hawk relaxed his grip and lifted his head, drawing in a steadying breath. "Ah, sweetheart," he murmured, "forgive me. I am a hasty brute."

Looking up at him, her fingers clutching at his firm, muscular waist, Mollie protested. "Don't stop," she begged. "Please, don't stop now."

Hawk's eyes began to twinkle, and he scooped her into his arms. "I won't stop, Mollie, but I never intended this to be a rape, and if I don't exert a bit of control, that's exactly what it will be. Come to bed first, sweetheart."

He carried her over to the massive four-poster bed, with its huge carved tester, and sat down, still holding her gently in his arms. This time when his lips touched hers, there was a gentleness, a tenderness that hadn't been there before, but his kiss stirred her just as much as it had before. And when the pressure increased, when she felt the tip of his tongue against her lips, Mollie responded without hesitation, parting her soft lips and letting her tongue dart to meet his, teasing him, knowing instinctively that her actions were stirring his passions to greater heights than ever.

As he proceeded to undress her, fumblingly at first and then more easily when she helped him, she found herself delighting in the control he tried to exert over himself. Mischievously, she had an urge to see if she could make him abandon that control. As soon as her chemise drifted to the floor, leaving her naked in his arms, she moved her hands caressingly across his chest to the lacings of his shirt.

" 'Tis not fair that I be so vulnerable to your touch, my lord," she whispered.

"Go slowly, Mollie," he warned. "We've the entire night before us."

"Have we, indeed, sir? I saw you yawning with the others."

She slipped her hand inside his shirt, enjoying the feel of the soft, springy hair of his broad chest against the sensitive skin of her palm.

She heard him catch his breath as her fingers encountered one rising nipple. So, she thought, she could excite him with her touch just as easily as he excited her with his. She smiled at him. But to her astonishment he pulled her hand away and dumped her off his lap onto the bed.

" 'Tis not sleep that will overcome me, sweetheart, if you intend to play that game," he said with a chuckle, standing to shed his clothes. "You've changed, Mollie."

She wasn't sure what he meant, but she was suddenly extremely conscious of her own nakedness, and though she was fascinated, she didn't want to stare at him while he undressed, so she scrambled under the thick, eiderdown quilt before she answered him.

"I haven't changed, sir. I have merely grown up a little, I think. I have thought often about you, you see, so . . ." She faltered, not really certain she wanted to continue, to tell him of her fantasies in the long, lonely nights since he had gone. But he seemed to understand. The look in his eyes was a warm one when he joined her beneath the quilt, gathering her once more into his arms.

"I know, sweetheart. I thought of you, too. But my memory played me false. I'd forgotten how beautiful you are. Or perhaps you have grown more beautiful in my absence. And I'd swear your skin is softer, your hair more silky. The air of Kent seems to have agreed with you, Mollie."

He had been caressing her while he talked, and Mollie found herself incapable now of coherent speech. His hands roamed everywhere, and her body responded instantly to his lightest touch. Then his lips followed where his fingers and hands had gone before, while his hands began to guide hers, urging her to explore his body to her heart's content.

Only once, just before he reclaimed her as his own, did it occur to Mollie to wonder why she had allowed herself to submit to him so easily. But then he was inside her, and it didn't matter anymore. She lifted her body to welcome him, finding that the initial awkwardness in their rhythm soon faded, letting them move in harmony until the world seemed to explode within her. She was conscious then of a small sense of irritation when he did not stop. Instead, he moved faster and faster until she thought she could tolerate no more. But then the feeling inside altered again, and she didn't want him to stop. She felt herself climbing higher and higher. He made a sound deep in his throat, halfway between a moan and a groan, and then it was over. The tension drained from his body, and he collapsed on top of her.

"Oh, Mollie," he said softly.

Mollie sighed. But when he rolled off her and plumped the pillows up behind himself, she smiled at him. And when he seemed to draw pleasure from looking at her slim body, rosy now from exertion, she made no move to draw the quilt up again. Hawk pulled her into his arms, and she nestled there, content. Perhaps his return would not make difficulties, after all. She certainly had not expected their first private interview to be like this.

The thought brought a niggle of doubt with it, however. Perhaps he had merely wanted to assuage his lust before getting down to more serious matters. To be sure, it had not seemed that way at the time, but how could she possibly trust her own judgment when she had so clearly let her passions run away with her good sense. Was it possible that she had submitted without the briefest of protests in order merely to please him, hoping that her submissive attitude would mitigate his displeasure later? She stiffened slightly. Surely not. Surely she was not such a coward as that.

Hawk looked down at her, his brow furrowing a little when he saw her expression. He reached down with his free hand and pulled the quilt up, covering them to the waist. Then he gave her a little hug.

"Why the frown, Mollie? I didn't hurt you, did I? I was careful."

She looked up from under her thick, dusky lashes, touched by his concern. "No," she said, low, "you didn't hurt me. I liked the things you made me feel."

"Did you? You didn't like them four years ago."

"That's not quite true," she said slowly. "I think perhaps I was a little afraid of the feelings then. I was so young and I didn't know what to expect, you see."

"But you know now?" His voice had hardened noticeably, and she swallowed carefully before answering him, knowing that she walked a thin line.

"I believe I know what you are thinking, sir, and that is

not what I meant at all. 'Tis only that I am a deal older now,
and I have learned much more about the ways of the world.
Then, too, you had magic in your hands tonight,'' she added,
smiling. "I felt no fear, only desire."

His fingers played lightly along her forearm, and she could
feel him relax beside her, but she could not let the subject drop
entirely. Not without discovering what things he had been
told and what he meant to do about them. Not for a moment
could she make herself believe he had heard nothing. The
silence lengthened until she could stand it no longer.

"Sir?"

"I have a name, sweetheart."

"I know you do, but 'tis so long since I last used it that it
sits strangely upon my tongue."

"You haven't referred to me by name in four years?" He
was indignant.

She grinned at him, enjoying this interlude, hoping his
mood would not alter too drastically after she had said all she
had to say. "I called you Hawk," she told him, "like your
father did, and like Ramsay and Harry. Only Lady Bridget
calls you by your Christian name, and she does not do so
except when you are with her. She is more likely to call you
Hawkstone, you know."

"Well, I should like to hear you say my name, but I shan't
press you. And I didn't mean to turn the subject. I feel certain
you've a number of things you'd like to discuss with me."

Mollie swallowed again, this time with more dififculty.
What had he meant by that? Did he expect her to enumerate
each incident and beg his forgiveness for each slip, each step
she had taken beyond the line of propriety. She'd be damned
if she would!

She glanced up at him. He was staring straight ahead,
waiting. His lips were pressed tightly together, as though it
was only by exerting an effort that he was able to let her have
her say first.

"It was not so bad as all that, Gavin," she found herself
saying defensively.

He looked down at her, his expression making it clear that
her words were not the ones he had expected to hear.

"What was not so bad?" He seemed to choose his own
words carefully.

"Whatever it is you think I have done. Whatever it is they

wrote you about." She went on in a rush before he could reply, "I know I should not have done some of the things I did, but truly they were not so dreadful; and while it is not the fairest thing in the world that Lady Margaret Hazeldell or the Marchioness of Hawkstone can get away with things that would be condemned out of hand in a Miss Nobody, still that is the way of the world, and I see no reason not to take advantage of the fact when the alternative means living like a recluse."

"What things?"

The words brought her up short. "Why, whatever Lady Andrew and the others wrote you," she said more hesitantly, confused by the fact that he seemed not to know what she was talking about. "I know they must have written, for they were forever reading me lectures and saying it was their duty to inform you, but please, sir, I am quite certain they exaggerated everything out of . . . of . . ."

"Out of spite," he finished for her. "Good Lord, Mollie, you don't think I believed that fustian. I don't give a tinker's damn for anything Aunt Trixie or the others might tell me. I know you better than that. When I said you'd changed, I didn't mean anything like that, just that you seemed more relaxed, more sure of yourself. You're still the same serene, ladylike wife I left behind. Certainly, too much a lady to risk cuckolding your husband before the succession is secured."

Her eyes flashed at the implication in his words, but she knew well that he still had little notion of how much truth there had been in some of the things his aunts had written.

"Of course I would never do such a thing," she said finally, through gritted teeth, "but . . . but there were things that were not quite . . . well, that went beyond the line of being pleasing."

"Pleasing to whom? My aunts?" He shook his head when she opened her mouth to explain. "Never mind. Perhaps there were things you are not proud of, Mollie, but I have no intention of cross-questioning or laying blame. My behavior these past years has not been entirely unexceptionable, either. I confess, I had thought you meant to make that the subject of this conversation." The smile in his eyes was a rueful one.

"You thought I meant to take *you* to task over *your* behavior?"

"Is it so odd that I might believe you would be angry?"

She gazed at him thoughtfully. "I was angry when you left. And hurt, too. I thought I'd been nothing more than a challenge to you, that once you'd got me riveted, you simply went on to the next challenge, that you didn't care a pig's whisper about me."

He sighed. "I was a pretty frippery fellow, sweetheart, but not quite so frippery as that."

"Then, why?"

"Why did I go?" She nodded. "Many reasons. I was too young to know better. I wanted to get out from under my father's thumb. The excitement of military life called to me. And there were other things."

"With me?"

"With you." He looked down at her. "Did you ever know my mother?"

"No, but I've heard a deal about her from your father and from Ramsay. She was ill a great deal, and I think your father had a rather poor opinion of her. Ramsay seems to have had a fondness for her, but he loves Lady Bridget more."

Hawk grimaced. "She suffered a great deal with my father. I was afraid I might be like him." Shaking his head, he pulled her closer to him. "There is too much here to try to explain all at once, but I know now that I am no reflection of Thurston Colporter. That part of the fear is gone. There are still shadows of other fears, but one at least seems to have had little foundation in fact."

"What's that?"

"That you would still be so angry that you wouldn't even talk to me. I think that is a large part of why I have put off coming home for so long. I made every campaign, every least reason, an excuse for delay. I'm sorry now that I didn't have the courage to face you before now."

"Why did you come now, my lord?" she asked, trying to digest the things he was telling her. A fearful Hawk was the last thing she had expected. It put a different light on things. He still hadn't answered her, and she had the feeling that he didn't want to answer her. She lifted an eyebrow, questioning his reticence.

"I was ordered home," he said at last, reluctantly. "Wellington said it was time I attended to my duties and quit playing soldier with the other lads. He said I ought to have come home when Father died, and he is right. But the guilt just grew and grew, Mollie. I was ashamed of myself for giving in to fears that now seem like the most childish of motivations. Can you understand? Does what I'm saying make the least bit of sense to you?''

His gaze was penetrating, and she knew her answer was important to him. It gave her a sense of power she hadn't felt with him before. Hawk was vulnerable. But she had no wish to take advantage of the fact. She smiled softly. ''I don't know that I understand it fully,'' she said, ''but I'll try.''

He bent to kiss her. ''We'll both try, sweetheart. I think perhaps we have a chance to make something of this marriage of ours, don't you?''

4

When Mollie awoke the next morning, she was alone in the huge bed. The curtains had been opened and a small fire crackled in the stone fireplace. Sunshine streamed in through the two tall, narrow windows, laying golden rivers of light across the dark Turkey carpet covering the cold stone floor. Stretching lazily, she wondered where Hawk had gone.

Ordinarily, Cathe brought Mollie her morning chocolate at half-past seven. Surely, she thought, it was later than that by now! She glanced around the room, looking for a clock. There was none. Well, no matter, she decided. She wanted her breakfast, and she wanted her clothes. The ones she had taken off the night before were no longer lying on the floor where she had left them. Unless she wished to wear one of Hawk's shirts, she would have to ring for someone. The bellcord hung beside the bed. After a pause during which she wondered who would respond to her ring, she tugged firmly on the cord. Then, just in case, she pulled the eiderdown up to her chin.

But it was Cathe who entered a few moments later, carrying a tray bearing a pot of hot chocolate and fluffy Scottish scones with honey and marmalade. Mollie sniffed appreciatively, and Cathe grinned at her.

"Good morning, m'lady. 'Tis a fine spring day."

"What time is it, if you please?"

"Why, 'tis gone nine, m'lady, but the master said we was t' leave ye be. Said the sleep would do ye good, 'e did."

"Did he now?" Mollie murmured with a smile as she shifted the tray more comfortably across her lap.

Cathe plumped the pillows behind her. "Aye," she said, "and 'e said ye wasn't t' bother yer 'ead about Mr. Troutbeck, neither."

"Mr. Troutbeck! Oh, good Lord. I told him I'd meet with him at half-past nine. Get my clothes, Cathe."

"But the master said—"

"Hang the master! Get my clothes!"

Cathe fled and Mollie shoved the tray away, flinging the coverlet over it in her haste. Without a thought for her nakedness, she hastened to the washstand and splashed cold water on her face, drying herself with the slightly damp towel hanging on a nearby hook. His towel. And his brushes and combs on the dressing table. She snatched up one of the brushes and tried to drag it through her long curls. How could she have forgotten about her meeting with Troutbeck? There were a number of details to be discussed and arrangements to be made before she left for London. For one thing, the road to the valley floor from the lake was a mess after the heavy rains. A party of men must be sent out this very day to begin repairs, or every bone in their bodies would be shaken when they traveled over it by carriage next week. As it was, the men would barely have time to repair the deepest ruts and the worst of the chuckholes.

The oblong brush was too large for her hand and she could not manage it easily enough to bring any order to her tangled hair. If only he had allowed her to prepare properly for bed! Normally, she plaited her hair before retiring, which made it much easier to manage in the morning. His combs weren't much better. Fine-toothed, they only became enmeshed in the snarls. Flinging them back onto the dressing table, she turned impatiently when Cathe entered.

"My hair is a mess. It will take forever to put it right."

Cathe grinned at her but said nothing, merely handing her a clean chemise and moving to lay a lilac sprigged round gown across the bedclothes.

"Don't put it there," Mollie warned. "The tray's still there somewhere."

Obediently Cathe put the dress on the chair back and then pulled the quilt forward. "Oh, m'lady, ye've gone and got chocolate and 'oney all over the quilt. And this cover only just washed yesterday."

Guilty color flooded Mollie's cheeks, and with a rueful smile she said she was sorry. "I was in a rush and didn't think, Cathe. You'll just have to see that the quilt cover's washed again."

"Yes, m'lady, and we'll 'ave to 'ope the chocolate don't stain it and 'asn't gone through to the down," Cathe replied.

"But I expect Mrs. Bracegirdle will know 'ow to turn the trick. She be right deedy about such stuff."

Mollie agreed that the housekeeper was indeed a treasure, then pointed out that she was waiting for her gown, and Cathe, after removing the tray to a safer location, hastened to assist her. The simple gown was quickly fastened up the back, and the narrow muslin sash was tied becomingly under Mollie's left breast. Her hair took as long as she had feared it would to comb into a braided twist at the nape of her neck, but at last she was ready. Instead of slippers or sandals, she wore a pair of sturdy leather half-boots, so she scarcely noticed the cobblestones underfoot when, having run down the back stairs and through the rear hall, she hastened across the stableyard to the estate office. The little bitch, Mandy, followed her excitedly across the yard, coming to a panting halt on the stoop.

Mollie pushed open the door into the cluttered little office, talking as she hurried inside. "I'm dreadfully sorry to be late, but here I am at last, so—" She broke off as the two men on opposite sides of the paper-strewn desk came hastily to their feet.

"My lady!" exclaimed the round-faced little man behind the desk, straightening his dun-colored jacket over a round little paunch and pushing his wire-rimmed spectacles higher up the bridge of his button nose.

"Good morning, sweetheart. I trust you slept well."

She glared at Hawk, remembering only as he spoke that Cathe had said he meant to see Troutbeck. She had been too concerned about her own appointment with the bailiff to think much about anything else.

"Good morning, Hawkstone," she said formally. "I see you have made yourself known to Mr. Troutbeck. I am sure there are a great many questions you will wish to ask him about the estates, but I trust you will not object if we attend to some trifling matters of business first."

"Not at all," Hawk replied politely, glancing quickly around the tiny office, then pushing his own chair toward her. "Sit here, my lady. You will not mind if I remain. I should like to know what is taking place here in future. The reports I've received have been few and far between to put the matter lightly. The result of the war, no doubt."

"No, sir," Mollie answered frankly. "You rarely responded

to anything I wrote, except when I informed you of Mr. Brewer's reluctance to authorize funds for refurbishing Lady Bridget's rooms. On that occasion you addressed your reply to him, so I assumed thereafter that when you wished to know about something you would correspond directly with your bailiff.''

She saw his jaw tighten, but she was angry herself and didn't care. When she continued to glare at him, he met the look steadily and with a hint of ice in his gaze. ''I should no doubt have been more responsive when you wrote about such things as having the causeway repaired or a new field planted. However, things were a trifle heated at my end at the time, and it sounded as if you had matters well in hand here, so I did not. I did, however, expect you to request my bailiff to send me regular reports.'' He glanced at the uncomfortable Mr. Troutbeck.

''Well, don't blame him,'' Mollie retorted. ''Very likely I would have requested such a thing had I chanced to think you would be interested, or if you had ever asked for such reports. But you did not, and I, too, was busy, sir, just trying to keep up with what needed doing and trying to keep poor Lady Bridget from going into a decline.'' She stopped, warned by his sudden frown that she had gone too far. She ought not to be discussing Lady Bridget in front of Mr. Troutbeck. It occurred to her then that she had no business to be scolding Hawk in front of his bailiff either. ''I . . . there was a great deal to be done,'' she ended lamely.

''I don't doubt it,'' Hawk said quietly. He still held the chair for her. ''We should not be discussing issues from the past, however. I believe you said there were a number of things you wished to talk over with Troutbeck.''

Feeling a little less confident, Mollie glanced at Hawk searchingly, but she saw nothing in his expression to tell her if he was still angry. He ought to be, she thought. Any man would be whose wife had just ripped up at him like a shrew. Not that he hadn't had it coming, of course. Still, he hadn't merited such a dressing in front of a man who until that morning had been a total stranger to him. However, an apology now would only make matters worse. She took the chair he offered her, then glanced at him again over her shoulder.

''Should you not be attending to your guests, sir?''

''They left for London earlier this morning,'' he said,

boosting himself back onto a side table piled with ledgers, account books, and other such paraphernalia. "My time is yours, my lady."

She turned pointedly to the expressionless bailiff. "First of all, Mr. Troutbeck, we must make arrangements to repair the road."

"Yes, my lady," the round little man agreed, casting a glance at Hawk. "His lordship sent out a work party first thing this morning to attend to the matter. And to examine both causeways for any sign of damage as well," he added.

Mollie retained her businesslike air with difficulty. "Good," she said. "No doubt, after traveling that road only yesterday, his lordship would assume it to be our most pressing business. However, the young trees in the north orchard must be checked as well. Their roots are not yet very deep, and what with the heavy winds and all—"

"Indeed, my lady, his lordship . . ." Mr. Troutbeck's high-pitched voice trailed off unhappily, and Mollie glanced over her shoulder to find her husband regarding her with a touch of amusement in his eyes.

"I rode across to look at the orchard myself when I saw the others on their way," he said. "There were two trees at the upper end that looked a bit wobbly at the knees, so I sent a man to stake them when I came back."

"But we planted that orchard only two years ago," Mollie said, eyes narrowing. "How did you even know it was there?"

Ramsay mentioned it at supper yesterday. Said he'd meant to have a look at it but had gotten sidetracked by business in Gill's Green early in the day. Didn't say what business, of course, but I daresay I could hazard a guess," he added with a grin. "If it wasn't a bearbaiting or a cockfight, I'd warrant it was a mill. Seems to me we heard rumors to the effect that there was one hereabouts somewhere."

Mollie could feel the telltale color creeping into her cheeks, and to cover her confusion, she turned sharply back to the bailiff. "Is there anything you have not already discussed with his lordship?"

More unhappily yet, Mr. Troutbeck shook his head. "Nothing urgent, my lady. There are still a number of details we will want to discuss, of course. Things that have happened, changes that have been made in his absence. But as to storm damage, I think we've pretty well attended to that. I might add, ma'am, that I sent a lad yesterday as soon as the rain stopped, to have a look at that young orchard. He said the trees were fine. If his lordship hadn't checked again today, we might have lost two of them."

"Not the lad's fault," Hawk said. "Takes a while to assess damage like that. The water soaks in and makes the ground like so much mush. But it is the wind that does the real damage. Have someone take a look every day until the ground dries out."

"Yes, my lord."

"Mr. Troutbeck, there are still a number of arrangements to be made before I leave for London," Mollie said with a hint of desperation in her voice.

"Indeed, my lady, his lordship and I were just discussing them when you came in. Teams will be taken on ahead, so that you will have your own horses for the entire trip. His lordship means to stable his own cattle on the Croydon and Hastings roads henceforth. Naturally, orders have already been given to open the London house, but his lordship informs me that we have a slight problem in that Bracegirdle and his missus would prefer to remain here at Hawkstone this year."

She looked again at Hawk, and he nodded. "I asked her at breakfast, and she said if it was all the same to me, they'd just as soon stay. Seems they haven't had a vacation in a good many years, and Bracegirdle has been feeling his rheumatism. She recommended Mary Perfect, the head chambermaid, to take her place, and she thinks Ned Lofting will do for a butler. He's been acting as underbutler, she says, and has done well enough that Bracegirdle would not be shamed to entrust us to his care. Or, if you prefer," he added tactfully, "we can interview for a new housekeeper and butler when we reach London."

The prospect was an appalling one. "No, no," Mollie said, "Lofting and Perfect will do very well." Nevertheless, the wind had gone out of her sails. Not only had he attended to everything she had meant to do herself—and would have done the day before, had she not chosen to play truant with Ramsay instead—but he had learned more about her household than she had known herself. It had never once occurred to her to *ask* the Bracegirdles if they wanted to go to London. She had merely assumed that they would go.

"Is there anything else, my lady?" Mr. Troutbeck asked diffidently, interrupting her thoughts.

She gazed at him blankly for a moment, then gathered her dignity. "I think not at the moment," she said. "If I should think of anything further, I shall let you know."

"Good enough," Hawk said, getting down from his perch on the side table. "In that event, Troutbeck can continue instructing me. I know you have things to attend to in the house, my lady, so I shall bid you adieu for now. I should like a small bite of something at one o'clock. I know I can depend upon you to arrange it."

"We keep country hours here, my lord, as you ought to remember," she retorted. "Dinner will be served at two o'clock, which is the time Lady Bridget prefers it to be served."

He bowed, and a moment later, seething, Molly found herself back in the stableyard. The shaggy little bitch had apparently been waiting for her, curled up on the stoop. She rose now and stretched, and Mollie bent down to pat her.

"Good Mandy. Would you like to go back inside now?" But the little dog stayed where she was when her mistress began to walk back across the yard. Mollie snapped her fingers. "Come, Mandy." Mandy curled back into a ball on the stoop in front of the office door, tucking her little black nose into her bushy tail. Mollie sighed. "First Troutbeck, now you," she muttered, turning on her heel.

Ramsay was seated at his ease, reading a newspaper, his booted feet stretched out before the crackling fire in the rear hall. He looked up when she entered.

"I say, Moll, is Hawk still cooped up with old Troutbeck?"

"He is." Her tone was bitter.

"What's amiss?" He folded his paper in his lap.

"Oh, nothing," she replied, moving to warm her hands. "He's merely taking over everything, that's all."

"But it is his duty to do so," Ramsay protested. "He ought to have done so last year when Father died."

She sighed. "Perhaps that's what's amiss. He ought to have come back, but he did not. Instead, he left it all to me to manage. And now he comes back—not because he wanted to, mind you, but because Lord Wellington ordered it—and he just takes over without so much as a by-your-leave."

Ramsay opened his mouth and shut it again, giving thought

to her words. "He hasn't behaved very tactfully," he said a moment later, "but perhaps he does not realize how involved you are with the management of this place. Most men, you know, would assume their bailiff handled everything in their absence. I doubt Hawk even realizes you routed Mr. Brewer last year after he refused to give you the money for Aunt Biddy's new curtains. But can't Troutbeck tell him everything he needs to know, Mollie? Seems a most capable fellow to me."

She nodded. Mr. Troutbeck was very efficient. She knew she had been extraordinarily lucky to find him when old Mr. Brewer had announced his intention to retire after the matter of Lady Bridget's redecorating had been settled. But she *had* found Mr. Troutbeck, and she had likewise convinced the crusty Mr. Brewer to stay on long enough to train him. Troutbeck could run the place now, with or without her, but he knew perfectly well that she liked to know about everything that went on. He was her retainer, and she felt betrayed by the fact that he had so readily confided in Hawk without at least waiting for her to join them. She tried to explain her feelings to Ramsay without sounding like a child or an idiot, but she could not feel that she had succeeded very well, because for once he seemed unable to comprehend her point of view.

Indeed, he was more taken up with his own concerns. After some moments of halfheartedly attempting to make her understand that Hawk was not usurping her powers but merely asserting his rightful authority, Ramsay asked hesitantly if she had chanced to mention his intention to spend the Season in London with them.

"For he hasn't said a word, you know, not even to ask why I'm not at school now."

"Well, I haven't told him, though Harry may have done so," Mollie replied.

"He hasn't. Told me that whatever I thought of him, he wasn't in the habit of carrying tales."

Mollie smiled. "I hope you begged his pardon for doubting him yesterday. You ought to have known he'd never betray me to anyone—and certainly not to Hawk, whom he scarcely remembers."

"So he told me when I did beg his pardon. Top-lofty little beggar had the nerve to look down his nose at me as if he had to decide whether or not he'd *accept* my apology. Say what you will, Mollie, that brat *needs* a term or two at Eton. They'll soon teach him proper respect for his elders!''

She chuckled, her usual good humor restored, and sat down to chat with him for a few moments before getting on with her normal duties. They discussed the advisability of mentioning Ramsay's decision to Hawk at once and came to the conclusion that perhaps the moment was not the most propitious one. In any event, the matter was taken out of their hands some hours later at the dining table when Ramsay asked Hawk if he'd like to ride with him to look over the cut through the western ridge, which led into East Sussex, through Cross-in Hand, to the Eastbourne highroad.

''You won't want to drive all the way to Hurst Green and up the Hastings Road unless it is absolutely necessary,'' the younger man pointed out.

''An excellent notion,'' Hawk agreed approvingly as he helped himself from a platter of carved mutton. He passed a boat of mint sauce to Lady Bridget, on his right, then turned back to his brother. ''By the bye, I have hesitated to ask while others were about, but I never find you alone. Have you been rusticated?''

''Oh, no,'' Ramsay answered carelessly, flicking a glance at Mollie, ''nothing like that.'' He turned to accept a dish of boiled squash from the serving maid, and a small silence fell. Lady Bridget seemed preoccupied with her serviette, and Mollie was glad Harry was dining with Mr. Bates in the schoolroom.

''Perhaps you will elucidate,'' Hawk prompted gently.

''Oh, well, I had meant to discuss the matter with you, of course, since you are here,'' Ramsay replied, still carefully offhand, ''which is one reason I suggested riding to the cut.''

''The matter is one of some delicacy, then?'' Hawk's eyebrows lifted, and Ramsay moved a little awkwardly in his chair.

Mollie couldn't stand it any longer. ''You are making a great piece of work about nothing, the pair of you,'' she said tartly. ''Ramsay has merely decided that the time has come for him to acquire a touch of town bronze, sir. He came down when the half ended, and he does not intend to return until Michaelmas term begins.''

''I see,'' Hawk said, looking at his brother. Ramsay met

the look, but there was a trace of guilt in his eyes, and wariness, too. "You don't think that perhaps you have been a trifle hasty?"

"You cannot send him back now," Mollie put in. "The term is two weeks gone. Moreover, I see nothing wrong with his decision. Perhaps you will say that since the long vacation begins the first week of June this year, that will be soon enough for him to see a bit of London, but it is not, sir. He is quite old enough to have an entire Season—yes, and to go to Brighton with us in August as well. Two or three weeks in June would not answer the purpose at all."

"What purpose is that? Do you wish to find him a bride, my dear? I feel sure he is too young for that."

"Oh, yes," interjected Lady Bridget hastily. "Indeed, he is, Mollie, for a gentleman, you know, must have time to learn about the world before he takes on a wife."

"Exactly so," Mollie agreed, "and he can learn a great deal in London."

"You don't think he ought to finish his education first?" Hawk asked her.

With a light gesture Mollie waved aside the benefits of an Oxford education. "There is nothing he cannot learn later when he returns at Michaelmas," she said grandly.

"Then there is nothing further to be said," Hawk replied. "When do you wish to ride, Ramsay?"

Astonished to think his brother meant to make no further comment on the issue, Ramsay stammered out that he would be ready as soon as they had finished their meal. Conversation turned to other matters after that, and Mollie was left to her own thoughts.

She had seen Ramsay look at her oddly when she had taken up the cudgels in his defense, and she knew he was remembering that she had raised a good many objections to his decision only two weeks before when he had turned up at the castle. But that had been different, she told herself. Besides, the matter had been decided before Hawk ever put his foot over the threshold. It occurred to her that her husband had given in rather easily, and she wondered if perhaps he meant to say more to Ramsay during their ride. However, there was nothing she could do to stop him if that was his intent, so she turned her thoughts to the list of things still left to be accomplished before the family could leave for London.

When she went upstairs after the meal, she found Cathe carrying clothes out of her bedchamber. "What on earth! Where are you taking all this lot?"

" 'Is lordship said to move your things to the room next to 'is, m'lady. 'Tis the old mistress's suite, and 'e says it be more convenient for ye, now 'e be in the master's rooms."

"Oh, he did, did he? And I suppose I've nothing to say in the matter." But she could scarcely order Cathe to ignore Hawk's direct command, and he had already departed with Ramsay, so she spent the next two hours helping to arrange her belongings in the new rooms. The time passed quickly, and at five o'clock Mollie drew a hand across her brow and realized she was hot, sweaty, and tired. She had spent nearly the entire afternoon sifting through her wardrobe, taking the opportunity to select those things that needed mending and those that could be discarded. Now she gave a long sigh.

"I've got to go for a walk, Cathe, before I begin snapping. I don't want to look at another gown." The girl only grinned at her, so Mollie grabbed up a light shawl and flung it over her shoulders before hurrying down the back stairs, through the postern gate to the causeway. She saw a horseman approaching and recognized Hawk at once. He was alone. Wondering where Ramsay had gotten to, she raised her hand to wave. But he was not watching her. Suddenly, he stopped and slid out of the saddle, dropping the rein to the ground. Leaning over the low wall edging the causeway, he soon stood up again, dragging a wriggling, dripping Harry from the lake water. Mollie started to smile, then realized that Hawk's intention, at the very least, was to give the boy a good shaking. Grabbing her shawl firmly in one hand, she started to run toward them.

"Stop that!" she cried. "Leave him alone!"

Hawk glanced up at her, then turned to face her with Harry still firmly in his grasp. "Does he make a habit of swimming off the causeway alone?" he demanded when she was near enough so that he didn't have to shout.

"He is an excellent swimmer," she said defensively. "He has swum off this causeway since he was quite small."

"Alone?" Hawk repeated, his gaze direct.

Mollie looked away. "He is an excellent swimmer," she repeated. "I see no reason for you to be so cross with him."

Harry was standing silently beside his brother. He looked

now from one adult to the other, and when Hawk turned that steely gaze upon him, the boy bore up well under it.

"Well, Harry, do you make it a habit to swim here alone?"

There was a small silence. Hawk waited. Finally, Harry blinked and said, "No, sir. I am supposed to have someone with me. I just didn't think about it this afternoon, because I meant just to jump in and out again, and I thought it wouldn't matter just this once. Only then it felt good, and I just stayed. I won't do it again."

"Did Mollie make the rule?"

Harry shifted his feet, then glanced apologetically at Mollie. "Yes, sir."

"Very well, Harry. Go up and get dry clothes on now. And don't ever let me catch you doing such a foolish thing again unless you want to feel my hand where it will do the most good."

"Yes, sir. I-I mean, no, sir!" And Harry fled, clearly grateful at having gotten away so easily.

Mollie looked at her husband. "All right, so he's not supposed to swim alone. It just made me angry to see you shaking him."

"I meant to do more than shake him," Hawk told her. "Swimming alone is a dangerous thing, Mollie, and I've a strong notion this isn't the first time. That boy wants a stronger hand, but at least he's got integrity. You've taught him that much."

"There's nothing wrong with Harry," she said firmly.

"No," he agreed. "Nothing that a little maturity won't cure. Will you walk with me?"

She nodded, and picking up the dangling reins, he walked beside her to the stableyard. His groom was waiting. Hawk told the man to let Lord Ramsay's Bill know that his lordship would be along directly.

"He stopped off to speak to Haycock," Hawk told Mollie. "Seems he'd said he wanted to go hunting for poachers tonight. I discouraged it."

"Oh, good," Mollie said without thinking. "I knew he had hoped to do so, but I couldn't help thinking it would prove to be a dangerous business."

"Just so. Mollie, why do you persist in fighting me?" he asked as he held open the door into the rear hall.

"I don't persist," she muttered, not looking at him. "You just take too much upon yourself too soon."

He was silent, but his hand was at her waist, and she made no objection when he guided her to the stairway. Then Hawk said, "You were angry this morning when you found me with Troutbeck. Why?"

They had started up the stairs, and she held her skirt, concentrating upon the steps in front of her, feeling the resentment rising again even as he spoke. "You should have spoken with me first," she said, and the fact that the words sounded petulant in her own ears did nothing to assuage her temper.

"I thought you would rather sleep. Can Troutbeck not tell me all that I need to know?"

"That's not the point."

They had reached the gallery, and they turned toward the master's suite. "Is it not important that I learn as much as I can, as quickly as I can? Hawkstone is my birthright, after all."

"So it is, my lord," she said, her anger increasing, "but that does not give you the right to treat it like some toy, tossing it aside when it bores you, then snatching it back when someone else is playing with it."

"I haven't!"

"You have!" She pulled away from him, turning to face him, hands on her hips. "You have done just as you pleased, sir, while the people you left behind till the whim struck you to return—ah, no, till you were *ordered* to return—well, those people's feelings ought not to be trodden upon by you so callously now! You have condemned Ramsay's behavior, my behavior, and now poor Harry's. You come home and just think you can take over everything as though you'd never—"

"Enough, Mollie!" Hawk snapped. Then, when he realized Cathe was standing upon the threshold of Mollie's new bedchamber, staring openmouthed at them, he controlled himself with a visible effort. Pushing open the door to the sitting room that connected the two bedchambers, he looked sternly down at his wife. "Step inside, madam."

5

Casting a glance at the fascinated Cathe, Mollie lifted her chin and swept past her husband. She heard the door snap shut behind her.

"By God, Mollie," Hawk said furiously, "you'd be well served after that little display if I put you straight across my knee."

"You'd not dare," she snapped back, conscious of a devout hope that she was right as she turned to face him.

"Wouldn't I?" He stayed near the door, his big hands firmly at his sides. "You can have no notion of how tempting the thought is, or you'd be doing your best to pacify me." Her chin rose a fraction higher, and he took a deep breath. When he spoke again, his tone was more even. "Do you think I don't know how you feel? I've been well nigh wallowing in guilt, believing I deserved your anger. I was wrong to stay away so long. I know that. But it's done. It's over. And I've come home, where I belong. I let you tear a strip off me in Troutbeck's office, and I let you have your say about Ramsay, and even about Harry. That boy knew what he deserved as well as I did, but I let him off to please you." He paused, taking a step toward her. "I want to please you, Mollie. Truly, I do. But I've been so conscious of my guilt and so worried about your anger that in a day's time I've nearly lost sight of who I am. If I continue bowing and scraping to your every wish, trying to make amends for the past, I soon won't be able to stomach the sight of myself in the glass when I shave."

"But you don't—"

"Hush," he said, gently now. Moving forward, he placed both hands lightly on her shoulders. "You were right about one thing, and that is that we must give ourselves time. We can't expect our world to right itself in a day or a week. If I had strutted in here and demanded sweeping changes, I'd have set up everyone's back. But I haven't done that, and I don't intend to. Nonetheless, you might as well acknowledge, to yourself at least, that if I did intend such a course, it would be well within my rights."

Mollie wished he would take his hands away, because the feeling of them, warm upon her shoulders, was making it hard for her to think properly. There were so many things she wanted to say to him, so many things that had built up inside her, but they seemed tangled all together in her mind, and when she looked up at him, wanting to speak, she could think of nothing at all to say. She remembered, instead, the look on Cathe's face as she stood there watching them. Somehow, she thought, there always seemed to be an audience.

"I shouldn't have shouted at you in the gallery," she said finally. "Not with Cathe standing there."

"A proper wife," he retorted with mock sternness, "does not shout at her husband at all."

"You made me angry," she said simply.

"I know," he replied, "and I shall no doubt do so again, particularly if you insist upon denying my authority. Don't shut me out, Mollie."

"I don't—"

He put two fingers over her lips, silencing her. "You do. It is as much my fault as anyone's, for you've had no one to look to but your efficient Mr. Troutbeck. Yet you've kept this place running smoothly.

"Only since your father died."

Hawk smiled. "You must take me for a nodcock if you think I'll swallow that whisker. You've been managing things here a good deal longer than that. His death merely gave you the freedom to do so openly. His death and Brewer's departure, that is."

Mollie bit her lower lip and stared at his waistcoat buttons. "That was one time when you were very helpful, my lord."

He chuckled. "Nevertheless, you were annoyed with me for writing to Brewer directly."

"I wanted to know what you wrote, and he refused to show me."

"Can't say I blame him for that. I was a trifle severe with the old gentleman." Hawk's hands tightened on her shoulders, and the look in his eyes grew more intent. "Look here,

Mollie, can't we put this business all behind us? We'll be leaving for London soon and putting things here in Troutbeck's care, anyway.''

"But even in London you will want to rule the roast, sir, and I have been used to doing as I please."

There was a small silence, and Mollie stared harder at those waistcoat buttons when she realized how the words might be interpreted.

Hawk gave her a little shake. "I have business of my own in London, sweetheart, so I daresay I won't interfere as much as you seem to think. If it is money you're concerned about, I've no intention of drawing the purse strings tight. I shall enjoy seeing my lovely wife cut a dash."

Mollie took a deep breath then and looked up into his eyes. The warmth she encountered there was encouraging. "I wasn't afraid you would cut me off," she said, "only that it might not be so much easier for us there as you think it will be. I know you have the right to do the things you do, and I can see now that you don't mean to ride roughshod over us. But I can't help it when my feelings just fly out and express themselves."

"Will you try?"

She nodded, still looking into his eyes. He smiled and she had the feeling that she had pleased him. A sense of contentment washed over her suddenly and she put her arms around him. "I'm glad you've come back," she said.

He drew her close in a hug that seemed destined to crush the breath from her. "I, too," he said quietly against her curls.

His arms relaxed, but he didn't let her go, and Mollie had no wish to move away. She felt his hand lightly caressing her back, and it felt good. The silence between them felt good, too. She didn't want the moment to end. But at last Hawk's hands came to her shoulders again, and he stepped back, smiling down at her.

"I promised Ramsay a game of chess before supper," he said. "Shall I send a message instead, telling him to go to the devil?"

She shook her head, blushing a little at the thought that he would like to stay with her. "I must change my gown, sir. I'm all over dirt from——" The thought of how she had gotten mussed brought with it a niggling of her earlier resentment, and though she managed to stop herself from saying anything, her eyes glinted when she looked at him.

His smile was rueful. "Do you like your new rooms?"

She opened her mouth, closed it again, then sighed. "They are very nice rooms."

"And they are the rooms that rightfully should belong to the Marchioness of Hawkstone." He paused, waiting until Mollie nodded, whereupon he added gently, "But I should have consulted with you before I ordered Cathe to move your things."

She glanced up at him hesitantly. "I did think it was the least you ought to have done," she admitted.

"The very least," he agreed, kissing her forehead gently. "I, too, must learn to take matters slowly. Forgive me?"

She smiled then, her spirits rallying. "I shall certainly forgive you this time, sir. But I warn you to have a care in future. I've no intention of dwindling into the sort of milksop wife who never shouts at her husband."

Hawk chuckled. "We'll just see about that." He turned her toward the door to her own bedchamber and gave her a light smack on the backside to speed her on her way. "Now, you go change, and I shall do likewise before I teach that young fellow below how to play chess."

"I hope he beats you soundly," Mollie said, laughing as she went into her new bedchamber.

It really was a far nicer room than her old one. Still smiling, she remembered how angry she had been before. He had stirred her temper easily, she thought, and other emotions as well. Quickly, she washed and changed her clothes.

When she went downstairs later, Ramsay and Hawk were hunched in silent concentration over the chessboard, and Harry lay sprawled on the hearth rug, watching the fire, with Mandy curled up at his side. The boy glanced up when Mollie entered, then got to his feet and came to meet her, his eyes wide and apologetic.

"Mollie, I'm sorry," he said quietly.

She ruffled his light-brown curls. "It's all right, Harry."

"Was he angry with you? You shouldn't have tried to protect me, you know. Not after all the times you've threatened to snatch me bald-headed if I went alone."

She grinned at him. "He knows I care about you," she said, "but you didn't pay me much heed before today, did you?'' Harry looked at his feet, and she added gently, ''I daresay you won't be quite so haphazard about obeying your brother.''

He looked up again, grimacing expressively. ''I should think not. He scared the liver and lights out of me when he hauled me out like that. I hadn't even seen him coming! I can tell you, I'd by far rather have Ramsay angry with me than Hawk. I say, Mollie, Hawk's a bang-up fellow, isn't he?''

''He certainly is, Harry,'' she agreed, chuckling.

Lady Bridget entered some moments later, and the gentlemen finished their game. The conversation became more general in the dining room, and the rest of the evening passed quickly and pleasantly.

The following morning Mollie awoke in Hawk's bed to find him gone again. Cathe was just entering with her chocolate tray.

''Good morning, m'lady. 'Tis nigh onto eight o'clock, but the master insisted ye'd not wish t' be wakened earlier.''

''That's all right, Cathe,'' Mollie assured her, stretching. ''Now that he's here, I don't have nearly so much to do every day. An extra half hour's sleep is most welcome.''

''Ye'll be wanting more than that once we reach London, m'lady. I 'ear the grand folks be out the 'ole night long during that Season they speak so much about.'' It was to be Cathe's first trip, and she was increasingly excited as the day of departure drew nearer.

''I sometimes sleep till noon,'' Mollie confessed. ''There are nights when we go to five or six different entertainments. 'Tis a most exhausting business.''

''It must be a wondrous thing, surely,'' Cathe said.

''You'll see,'' Mollie promised.

She took her time over her chocolate, then dressed at a rather more leisurely pace than was her wont. It was nearly ten o'clock before she went downstairs, to find Lady Bridget working at her secretary. The elderly lady looked up, peering at Mollie over a pair of round, wire-rimmed spectacles.

''Oh, there you are, my love,'' she said. ''I have just been writing to Gwen to let her know we mean to be in Grosvenor Square on Monday. She and Worthing don't intend to leave for town until the eighth, I believe. Have you any message you wish me to include?''

''Just tell her we look forward to seeing her,'' Mollie said.

She liked Lady Gwendolyn Worthing. Hawk's sister was some few years older than Mollie, but she was an amiable person, always ready to share wickedly amusing gossip, and Mollie would indeed be glad to see her.

Lady Bridget agreed to include her message, and Mollie went in search of other tasks to attend to. Though she found many, by noon she was restless, wanting to get out into the sunshine. On any other day, she might have used the feeling as an excuse to ride out to inspect a field or an orchard, or perhaps to visit tenants and listen to their complaints. But after her discussion with Hawk the day before, she knew those activities would be frowned upon unless she talked to him first. And he was cooped up with Troutbeck again, determined to learn all he could before they left Kent.

Finally, with a widening smile, Mollie slipped back up to her bedchamber, and after a hasty search through the French garderobe that took up most of the gallery wall, she found what she was looking for. Quickly stripping off her dress, she changed into a pair of buckskin breeches, a white shirt with lacing and a soft collar, dragged a pair of leather top boots on over thick wool stockings, and then, snatching up a leather waistcoat, slipped back downstairs and out to the stables.

Her groom saw her coming and hurried to greet her, a broad grin on his weathered face. "Where ye headed this fine day, m'lady?"

"Fetch Baron, Teddy. And send one of the lads for my bow and quiver. I've a mind to practice a bit."

"Want I should come along, me lady?"

"No, I'm going no farther than the butt we set up in the south-shore meadow. I'll come to no harm."

A few moments later, her quiver and bow slung across her back, Mollie cantered across the causeway and along the lake trail to the south shore, where some years earlier she and Ramsay had set up a target range. At first he had been by far the better shot, but Mollie had practiced diligently, and as time passed, her skills had first equaled and then surpassed his. Now, she could beat him easily. At distances of under one hundred yards, she was a better shot even than Haycock, whom many believed to be the best man with a long bow in seven counties.

Sliding down from the saddle, Mollie twisted Baron's reins around the low branch of a tree. He had learned to stand with his reins grounded, but he had a tendency after a while to graze and eventually to tread upon the dangling rein. After three broken reins, Mollie had ceased to leave him for longer than a moment or two without tieing his rein properly.

She ran to look at the straw-filled butt with the target circles painted on its canvas face. There were five rings. The outermost was white, then blue, green, red, and gold. The paint was faded, and the cover itself was thin and needed replacing. Making a mental note to have it attended to while they were in London, she straightened the butt, which had been blown a little askew by the heavy winds. Then she paced off the yards and took up a position at a distance that was, for her, point-blank range.

First she removed her riding gloves and replaced them with the soft, well-fitting kid gloves she kept in her quiver. She had put on her long-sleeved leather waistcoat before leaving the stable. It, too, fit her snugly, and the sleeves would protect her soft inner forearm from the bowstring. Stringing her bow was a matter of but a few seconds' work, so it was not long before she was nocking her first arrow to the string. With a motion swift and sure, she drew back and let fly.

It had been some time since she had last practiced, so she was not astonished when the arrow settled low in the red circle. She nocked the second arrow. Again, the movement was swift, graceful, and confident. And this time the arrow went straight and true to the gold. Mollie let out a little sigh of satisfaction. She finished the round, then gathered up her arrows and paced off another ten yards.

Now she would be shooting by point of aim, so it was necessary first to send a practice shot to the target, aiming above where she aimed point-blank. Her first shot landed high, in the blue. She corrected, and once again her second shot was in the gold, a little higher than she would have liked it to be, but nevertheless in the gold. She continued with the round, and when she nocked her last arrow, eight of its brothers were clustered in the gold. Two had struck the red. Mollie drew the bowstring swiftly to her cheek and let fly. Gold again. She let out a long breath.

"Well done!"

Startled, Mollie whirled to see Hawk leaning against a tree watching her. She smiled at him. "I was restless, so I decided to try my skill. It has been a while, as you can see."

"Good Lord," he said, chuckling. "I see a veritable Diana, sweetheart." He let his gaze drift from her plaited hair to her leather top boots. "Do you often leave the castle in such apparel?"

Stricken, she looked down at herself. She had forgotten he knew nothing about her unconventional clothing. Everyone else was pretty well accustomed to it, although she made it a practice to keep out of Lady Bridget's way when she was so attired. Lady Bridget did not approve, and Mollie had no wish to distress her. But now she looked warily at her husband, wondering what he would make of her breeches.

"Skirts get in my way when I shoot," she said.

"I see." A smile teased the corners of his lips. "Under the circumstances, I think I prefer that only one of us shall wear the breeches in this family."

"Must I take them off, sir?"

"Not here, you mustn't," he replied hastily. "But I prefer you in skirts, my lady. Or without skirts. But without breeches altogether."

She gazed at him speculatively. "I have said I would make every effort not to flout your authority, sir. But I truly prefer breeches to skirts when I am shooting. Would you be opposed to a small wager?"

"What sort of wager?" he asked, amusement in his eyes.

"Why, purely a sporting sort," she assured him. "If I can outshoot you, I get to keep my breeches. If I cannot, I'll shoot in skirts hereafter."

Hawk cocked his head, his amusement deepening. "Perhaps no one has told you, but I am accounted to have a deft hand with a bow."

"I have heard, sir. But we've only the one bow, which will give me the advantage, for I am accustomed to it, while you are not."

"A lady's bow is not my fancy," he admitted, "but I daresay I can adjust to it rapidly enough."

Indignation lit a spark in her eyes. "This is not a lady's bow, sir. It has a fifty-pound draw. Haycock made it for me."

With drawing respect, Hawk glanced at the target, where her arrows still lodged, one in the blue, two in the red, and the other nine in the gold. "Let me see that bow," he commanded, holding out his hand. She gave it to him, and he tested it lightly, then held it out and drew the bowstring to his cheek. He did not attempt to hold it there, nor did he let it snap. He merely relaxed, turning to face her. "How shall we determine the winner, and what point advantage must I cede to you?"

"No advantage, sir."

"Nonsense. I am quite willing to give you ten points, Mollie. I haven't had a bow in my hand for a month or two, but if you will allow me two shots to find my point of aim at thirty yards, a ten-point advantage will soon disappear, I promise you."

"If, at the end of this contest, you still wish to award me ten points extra, I shall accept them, sir. But I will not begin with an advantage merely because you are so foolish as to doubt my skill. We shall each shoot six arrows from thirty, then forty, then fifty yards. The one with the highest score at the end of the third round shall be the winner. Fair enough?"

"More than fair," he said, a little grim now.

"Will two shots be sufficient to find your point of aim?" she asked sweetly. The only response being a sound more akin to a grunt than to human speech, she grinned to herself and went to collect her arrows.

Hawk took one from her, nocked it to the bowstring, drew swiftly, and let fly. The arrow lodged to the right in the red. His second shot also landed in the red, but it was much closer to the gold. Mollie's eyebrows lifted slightly. Not bad for a man who hadn't handled a bow in several months. He strode forward, pulled the arrows loose, then walked back to her.

"Shoot," he said, handing her the bow. "We'll each shoot two arrows at a time."

Obediently, she took the bow from him and let fly her first two arrows. To her quiet delight both struck gold. Hawk's first lodged near one of hers, but the second was a hairs-breadth inside the red circle. His jaw tightened a little. By the end of the round, Mollie was three points ahead. Her first shot from forty yards landed near the outer edge of the red circle, however.

"Damn," she muttered. She heard a low chuckle beside her.

"I know grown men who would be glad to hit that mark from such a distance," Hawk said.

"I do not generally shoot so wide," she retorted. "Your

presence is making me nervous for some reason. Or fear that
I might lose my breeches. I did not think you would be so
good." He only chuckled again, and she turned back to the
target, taking a moment to steady her concentration. Then,
nocking her arrow, she lifted the bow, drew, and released as
she exhaled. The second arrow sped straight to the center of
the gold. She handed the bow to Hawk.

When they moved back to fifty yards, Mollie was still
three points ahead, but once again her first shot struck red.
Though her second went true, when Hawk's first shot sped to
the gold, she grimaced, barely refraining from stamping her
foot. But he had already nocked his second arrow and she
didn't dare make the slightest noise. It, too, struck gold. The
match was now dead even, and it stayed that way until they
each had only two arrows left to shoot. Mollie took the bow
from Hawk, nocked her first, and sped it on its way. It went
true. Breathing a little easier, she nocked the second. When
it, too, lodged in the center circle, she handed the bow to her
husband.

Hawk's first arrow landed beside Mollie's. She gritted her
teeth. A tie would be as good as a loss to her, for had she not
said she would put off her breeches for good if she did not
win? Hawk's last arrow thumped into the target. He let out a
long breath, and Mollie swore.

"I won't take your ten points, either, damn you," she
said. He flicked a glance at her, his lips drawn together.

"I thought your eye was better than that," he said.

"What do you mean?"

"That last shot of mine is out."

As they drew nearer the target, she could see that he was
right. The arrow had lodged in the target at an angle. From a
distance it had looked to be in the gold, but it was not. It was
on the line between the two colors instead. Mollie chuckled.
"Perhaps I will accept your ten points after all," she said
sweetly.

"We'll have no gloating if you please," Hawk said, grinning back at her. "A wife who wears pants is enough punishment for any man."

"Well, you shoot better than I expected," she confessed.
"I was afraid for a moment or two that I should have to give
them up."

"You needn't. I make good my wagers, though I'd take it

kindly if you would refrain from coming here alone after this. You may keep your breeches, but next time you come out to practice, bring your groom." He turned away, striding toward the butt to collect their arrows, leaving Mollie to stare after him, half-amused, half-angry. Her first inclination was to point out to him that he was dictating to her again, but she thought better of it. It was well within his power to forbid her coming to the meadow at all. Besides, she had won a victory, and it was no small victory at that. She suspected that it went much against the pluck with him to give in to her so gracefully, especially since he had clearly thought he was merely humoring her.

Chuckling a little to herself, she followed him and took the arrows as he handed them to her to replace in her quiver. Then, when she would have turned toward the horses, he stopped her with a hand on her shoulder.

She looked up at him, puzzled. "Sir?"

"Don't go yet, sweetheart."

"Was there something more you wished to say to me? You never said why you came after me."

"I merely grew weary of accounts and crop yields and wished for pleasanter diversion. Your groom said you were here." His voice had lowered, and there was an intimate note in it now that brought warmth to her cheeks. Her eyelashes fluttered a little, as though she would look away from him, but his hand cupped her chin. "Have you any notion what the sight of you in that outfit does to a man?" he asked gently.

"It has never seemed to disturb your brothers," she replied, deeply conscious once again of the way his voice and touch stirred her blood.

"They both regard you as a sister," he pointed out. "I am glad, however, that neither Jamie nor Breck has been privileged to see you so attired. And I confess it does not please me overmuch that you appear this way before servants and stableboys."

"You won't change your mind?" Her eyes widened now at the thought that he might.

"No," he said, pulling her closer. "I'm a man of my word, sweetheart. But I cannot deny that I'm glad we'll be in London soon, where you won't be tempted to dress as anything but the beautiful young woman you are."

"Well, I might grow bored in London, too," she teased,

resting her cheek against his broad chest. "And there are butts in Hyde Park, you know."

He gave her a shake. "Not for the likes of you, there aren't. And I warn you, Mollie, it will be much the worse for you if I find—" He broke off, glaring, when he realized she was gazing up at him in wide-eyed innocence. "You little minx, you're merely trying to find how far you can push me, aren't you?"

"Well, you do have a tendency to come over dominating at the shake of a straw in the wind, sir, for all you think you're the reasonable, fair-minded sort."

"I *am* a reasonable man."

"Only until your will is crossed," she said, twinkling. "You will coerce me shamefully, sir."

"Then it would behoove you to see that my will is seldom crossed," he replied, smiling again.

Mollie shook her head, and her mouth turned down at the corners. "I foresee difficulties ahead."

Hawk captured her chin again and tilted her face up. "Not if you begin as you mean to go on," he said gently, lowering his lips to hers. His kisses were light ones at first, moving from her lips to her cheek, her eyes, the tip of her little nose, and then back to her lips again. But then, as the pace of her breathing began to increase, his touch became more demanding, more urgent. His tongue probed between her lips, and when hers darted to meet it, his hands slid to the buttons of her leather waistcoat and then to the lacing of the soft cotton shirt. Within moments her smooth, firm young breasts were bared to his touch. His fingers skimmed across their tips before his hand moved beneath the right one as though to test its weight.

Mollie stood on tiptoe, her hands moving across his chest, her passions leaping to respond to his every desire. Within moments, he had lowered her to the soft grass of the meadow, and his lips had moved from her mouth to her breasts, his fingers to the fastening of her breeches. For some moments she gave herself up completely to pleasure, but it soon became difficult to keep her mind on the business at hand. Suddenly, irrepressibly, she chuckled. Hawk lifted his head, looking at her curiously.

"My lord," she said, grinning at him, "I've no objection to your choice of activity, but this location leaves something

to be desired. Two days of sunshine have not been sufficient
to dry this meadow. In truth, sir, my buckskins are already
damp, and I shall soon be soaking wet!''

He grinned back. ''I see no difficulty. We'll simply return
to the comforts of my bedchamber, where we will bring this
delightful interlude to its proper conclusion.''

''In broad daylight?''

''We'll draw the curtains.''

''But the servants will think we're addled!''

''Nonsense. The servants will be envious.''

Mollie chuckled. ''I begin to agree that the sooner we
reach London, the better, sir. At least there you will be
forced to behave in a civilized fashion.'' But she made no
further demur when he pulled her to her feet and began, most
solicitously, to help her fasten her clothing.

6

London was gray and dismal when they arrived in Grosvenor
Square after a tedious, day-long journey, but Mollie was
nonetheless more than usually grateful to see the tall, elegant
town house. Hawk and Lord Ramsay had ridden, but Harry,
occupying the forward seat in solitary splendor, had chattered
incessantly about all the sights he expected to see once they
reached the metropolis. Between his excitement and Lady
Bridget's idle conversation, Mollie had soon been heartily
bored and had found herself wishing that she might have been
born a gentleman just so that she could ride alongside the
carriage with the others.

She had no wish to dampen Harry's enthusiasm or to
offend gentle Lady Bridget, however, so she exerted herself
to attend to them. At the second change, which was made in
East Grinstead, she greeted Hawk's invitation to take Harry
up behind him with mixed emotions. Though grateful for the
respite, she was conscious of a strong wish that it could be
she, rather than Harry, who scrambled up to ride pillion
behind the broad-shouldered marquess.

But now they were in London at last, and Harry could be
turned over to his tutor, traveling with Hawk's and Lord
Ramsay's men in the third carriage, behind Cathe, Mathilde
du Bois, and Lady Bridget's Prentice in the second. The
spacious Hawkstone House entryway was warm and inviting.
Ned Lofting, having traveled up from Kent with Mary Perfect
the previous Friday, was there to greet them, impeccably
attired in a long-tailed gray coat, well-pressed knee breeches,
and a neatly tied cravat. Leaving the butler and his minions to
attend to the baggage coach, the gentlemen went upstairs to
change out of their riding dress, and Mollie and Lady Bridget
retired to the first-floor drawing room, having first given
orders that tea should be served to them there at once.

Mollie was amused to hear that since *Mrs.* Perfect had foreseen the request, tea would be immediately forthcoming. Mary Perfect was not married, but her elevation to the post of housekeeper had evidently made the change of title a necessary one—in her eye, at least. The housekeeper came herself to be certain their tea was all it should be.

She was a tall, slender, middle-aged woman with light-brown hair brushed severely off her forehead and confined in a neat coil at the nape of her neck. Her eyes were hazel, and her complexion unlined, despite her years. In black bombazine with just the smallest hint of a ruffle at collar and cuff, she presented the picture of efficiency. Her firm expression softened slightly when Lady Bridget complimented her on the appearance of the house.

"There was little enough to do when I arrived, my lady," she said in her clear voice. "The town staff is very competent. I trust everything is to your satisfaction."

Detecting an anxious note beneath the calmly spoken words, Mollie smiled. "We have every confidence in you, Perfect. The Bracegirdles would not have recommended Lofting or you, had they not believed you both completely capable."

"Thank you, my lady."

The door opened just then, and Lofting entered. "Begging your pardon, m'lady," he said, "but Lady Andrew is below and wishes to know if you and her ladyship are at home."

"Oh, for heaven's—"

"Oh, dear," said Lady Bridget in the same breath.

Lofting controlled his features admirably, but it clearly required an effort, and Mollie grinned at him. "I suppose you couldn't simply tell her we've not arrived yet?"

"Mollie . . . dearest," protested Lady Bridget in feeble accents.

"The baggage be scattered all over the hall, m'lady," said the butler apologetically.

"And she would never believe we'd sent it on ahead," Mollie sighed. "Very well, where have you put her?"

"In the main saloon, m'lady. She went in there herself. Just said she knew you was here and would want to see her."

"Takes a deal for granted, does she not?" Mollie muttered. Then, seeing Lady Bridget's shocked expression, she smiled. "Don't fret, ma'am, I shan't deny her. I suppose you'd better

bring her up, Ned, but first send a man to inform the master
of her arrival.''

''I sent Michael up immediate, ma'am, thinking if you
wasn't wishful to, perhaps the master would handle matters.''

"Very well," Mollie told him, slightly nettled that he had
sent for Hawk before coming to her. But she controlled her
irritation, recognizing it for what it was. She and her husband
had continued in charity with each other for some days now.
It was a state she enjoyed, and she had no wish to allow her
own, admittedly often foolish little resentments to upset their
good relationship.

"I dislike meeting Beatrix in all my dirt," said Lady
Bridget fretfully.

"Don't bother your head about it, ma'am. It may prove to
be a blessing in disguise. We can always tell her that, much
as we enjoy her company, we simply must retire to refresh
ourselves after so long and tiresome a journey. She detests
traveling, you know, and so is very likely to believe us."

Lady Bridget brightened considerably and was able to greet
Lady Andrew's sweeping entrance some moments later with
all her natural graciousness. A tall woman, Lady Andrew
Colporter carried herself with all the regal hauteur of a queen.
Her salt-and-pepper hair was skillfully arranged in coils and
twists atop her head, and her blue cambresine walking dress
had been cut by a master hand. The dress was trimmed with
sable, and she carried a large, matching muff over one hand.
Her grande-dame attitude and the way she paused on the
threshold when Lofting announced her almost brought Mollie
to her feet as she had been trained to do as a child. Repress-
ing the urge, not without a certain amount of pleasure, she
greeted Hawk's sharp-faced aunt with a nod as regal as the
one returned to her and invited Lady Andrew to take a seat
and join them in a dish of bohea. There were moments, she
reflected as the older woman passed her to sit near Lady
Bridget, when being a marchioness was truly stimulating.

It had been said of Lord Andrew Colporter's wife by those
who liked her least that marriage into the Colporter family
had caused instant amnesia with regard to her antecedents.
Lady Andrew never made mention of her own family, though
Mollie knew she was a Wantage and therefore sprang from
perfectly respectable roots. Nevertheless, Lady Andrew seemed
to have put her family behind her, and when she spoke of

"the family," she referred, as everyone knew, to the Colporters. Indeed, Mollie believed that Lady Andrew was a good deal more conscious of what was due "the name" and Hawk's position than Hawk was himself.

"Merciful heavens, Biddy!" Lady Andrew said as soon as the amenities were over and Lady Bridget had handed her a cup of tea, "I certainly hope you mean to furbish yourself up before you go into company. Your hair and that gown are sadly out of date!"

"Really, Beatrix," Mollie said sweetly before Lady Bridget could gather her wits to reply to the stricture, "it is scarcely fair of you to descend upon us the moment we arrive and declare our appearances outdated. We have, as you well know, been on the road all day. And considering that neither of us has been cutting a dash for a good year or more, it is outside of enough to condemn our lack of à-la-modality."

"I'm sure I never meant to criticize," replied Lady Andrew, looking down her nose. "However, I for one do not consider mourning an excuse to fall into disrepair, Margaret. And I notice, moreover, that your hair is becomingly styled. Not, of course, that you will dare pretend a lack of social activity on your own part this past year. You have not behaved, as I have mentioned on several occasions, in a manner befitting a Colporter. One can only hope, my dear girl, now that Hawkstone is safely returned to us, he will see that you do nothing further to disgrace the family name."

"Beatrix, you ought not to speak of things you can know nothing about," Lady Bridget said, rallying with unaccustomed vigor to defend Mollie.

"I know a good deal more than you might suspect," Lady Andrew told her ominously. Then, as the door opened, she looked up and smiled with something more nearly resembling warmth. "Hawkstone, how good to see you. We were just speaking of you, my lord."

Dressed now in the dark-blue coat and cream-colored breeches that were normal daily attire for a London gentleman, Hawk strolled forward, lifting his eyeglass to peer first at his guest, then at his wife, whose cheeks were red with anger, and lastly at Lady Bridget, whose pale-blue eyes sparkled with indignation. Lowering the glass, he returned his gaze to Lady Andrew, a smile just touching his lips. "How do you do, Aunt Trixie? Been setting the cat among the pigeons already, have you?''

She set down her cup and pulled off her gloves. ''I have merely been telling Mollie that it is too long since you have been among us, Hawkstone, that it is time and more you took up your proper role as head of the family.''

''Have you, indeed?'' His tone was gentle.

''We must all be glad to have him home again, Beatrix,'' Lady Bridget said pacifically, regaining her composure now that Hawk had come into the room.

''Yes, well, 'tis time and more that he gathered the reins, as I was only this very morning telling Andrew. As your aunt, Hawkstone, and one who cares for the good name of this family, I do not scruple to tell you that you have shirked your responsibilities most shockingly. I have no wish to say more on that head, however.''

''Do you not?'' The gray eyes were chilly now.

''Indeed, it is of little use to poker up like that with me, young man,'' she informed him. ''Though I daresay you like hearing criticism as little as your misguided wife does—''

''Have a care, Aunt,'' Hawk warned.

''Yes, well, I'm sure I mean no offense, Gavin, but I believe in plain speaking. No one has ever yet accused me of beating about the bush when there was something unpleasant to be said. However, I shall say nothing further about Margaret's behavior, for no one is more certain than I that with you at home again, we shall have no further cause to blush for her. However, I take the liberty of hoping that you will take immediate steps, if you have not already done so, to find a sterner man to deal with Henry!''

''What has Harry got to do with anything?'' Hawk asked, genuinely bewildered.

''Yes, well, I thought as much,'' Lady Andrew stated, casting an accusatory look at Mollie. ''I told Andrew precisely how it would be if he did not take it upon himself to write you an account of the whole. But he said there would be time and more to discuss little Henry upon your return. I daresay they've been filling your head with rubbishing nonsense about sending the boy to school!''

''I fail to see what concern that matter is of yours,'' Hawk said, his lips thinning as his heavy brows drew together.

'' 'Tis simply that I knew no one else would tell you how

abominably he behaves," she said righteously. "They all cosset and spoil him to death, but I suppose I know my duty better than that. He's no more business to be sent off to school, where his behavior will disgrace the family name, than . . . than . . . well, he oughtn't to be, and that's all I shall say," she ended, faltering at last as the glint in Hawk's eyes became undeniably glacial.

"Are you sure you wouldn't like to tell me more, Aunt?" His tone was not in the least encouraging, and a small, leaden silence followed his invitation.

Then, with a self-conscious laugh, Lady Andrew said, "Well, to be sure, I never meant anyone to take offense." She reached for her cup and took a small sip, then looked up brightly and said in a tone she might have used to comment upon the weather, "I daresay you have all heard by now about the dreadful attack on Queen Charlotte, have you not?"

As a diversionary tactic it was entirely successful. Lady Bridget uttered a cry of dismay. Mollie quite forgot her indignation, and even Hawk's expression changed almost ludicrously to one of astonishment. He lifted his glass again and peered at his aunt.

"We certainly had not heard," he said. "Where did you come by such a tale?"

"Why, 'tis all over town," she insisted. "Surely, your servants know. I am surprised your man didn't tell you, Hawkstone."

"We don't encourage our servants to gossip," Hawk said repressively, then spoiled the effect entirely, eliciting a choke from his irrepressible wife, by adding, "Besides, like us, Mawson has only just arrived."

Mollie stifled the bubble of mirth and returned her attention to Lady Andrew, for once finding herself interested in something the woman had to say. "Tell us," she invited.

"Yes, well, it happened only yesterday. Her poor majesty was awakened out of a sound sleep at five o'clock in the morning by the assistant mistress of the robes, who was shrieking and screaming at her from just outside her bedchamber door about some imagined wrong or other."

"How frightening," Lady Bridget said.

"Whatever possessed the woman?" asked Mollie.

"No one knows for certain, though Miss Davenport—for such is the unfortunate young woman's name—was born and

raised in the queen's palace. Her mother was rocker to the
infant princesses, and in consequence, Miss Davenport became
inordinately fond of the Princess Amelia. It is thought that her
mind was unhinged by the princess's death. They believed she
had recovered, though she is still subject to fits of melancholy.
Nevertheless, it was deemed safe for her to return to her
old rooms in the tower above the queen's bedchamber.''

"Clearly an error in judgment," Hawk observed dryly.

"Yes, well, it took a page, two footmen, and a porter to
subdue her," said Lady Andrew, ''and that only after she had
smashed through the outer door to the queen's chamber and
was endeavoring to force the inner door. Then Dr. Willis,
who was in attendance upon the king, was sent for, and Miss
Davenport was got into a straightjacket!''

"Merciful heavens!" exclaimed Lady Bridget.

"Poor woman," said Mollie sympathetically, but though
she spoke of Miss Davenport, Lady Andrew assumed she
meant the queen and replied accordingly.

"Yes, well, you may well say so. I have it on good
authority that her majesty was so overcome by fright that she
actually sent for the Regent!''

As Mollie, and indeed everyone else in England knew,
there was no love lost between Queen Charlotte and her
eldest son. If she had sent for him, clearly she had been
frightened out of her wits.

"What became of poor Miss Davenport?" Mollie asked.

"Oh, they packed her off to a private lunatic asylum. I
daresay she'll be well enough cared for." Lady Andrew dismissed Miss Davenport. "I only hope this don't spoil the grand
dinner his highness is giving at Carlton House tomorrow in
her majesty's honor. You mean to attend, do you not?''

Mollie opened her mouth to deny any such intention, but to
her astonishment Hawk nodded. "We are. And if I know her
majesty, she will recover her nerves quickly enough. There is
nothing she delights in more than an entertainment devised
solely to honor herself.''

Lady Andrew took her leave a short time later, and even
Hawk breathed a sigh of relief.

"That woman!" Mollie muttered between her teeth. Then,
realizing she had spoken aloud, she looked up at her husband
guiltily. "I'm sorry, sir, but I cannot like your aunt.''

He winked. "You've no need to apologize for showing the

good sense to dislike her. A thoroughly detestable woman in my opinion. What on earth did Harry do to set up her back?''

Mollie looked quickly at Lady Bridget, and when she saw the pale eyes begin to twinkle, she allowed herself a gurgle of laughter. ''I'm afraid your abominable brother smeared honey in her best bonnet the last time she paid us a visit at Hawkstone. Lady Andrew had set it to one side in order to enjoy a dish of tea before they took their departure, and Harry—''

''Say no more,'' Hawk said with a chuckle. ''I'll wager I can paint the full scene for myself. She didn't chance to notice before she put on the bonnet, and when she did, all the furies of hell descended upon your heads.''

''Gavin!''

''Sorry, Aunt Biddy, but wasn't that the way of it?''

''Indeed it was,'' Mollie told him, grinning, ''and what with Lady Andrew shrieking for her dresser and your uncle commanding in stentorian accents that Harry be brought to him at once for punishment, it was as good as a play.''

''Oh, Mollie,'' wailed Lady Bridget, ''how can you say so? It was dreadful.''

''Only at the moment, ma'am,'' Mollie replied, patting her hand, ''and it was soon over, for all that.''

''I take it Harry had the good sense to play least in sight?''

''Yes, and they couldn't remain long enough to rout him out, because they had sent word ahead to Oatlands that they meant to arrive that night. As it was, they were delayed while Lady Andrew's dresser washed the honey from her hair. It was a wonder her ladyship didn't catch an ague, too, for her hair was still wet when they left.''

''Perhaps she hung her head out the window of the coach to dry it,'' Hawk suggested, his expression showing clearly how much he enjoyed the vision thus brought to his mind's eye.

Mollie chuckled.

''But it was a dreadful thing,'' Lady Bridget observed. ''Harry had no business to have done it and ought to have been punished.''

Hawk raised his eyebrows. ''Do you mean to say he was not?'' He looked at his wife, who returned his gaze defiantly.

''No, sir, he was not, because I took it upon myself to countermand your uncle's orders to Mr. Bates. Lord Andrew had already thrashed Harry himself earlier in the week for the merest trifle, and the poor boy could never so much as show his face without either your uncle or Lady Andrew cross-questioning and criticizing him. Nothing satisfied them. If his nails were not dirty, his hair was not combed to her ladyship's satisfaction. If he spoke to anyone, either his grammar was corrected or his tone was declared to be impertinent."

"They said he must not call me Aunt Biddy," said her ladyship in a puzzled tone. "I must say, Gavin, I thought it was going a little beyond what was necessary to insist that he call me ma'am when no one but dearest Mollie ever does so."

"It was, indeed," Hawk agreed, "but you ought not to have let him off scot-free after such a prank, Mollie, no matter what provoked it."

"Well, I did tell him he ought not to have done it," Mollie said, looking up at him from under her thick lashes. A small, choking sound came from Lady Bridget, and Mollie's gaze shifted. "I did, ma'am. You know I did."

"To be sure, you did," Lady Bridget agreed, "but I cannot think you caused him to feel the slightest remorse, you know."

"Why not?" Hawk demanded.

Mollie looked at him, then back at Lady Bridget, whose lips were folded tightly, as though she felt she had said too much already. "Well," Mollie said, casting a wary eye back at her husband, "I'm afraid I found the whole episode a trifle amusing, sir. It was difficult to scold Harry when I kept . . . well, when it just seemed as if . . . ." She shrugged, unable to put the matter in words she thought would be acceptable to him.

Hawk's eyes began to dance. "Couldn't stop laughing long enough to give the boy a proper trimming. That's it, isn't it?"

Mollie nodded, her own eyes atwinkle. "I daresay it was wrong of me, sir, but they had both given him *such* a time of it. He'd managed on his own to pay off Lady Andrew, and somehow I felt that by telling Bates he wasn't to thrash Harry after all, I was helping him pay off his lordship as well."

"And not just for Harry's sake, I'll warrant."

His eyes were no longer laughing, but he was not angry with her either. That gentle, caressing note was in his voice, and Mollie felt the color rushing to her cheeks. Her gaze met his, and the understanding she saw in his eyes brought a sudden salty dampness to her own. She turned away and gave a small laugh.

"I daresay I handled it all wrong, sir. Perhaps they are right to say we've spoiled him."

"There's nothing amiss with Harry that a term or two at school won't cure."

"You don't think he will disgrace the family name?" Mollie asked, smiling more naturally now.

"I thought you said Andrew's reason for not sending him was that the boy was sickly?"

Mollie nodded. "And I can't think how he came by such a notion," she admitted. "I confess, her ladyship's reasoning makes more sense."

Lady Bridget gave a self-conscious little cough, and when they both turned their eyes upon her, a delicate shade of pink crept into her smooth cheeks. Flustered, she gave a deprecating little wave of her hand.

Mollie's eyes widened. "Surely, *you* never told them Harry was sickly, ma'am! Why, you've never in your life been able to tell a bouncer with any conviction!"

"No, no. Oh, no, of course I did no such thing," Lady Bridget said hastily, her cheeks darkening. "And I don't even know for a fact that Thurston did so. Only—"

"Of course," Mollie said quickly. "That is precisely how it came to pass." She looked at Hawk. "Your papa doted on the boy, but if he suspected anyone might accuse him of it, he went all brusque and crusty. I truly think he cared more about Harry than he ever did about anyone else. It is entirely possible that he complained of the boy's being sickly and spoiled rather than admit he merely wanted to keep him at home."

Agreement having been satisfactorily attained, the subject soon turned to those preparations still to be achieved before Mollie and Lady Bridget would be ready to be seen in company. In the days that followed they enjoyed themselves with an orgy of shopping. Neither had realized that Hawk meant to plunge them immediately into the social whirl, and they had come to London ten days prior to the opening of Almack's, generally the true beginning of any London Season, with the intention of replenishing their wardrobes. Not that they were totally unprepared, of course, for they had made a flying visit to London six weeks before in order to see their dressmaker. Still, there were final fittings to be seen to and a number of accessories to buy. Tuesday morning found them in Covent Garden bright and early to visit their dressmaker.

Having done a great deal of work for them in the past,

Mademoiselle Bertrand was happy to exert herself in order to provide both ladies with suitable gowns for the dinner that evening at Carlton House. The fittings were attended to, and Mademoiselle agreed to send the finished products to Grosvenor Square by four o'clock. Well satisfied, the Colporter ladies returned to their coach and directed the driver to Oxford Street and the premises of W. H. Botibol, plumassier, in order for Mollie to purchase a pair of ostrich feathers to wear in her hair that evening.

The dinner at Carlton House was as grand as Lady Andrew had promised it would be, and Mollie was fascinated, as always, by the opulent decor. She had attended several balls and musical evenings in the Regent's magnificent house, but because he lacked a suitable hostess—not being upon speaking terms with his wife, who was currently doing all in her power to undermine what little popularity he retained with the English people—Mollie had never before attended a dinner there. Six courses were provided, each consisting of three or four main dishes, as many as ten or twelve side dishes, and upward of twenty removes. The meal seemed to go on for hours.

It ended at last, however, and first the ladies and then the gentlemen, after their port, repaired to the Crimson Saloon, where musicians had been engaged to play for their entertainment. No one seemed to heed the music, however. Everyone was more interested in seeing and being seen. Mollie, looking for her husband when the gentlemen joined the ladies, was surprised to see him in conversation with the Regent and Lord Bathurst. They had moved a little apart, and their conversation appeared to be a serious one. She watched them curiously, having not realized that Hawk was on such terms with the secretary of war or with the Prince of Wales, who had become Regent, after all, in his absence. But then, she told herself, there were no doubt a good many things she did not know about her husband.

She asked him about the conversation when they were once again in their carriage on the way back to Grosvenor Square. Hawk smiled at her.

"His highness and Lord Bathurst were curious to hear what I might tell them about Wellington. I know little, of course, that they have not read in the dispatches, but I think Prinny, at least, liked talking to someone who has been there. He has always regretted not being allowed to take part in the action."

"It would scarcely be suitable for the Crown Prince to be sent off to war, Gavin," Lady Bridget said gently. " 'Tis no wonder his majesty would never hear of it."

"Well, Prinny resented it, nevertheless."

That was all he said on the subject, but Mollie's curiosity was unappeased. She was sure he might have said more if he had wished to do so.

Lord Ramsay had not been included in the invitation to Carlton House, and he had been displeased when Hawk decided he would be wiser to remain at home the first two nights. Having seen his tailor, arranged to have several pairs of boots made for him by Hoby, the fashionable bootmaker located at the corner of Piccadilly and St. James's Street, and having purchased several hats from Lock, the hatter in St. James's Street who provided hats for such fashionables as Lord Alvanley and Beau Brummell, Ramsay was ready to make his entrance to society. It clearly irked him to be left at home to kick his heels. However, Hawk was adamant, saying that he would make it up to him by taking him to White's the following day.

Mollie spent the rest of the week shopping with Lady Bridget, for there were still any number of necessary purchases to be made. Besides visiting the shops in Covent Garden, Mayfair, and Oxford Street, they visited the linen drapers, silk mercers, haberdashers, milliners, and corsetiers situated around Leicester Square. Not only were there items to purchase for themselves, but Mollie, after a long conversation with Mrs. Perfect, had decided to redo the ground-floor saloon as well. Thus it was that Lady Gwendolyn Worthing, arriving in town the following Monday, found her sister-in-law sitting on the floor in the midst of a pile of silks and brocades on Tuesday morning.

"Gwen, how perfectly delightful!" Mollie exclaimed, jumping to her feet to greet the smiling, smartly dressed, auburn-haired young woman, whose speaking gray eyes at once proclaimed her to be a member of the Colporter family. "Aunt Biddy and I intended to call later in the day to welcome you to town."

"We have already been welcomed, I thank you," said Lady Gwendolyn acidly. Then her eyes twinkled, and her tone changed to a teasing one. "As I understand you were welcomed, immediately upon your arrival last week."

Mollie chuckled. "I hope she was more charitable toward you than she was toward me. But I know she was. She positively dotes on you, Gwen."

"I should live to see the day," Lady Gwendolyn said dryly. "She informed me that she knows to the penny what I laid out—or rather what Worthing laid out—for the new nursery at Pillings, and much as she detests criticizing, she felt it her duty to tell me she thought I had been a trifle extravagant. The inhabitant of said nursery being a mere female had a good deal to do with her sentiments, of course. And not even a Colporter female at that."

"Well, at least she did not feel it to be her duty to send detailed accounts to your brother for the last four years, telling him precisely what sins you were committing in his absence," Mollie pointed out.

"Not last year, at any rate. I was safely indisposed. The year before, however, when Worthing and I were at outs over that predatory opera dancer of his, and I let the handsome Lord Featherby squire me about to get even, I received the devil of a scold from Hawk. Two full pages, Mollie. I can tell you, I was glad he was on the Continent and not here at the time." Lady Gwendolyn smiled ruefully. "I know *you* didn't pass the word along to him."

"No, of course not. Though it might not have been Lady Andrew either, you know. You have other relatives nearly as busy." Lady Gwendolyn nodded, and Mollie added, "How is young Megan, by the bye? She must be nearly big enough to sit up by herself now."

"Indeed, she is, and a handful. I cannot tell you how grateful I was when she was old enough to be turned over to Nannie." Lady Gwendolyn ran a hand over a piece of green brocade. "Do you and Hawk go to Almack's tomorrow?"

Mollie agreed that they would be attending the first assembly of the Season, and from that point the conversation alternated between social events and upholstery fabrics.

7

Everyone who was anyone had arrived in London in time for opening night at Almack's, and Mollie, having already paid and received a number of morning calls, knew that most of her friends and favorite flirts were in town. Lady Jersey and the Countess de Lieven, wife of the Russian ambassador, had stopped in to see her. And she had met Lord Alvanley driving with the famous Beau Brummell Wednesday afternoon in Hyde Park. They created quite a picture—the one so short, plump, and ugly; the other elegant, slim, and well-favored. Rumor had it that both gentlemen were suffering from financial reverses, but one would never guess it to look at them, as Ramsay, riding beside her on a neat cover hack, had commented.

"Precise to a pin," he said, adding consciously, "Met them both when Hawk took me to White's, you know." Lord Alvanley drew up his rig at a sign from Mollie.

"Good day, Lady Hawk," said his lordship, adding with his customary lisp, "You look charmingly in that riding dreth, ma'am. Becometh you mighty well."

"Indeed," Mr. Brummell agreed, smiling slightly.

"I know better than to accuse either of you of flattery," Mollie replied with a laugh, "so I shall simply say thank you in a ladylike fashion and bring my brother-in-law to your notice. I fancy you have met Lord Ramsay?"

Both gentlemen having condescended to acknowledge the acquaintance, Ramsay was in excellent spirits when they rode on. But it soon became clear to Mollie that he had had a specific purpose in mind when he had invited her to ride out with him that afternoon.

"I say, Moll," he said at last after several false starts, "do you think perhaps you might have a word with Hawk on my behalf?"

She looked at him in surprise. She had thought the two brothers were getting on famously with each other. "What could I discuss with him that you cannot?" she asked.

"He don't choose to discuss the matters I wish to discuss." He looked at her in frustration. "Dash it, Mollie, the fact of the matter is I think he does not trust me. He's keeping me on a dashed tight leash, you know—not at all what I expected."

"He wants you to go carefully, Ramsay, not to make any errors before your good character is known to those who matter. If you do something dreadful, you might be denied tickets to Almack's. It is even more difficult, after all, for a gentleman to come by them than it is for a lady in her first Season."

"Much I should care for that," Ramsay muttered. "Devilish poor place to be stuck every Wednesday night, by what I hear. Cardplaying for chicken stakes with old ladies or being made to do the pretty with insufferably young ones. And nothing to wet a man's thirst but orgeat and lemonade. And knee breeches! I should much prefer to be denied admission to the place. Hugh Hardwick, that fellow I had the wager with in Gill's Green, invited me to go along to a bang-up affair tonight at a new gaming place in Cockspur Lane, but Hawk insists upon dragging me to Almack's. And Friday, when Hugh and a friend of his knew where there was some first-rate entertainment to be had, Hawk took me off to Boodle's for dinner instead."

"But you enjoyed that," she pointed out.

"That don't signify. It's all of a piece. I can do nothing on my own. He even refuses to increase my allowance to meet the added expenses of living in town. Says he'll spring for anything I really need, but that's a hum. I daresay he'll prove to be as much of a dashed squeeze-penny as Father was."

"Impossible," Mollie said, grinning at him. But when he only glared in response, she relented. "Very well, I shall speak with him. But I cannot promise it will do the least good, you know. You are the one who was telling me not long ago that he is merely exerting his rightful authority."

Ramsay sighed. "I know he is. But don't it seem a trifle unfair, Moll, after all those years of living under Father's thumb, finally to be free to cut a dash in the world, only to find oneself under Hawk's thumb instead?"

She agreed that it was difficult, but privately she was

alarmed by his artless conversation and found herself wondering what sort of larks he might be up to without Hawk's firm hand on the reins. Nevertheless, at the first opportunity, she broached the matter to her husband.

He had come into her room to visit with her while Mathilde du Bois was putting the finishing touches to her toilette. At last, when the imperious dresser indicated that she had done all she could, Mollie arose from the dressing chair and turned with a grin to her husband.

"Well, what do you think?" Her puff-sleeved, scoopnecked gown of lavender lutestring clung to her exquisite figure in a most alluring fashion. Her hair had been caught up at the back of her head in a cascade of intricate braids and curls, with soft tendrils wisping about her ears and the nape of her neck, and her cheeks were pink with the pleasure of knowing she looked very well indeed.

Hawk smiled back, looking splendid himself in a well-cut black coat and knee breeches, a white silk shirt, and white stockings. His cravat was tied in a simpler style than that affected by the swells, but Mollie thought he looked very handsome.

"Magnificent," he said in response to her question. "The other ladies will weep with envy when they see you."

Mollie chuckled, dismissing Mathilde du Bois. But when Hawk held up her sable-trimmed silk cape, she shook her head, deciding it was an excellent time to tell him of Ramsay's complaints. Hawk heard her out in silence. Then, when she paused, he merely looked down into her eyes as if he would read the very thoughts behind them.

"Well?" she demanded, raising an eyebrow.

His expression did not change. "Defending the young again?"

She opened her mouth to deny the charge, then closed it and turned away, thus missing the flicker of amusement in her husband's eyes. She thought about what she had nearly said, that he was wrong, both about her reasons and about the way he was handling Ramsay. He did not press her for an answer, and at last she turned back to face him again, a tiny frown creasing her brow.

"I do not think I am automatically defending him, sir," she said carefully. "I hope you will not always leap to that conclusion if I choose to disagree with you."

He nodded. "That's fair enough. Why did the lad not come to me himself?"

"He said you had no wish to discuss the matter," Mollie replied bluntly.

"He's right." The response was even more blunt.

"But don't you see how frustrating this is for him? He feels as if he cannot move without you at his side, overseeing everything he does."

"Better frustrated than over his ears in debt or lying on the floor in some gaming hell with his throat slit from ear to ear or killed in an alley by Resurrectionists to be sold to a medical school."

"For heaven's sake, Gavin!"

"I'm sorry if your sensibilities are offended by such talk, Mollie, but unlikelier things happen every day in this town. There are not enough bodies to accommodate the need, so the Resurrectionists, for a price, provide them, and a drunken young man weaving his way home from a gaming hell in the small hours of the morning is a prime target."

"Ramsay does not get drunk!"

"How do you know?"

"I . . . I don't." The tales she had heard of how Oxford students spent their time did not encourage her to pursue a blind defense. "I don't know what he does when he is away," she admitted, "but I've never seen him in his cups."

"No, nor have I," Hawk said. "I scarcely know the lad at all anymore. But I *am* responsible for him, Mollie."

She nodded, then looked up at him again. "Is it not unwise to stifle his high spirits, Gavin? Might he not do something foolish out of simple frustration?"

He did not speak immediately. Then, after a small sigh, he said, "I'll talk to Ramsay, sweetheart, and discuss my position with him. I ought to have done so before now. Perhaps I have been overly protective."

Mollie was satisfied. She was coming to believe that her husband had developed a strong sense of fairness, and she was certain that even Ramsay could not say she had not done her best for him. This time when Hawk held up her cape, she smiled and allowed him to arrange it around her shoulders before accompanying him down to the main hall, where the others awaited them.

Except for the previous Season, when old Lord Hawkstone's

untimely death had curtailed her activities, Mollie had refused to allow her husband's absence to interfere with her pleasures and had ruthlessly removed her household to London each spring in order to indulge herself, and Lady Bridget as well, in that whirlwind of social activity known simply as the Season. It occurred to her in the coach on the way to King Street to wonder how great a difference Hawk's presence would make to her pleasure.

So far he had not interfered with her in any way. She had spent a prodigious amount of his money on herself, on Lady Bridget, and, for that matter, on the ground-floor saloon. Since he had often met them upon their return from a shopping spree, he was not unaware of the vast number of packages that had been borne into his house. Yet he had not said a word in opposition to such expeditions. Ramsay might complain of his clutch-fisted nature. Mollie certainly could not do so.

Nor had he once questioned her comings and goings. If she chanced to mention paying a call upon Lady Cowper or receiving one from the Princess Esterhazy, he expressed an interest in hearing all about it. But if she didn't mention where she was going or where she had been, Hawk didn't press her for information.

Now she wondered if his presence alone would affect her popularity. Never before had she lacked a partner at a ball or an assembly. But some of her flirts might be put off by a husband's proximity, particularly when the husband was a gentleman as large as Hawk and had, moreover, a reputation for being handy with his fists. And if they were not put off, what, then? Hiding a smile, she remembered several gentlemen who were especially audacious. How would Hawk respond to their attentions toward his wife? A tiny thrill of anticipation shot up her spine as several potential scenes leapt to her imagination.

However, as matters transpired that evening, there was no cause for her to bother her head about such things. Not that she was ignored, for she was not. Hawk danced with her once, a country dance, then seemed content just to watch her enjoy herself while he introduced Ramsay to various persons who could be expected to provide the lad with unexceptionable entertainment in the days ahead. Despite his earlier complaints, Ramsay enjoyed himself hugely, and when Mollie caught

Hawk's twinkling eye upon her midway through the evening, just after Ramsay had led a pretty, lively damsel into an energetic round dance, she grinned back at him, knowing he expected her to be pleased by his efforts. He did not ask her to dance with him again, but she frequently saw him watching her while he conversed first with one old acquaintance, then another.

She had had a doubt or two earlier when Hawk had said he would enjoy watching her cut a dash, but it seemed now as if he had meant it. Lady Bridget preferred the cardroom, so Mollie saw little of her, and as time passed, the evening grew more lively. There were a number of scandalized exclamations when the Countess de Lieven and Cupid Palmerston took to the floor in a lively waltz, the first such occasion in the staid assembly room. They were soon joined by Lady Jersey and her partner, however, and then the Princess Esterhazy and hers, and before long many of those who knew the steps, including Mollie and Sir James Smithers, were whirling around the floor, laughing and exchanging comments about the controversial dance. Naturally, there were still many who disapproved, but their comments were kept to a minimum once it was seen that the haughty patronesses had decided to allow waltzing within the hallowed precincts. Indeed, the only sour note all evening, as far as Mollie was concerned, was provided by Lady Andrew, who, coming upon Lord Ramsay unexpectedly, demanded in carrying tones to know what he thought *he* was doing in town.

"I daresay you were sent down," she declared, lifting her chin. "Cutting scandalous capers, no doubt."

"No, ma'am," Ramsay answered politely. He was carrying two cups of orgeat, one for himself and one for Mollie, having been sent to fetch them by Lord Alvanley, who had given it as his opinion that Lady Hawk was in need of refreshment and a quiet sit-down. Mollie, sitting beside his lordship now, saw Ramsay's plight and excused herself to go to his assistance.

"Good evening, Beatrix. Is one of those for me, Ramsay? Perhaps her ladyship would like the other?"

"No need to put the boy up to politeness he hasn't thought for himself, Margaret. I have just been telling him he ought not to be here at all."

"I told her I wasn't sent down," Ramsay said, his tone

long-suffering, "but she will have it that if I weren't here under false pretenses, she'd have been informed of my presence in town."

"But how can you not have known?" Mollie asked, looking at the older woman in surprise.

"Because no one saw fit to inform me, and because this young man has not got manners enough to pay a proper call," Lady Andrew declared. "I've every intention of telling your brother just what I think of such rag manners, sir. I cannot imagine what he is about to allow you to leave school like this."

"It was not his decision, but mine," retorted Ramsay, goaded.

"Stuff and nonsense. As if you would be here if he disapproved."

That statement being unanswerable, Mollie and Ramsay both felt Lady Andrew had had the last word. They did not allow her to dampen their spirits, however, and greeted Lady Gwendolyn Worthing and her placid husband some moments later with enthusiasm.

Though neither Mollie nor Ramsay could think for a moment that Lady Andrew had not made good her threat to speak to Hawk, he said nothing of such a conversation to either of them. Indeed, in the days ahead, as their social activities increased, he often seemed uninterested in his wife's and his brother's whereabouts. As often as not, his pursuits did not march with theirs. He might begin an evening in their company, but later he would take himself off with one crony or another, leaving Mollie to the attentions of her favorite flirt of the moment and Ramsay more and more to his own devices.

Instead of finding herself at ease with the situation, Mollie soon discovered that Hawk's indifference became irksome, and she began to do what she could to bring him to his senses. She carried a fan and flirted outrageously with all manner of persons at Lady Sefton's ball. Then, later that same evening, at a rout in Berkeley Square, she singled out the elegant Mr. Brummell for a half hour's dalliance. He seemed amused by her efforts, and so, unfortunately, by the look of him, did her husband.

The following evening at a late supper following a play at the King's Theater, Lady Gwendolyn, who had sat beside

Mollie in the Colporter box, took her to one side and demanded to know if her wits had gone begging.

"I daresay I sound just like Aunt Trixie," she declared roundly, "but the way you were flirting over that ridiculous fan with the men in the pit tonight made me itch to suggest you sit with Harriette Wilson and her sisters!"

"Gwen!" Mollie was truly shocked, for Harriette Wilson was the most famous courtesan in London. It had been fascinating to see her in her own box at the theater, if annoying to see one's own husband among the cavalcade of bucks and dandies paying court to the woman during one of the intervals, but to have one's behavior compared to hers! Mollie's eyes flashed.

"Well, and so you might stare," Lady Gwendolyn said in a stern undertone, "but I saw you, and I'm persuaded that Hawk cannot have helped but notice, too. Whatever are you about, Mollie? Such behavior will infuriate him. I shouldn't wonder at it if he does not read you a thundering scold."

Mollie shrugged. "He pays me no heed," she said a little dismally. "He said from the outset that he would not interfere with me, and he does not."

"Poppycock," Lady Gwendolyn retorted. "He may not wish to put a rub in the way of your pleasure, but my brother will not stand idly by while you make a cake of yourself— and of him as well. Have a care, Molly. I know whereof I speak. Remember Lord Featherby? And Hawk was in Spain then, thank God."

Her sister-in-law's warning gave Mollie enough food for thought so that she half-expected Hawk to say something in the carriage about her behavior. She had no wish to make him truly angry, but had merely hoped to make him exert himself a little more to please her. He showed no sign of anger, however, merely speaking casually about the farce that had followed the play. From time to time he did regard her searchingly, as if he expected her to say something to him, and she wondered if he was giving her an opportunity to apologize for her behavior, which during the past week or so had admittedly been rather blatant. But since he did not seem to be angry and since she had no wish to stir his anger, she decided it would be foolish to introduce the topic at all.

Thinking over the past few days, she decided she had been a trifle heavy-handed in her efforts, and she determined to be more subtle in future. After all, her only intent was to make Hawk pay her more notice. Clearly, his sense of challenge was no longer stimulated by the mere fact of seeing her with other admirers. Indeed, it seemed to please him that the other men found her attractive. He spent his time renewing his old acquaintances and making new ones, always, she thought, in conversation with someone. And those conversations were not only with other men. There were women, too. Lots of women. There was nothing at all scandalous in his behavior, nothing even that could stir her jealousy. She knew that before their marriage he had been at least as popular as she was herself, so no one could wonder at the number of ladies he was acquainted with. But he seemed determined to renew his acquaintance with them all. He was invited everywhere, and if Mollie was otherwise engaged, he went alone, sometimes taking part in as many as six or eight entertainments in a single evening. Therefore, she was rather surprised a day or so after the news reached London of Wellington's victory at Vitoria when Hawk insisted that she accompany him to a rout at Ashburnham House, the London residence of the Russian ambassador.

"I am not overly fond of Monsieur de Lieven, sir," she told him when he casually informed her at the breakfast table, as she was looking through her morning post, that he wished her to accept the invitation for both of them.

"But you will not want to offend the countess," he responded, helping himself to buttered toast.

"No, of course not." One was very careful to do nothing to offend the haughty young Countess de Lieven. "But the invitation states that the rout is to be in honor of the newer members of Monsieur de Lieven's staff as well as Wellington's victory, sir. You know perfectly well that that means most of the guests will be members of the diplomatic and political set, and that the talk will be of dispatches and spies and treaties and such. Not the sort of thing to interest me or most of my friends. Her ladyship invites us merely to show off her *ton*-ish connections. Of course," she added on a brighter note, "no one will expect us to remain above fifteen minutes or so."

"Ah, but I wish to remain longer," he said gently.

"Then, you should go by yourself, sir, so that you may remain as long as you like," she replied.

"My prolonged presence might be remarked upon unless it is seen that my lovely wife is enjoying herself, as is her custom, with those of her cavaliers who chance to be present. And there will be a number of them, my dear, for the countess's entertainments are always devised with the utmost ingenuity.''

Mollie regarded her husband with astonishment, but since he seemed not the least inclined to further explanation, she let the matter drop, only to be even more surprised when he asked a day or so later if she would arrange a dinner party to be held the following week.

"Of course, sir," she replied, "only perhaps you have forgotten that we have already made plans for a similar evening the week after next."

"No, I hadn't forgotten, but the guest list for the first occasion will be somewhat different from that for the second," he answered cryptically. "I shall give you the list of those I want invited by Friday. You may make up the numbers with anyone else you choose. Oh, and, Mollie," he added, looking directly at her, "I shall want you to invite several persons who can be induced to sing or recite poetry or some such thing after dinner."

"What? I suppose you will next want Miss Aisling to play her harp for us! You are so fond of such entertainments. Coming it much too strong, my lord." She stared hard at him. "What game are you playing, Gavin?"

"None that need concern you, sweetheart. I have never hosted a soiree before, and I thought I ought to do so."

"Gammon. You have always said that the only thing such entertainments accomplish is to keep the gentlemen lingering over their port." She noted a flicker in his eyes that told her she had come nearer the mark than she had any reason to expect. Her own eyes narrowed, and she prepared to carry on the discussion. However, Hawk had other notions and made good his escape some few moments later.

The evening selected for the rout at Ashburnham House soon arrived, and proved to be a beautiful one with a myriad of stars and a full moon to help light their way to Dover Street. Lady Bridget had another engagement, but Lord Ramsay accompanied them, not because Hawk had demanded it, but because the Regent was likely to be present. Mollie had been amused by the young man's casual declaration that he supposed he ought to go along.

"I daresay I shan't stay long," he had confided, "but one ought to meet the Regent, after all, and Hawk has said he will present me."

He reminded his brother of that promise as the coach turned from Mount Street into Berkeley Square, where it fell in behind other carriages making for the same destination.

Hawk chuckled. "I remember. If Prinny makes his appearance before you desert us, I shall indeed present you."

"Thank you, sir. I'd like that." Ramsay had his voice under firm control, but Mollie knew he was excited by the prospect of meeting the Prince Regent. She had with her own ears, and upon more than one occasion, heard her young brother-in-law stigmatize the Prince as a wastrel and a brute, but nevertheless, she knew he was all agog to be presented.

Soon they could hear the musicians playing in the gardens that backed onto Hay Hill, and a few moments later the marquess's crested coach turned into Dover Street and drew up beside the canopied, red-carpeted walkway leading to the main entrance of Ashburnham House. A liveried flunky opened the coach door and let down the steps, and Mollie gave him her hand and descended to the walkway, followed by the two gentlemen.

After greeting their host and hostess and being introduced to the two young Russian gentlemen who were the guests of honor, the Colporters passed through to the ballroom, which was already teeming with a colorful array of guests. Lord Ramsay, espying a pretty young damsel whose acquaintance he had made at Almack's, hastily excused himself, reminding Hawk of his promise to introduce him to the Regent. Mollie looked up at her husband.

"What do you want me to do, Gavin?"

He smiled down at her. "Why, merely to enjoy yourself, sweetheart, like you always do. There is Jamie yonder, and I'll not be surprised if Breck and some of the others show their faces as well."

Sir James Smithers stepped up to them just then, looking comfortable, as he always did, even in full evening dress, and asked if Mollie would honor him with a dance. She accepted, wishing briefly that Hawk had asked her first, but soon enough she found herself being asked by other young men of her acquaintance as well as several she had never met before, including one who was actually reputed to be a spy for Napoleon. Mollie knew that Gaspard d'Épier came from a distinguished émigré family, so it was difficult for her to believe the rumors. Nevertheless, it was exciting to dance with him, and the others as well, and two hours passed quickly by before she found herself suddenly without a partner and glanced around the ballroom in search of her husband. He was nowhere to be found. Then she remembered hearing music from the gardens as they drove along Hay Hill. The embassy gardens were extensive, and often, she knew, as much activity went on under the open sky as in the house. Perhaps she would find Hawk outside.

Accordingly, she made her way to the rear of the ballroom, where a pair of French doors opened onto a broad terrace from which one had a fairy-tale view of the gardens beyond. Colored lamps glittering like jewels were concealed among the flowers, and the background of the garden on Hay Hill was hung with a transparent landscape of moonlight and water, with a real cascade flowing between mossy paths and Arcadian groups of scented shrubs. Truly the Countess de Lieven knew exactly how to stir the most jaded appetite for pleasure among those who were bored with too many parties every night of the Season. As the thought crossed Mollie's mind, she told herself she was not bored precisely. But she breathed deeply of the fresh air and felt revived by the lovely view below. There was, however, still no sign of her husband.

Just then she heard her name and turned to find her hostess approaching on the arm of a tall young man in a splendid uniform. At first Mollie had eyes only for the dark-green jacket with its red trim, the diagonal slash of a white sash, and the numerous medals clinking on the broad chest. As the couple drew nearer, however, Mollie's gaze moved upward, and her eyes widened as they encountered the gentleman's face. She found herself making a conscious effort to fold her lips carefully together, lest her jaw drop open in a most unladylike display, for the gentleman at the Countess de Lieven's side was quite the handsomest young man she had ever seen.

"Mollie, my dear," the countess said in her soft, slightly accented voice, "I beg leave to present his highness Prince Nicolai Stefanovich. Although he has been a member of my husband's retinue for quite some time now, he has been out of town and complains to me that he has never before been presented to your notice.''

Mollie dropped into a curtsy. He was a prince, after all. But his hand touched her arm, drawing her gently upright again, and she found herself looking into a pair of dark, luminescent eyes so intense that they seemed to strip the very clothes from her body as she stood there. Then he smiled, showing even white teeth behind full, sensuous lips.

"Lady Mollie," said his highness in a low voice throbbing with undisguised desire, "I saw you but for the briefest moment before I told Dasha it was her solemn duty to bring us together. Fate intended us to meet. Do you not agree?"

8

Mollie stared speechlessly at Prince Nicolai. He was neither as tall nor as broad as her husband, but he was possessed of a fine and manly physique that was accentuated by the magnificent uniform he wore. Besides the dashing red trim at collar and cuffs, the dark-green, close-fitting coat sported gold buttons, braid, and epaulets. The white sash was further ornamented with narrow gold stripes, and his well-pressed and tailored white trousers had a wide red stripe along the outer seam of each leg. The prince was altogether a magnificent creature, Mollie thought.

But it was not his colorful clothing that held her spellbound. Nor was it his lustrous black hair or the trim side-whiskers that framed that beautiful face. The spell was cast by a pair of liquid black eyes set deep under thick, black brows—eyes that challenged her to reply to his daring question.

Wrenching her gaze from his, she turned to the Countess de Lieven instead, hoping to display at least a semblance of her customary poise. The countess gazed back at her limpidly, an enigmatic half-smile playing at her lips. The look was as good as a warning, for Mollie knew well the woman's penchant for making mischief, and it helped her gather her wits.

"I am quite certain I should remember his highness if we had chanced to meet before," she said finally, allowing a touch of humor to enter her voice. She smiled then at the prince. "You flatter me shamefully, sir. You must know that gentlemen in England are not so outspoken."

"More shame to them," replied his highness promptly. "To be in the presence of extraordinary beauty and not to make mention of it is a crime in any nation, my lady."

The countess chuckled. "I can see that you two will get along famously together, so I shall leave you now. The

Regent will arrive at any moment, and I must be at my
husband's side to greet him.''

Mollie was not by any means certain that she wished to be
left alone in the garden with Prince Nicolai Stefanovich.
Already his eyes devoured her. The man clearly had no
qualms about allowing his gaze to rest wherever it pleased
him to rest it either, and she was unused to a gentleman's
gazing so raptly at her décolletage.

"Your Highness," she said gently, reprovingly.

It was more discomfiting when his gaze bored into hers,
for there was blatant invitation in the way he looked at her.
Mollie frowned.

"I have displeased you, my lady?"

"You make me feel uncomfortable," she replied frankly,
"as if I've got spinach stuck between my teeth or something."

With a rueful laugh, he gave his head a little shake and
rubbed his brow. "You must forgive me, my lady. I have
been in your so charming country long enough to learn that
English ladies are unappreciative of open admiration. Forgive
me. I am not usually so gauche. 'Tis simply that your beauty
swept my good sense away altogether."

Mollie swallowed carefully. Surely she should point out to
him that he was still being a trifle open in his admiration.
However, one must remember one's own manners as well.
The prince was a guest in her country. It was her duty to put
him at his ease, not to criticize his behavior. And if he
wished to go on paying her fulsome compliments, well, she
must simply bear up under the weight of them.

So it was that when he invited her to take a turn of the
fairy-tale gardens with him, she made no demur. There were
plenty of other couples enjoying the fresh air and pleasant
surroundings, and if several persons glanced curiously at
Mollie walking with the prince, she chose to assume that it
was because the two of them made such a good-looking
couple. A brief time later Nicolai suggested that perhaps she
might care to dance, and they went back inside, where the
musicians were just tuning up for a waltz.

"It pleases me that your country has recognized the waltz
at last," the prince said, smiling as he took Mollie's hand,
and placed his own firmly at her waist to lead her into the
dance. "I trust you enjoy it as much as I do."

"Oh, indeed, sir, 'tis all the rage this Season, you know. It is not entirely new, of course, but it has never enjoyed so much success before now. This year 'tis even the fashion to invite one's friends to morning balls, merely to practice the steps.''

"We must thank our hostess for bringing the dance into fashion, must we not?''

"Indeed, though it created a rumpus the first time we danced it at Almack's. Mr. Brummell calls it a riotous and indecent dance, and even the countess and Lady Jersey refuse to countenance its execution for girls in their first Season.''

"Foolishness,'' murmured the prince close to her ear as he whirled her successfully through an intricate pattern of steps. "In Europe it is quite commonplace.''

"I daresay, but this is not Europe, sir.'' Mollie caught a glimpse just then of her husband. He was not dancing but was standing with the Prince Regent, who had entered without his usual fanfare some moments before. She was sure Hawk had seen her. Moreover, there had been the slightest hint of a frown on his rugged face. She stiffened in Stefanovich's arms, nearly missing her step.

"Are you all right?'' he asked. "I did not tread upon your foot, did I?''

"No, of course not,'' she replied, looking around to find Hawk again. "But you are holding me too closely, sir. I cannot mind my steps.''

"Nonsense, my lady. If you will allow your beautiful body to melt itself against mine, you will find the steps take care of themselves, I promise you.'' Again his lips were dangerously close to her ear. Mollie took a deep breath.

"Highness, I should not like to create a scene,'' she said with grim meaning, "but if you do not loose your hold upon me, I shall tread upon *your* foot.''

He relaxed his embrace. "You must forgive me once more, lovely one. Your nearness makes me overbold. I hope my misbehavior will not cause you to forbid me to call upon you?''

Her eyes widened. "Of course you may call, sir. My husband and I would be pleased to offer you the hospitality of our home.''

"But I was hoping you would offer me that hospitality without the inconvenience of your husband's presence, Mollie,'' he murmured audaciously. "Are there not times when the estimable marquess spends his days at White's like the rest of England's milords?''

She knew precisely what he was asking her. It was a fairly common practice among the upper classes for ladies to entertain their lovers while their supposedly unsuspecting husbands were elsewhere. It was not common, however, for those ladies to entertain in their husbands' own homes.

The prince's invitation was scarcely the first of its nature that Mollie had received. Over the period of Hawk's absence she had received any number of them. Several had even come from men who professed to be her husband's very good friends, and many had come from gentlemen who clearly believed themselves to be offering to do her a favor. For the most part she had not been tempted by any of those offers. Nor was she tempted now. The only difference was that the prince's was the first offer to come on such short acquaintance. Then, too, the casual nature of his invitation and the calm assumption that she would consider it made her wonder what he had heard about her before the countess had presented him.

She said nothing until the music stopped. Then, resting her hand lightly upon his forearm and keeping her voice noncommittal, she said, ''I am flattered by your interest, Highness, but I fear I am the tiresome sort of woman who is devoted to her husband.'' She saw Hawk approaching, alone, and for once there was little warmth in his expression. When he stepped up beside Stefanovich, the prince suddenly seemed smaller, less magnificent, somehow. ''Have you been looking for me, my lord?'' Mollie asked, smiling up at him in what she hoped would look to the prince like a devoted manner.

''I was. If you wish to make an appearance at Emily Cowper's affair, we should take our leave now.''

She had made no such plans, but she knew better than to protest. He was ready to leave. Whatever purpose he had had in coming to Ashburnham House had been accomplished. She glanced toward the prince.

''Highness, may I present my husband, the Marquess of Hawkstone. Sir, this is his highness, Prince Nicolai Stefanovich, a member of Monsieur de Lieven's retinue.''

''We met briefly earlier,'' Hawk said. He spoke calmly enough, but Mollie was certain she detected an underlying

curtness. "Shall we go, my lady? Your servant, sir." He
nodded to the prince, took Mollie's hand, firmly placed it
upon his forearm, and led her away. Looking up obliquely
from under her lashes, Mollie noted the tightness in the
muscles of his jaw and the way his lips seemed to thin into a
straight line. A moment later they had found their host and
hostess and made their farewells. The carriage was waiting at
the end of the walkway.

"Where is Ramsay?" Mollie asked as her husband helped
her into the coach.

"Gone a half hour ago, as soon as he'd made his bow to
Prinny." A flunky put up the steps and shut the door, and the
coachman whipped up his horses.

"Gavin," Mollie said a few moments later when the coach
had passed through Berkeley Square without stopping, "are
we not going to Emily Cowper's?"

"No." Silence fell upon them again.

"Gavin?"

"What?"

"Have I done something to vex you?" Her voice was
small, surprising her. She hadn't realized until the words
were spoken how much the answer meant to her.

His hand found hers in the shadows and gave it a warm
squeeze. "Have you not meant to vex me, Mollie?"

"N-no."

"Only to punish me a little, then." He made it sound like
a statement of fact. In the glow cast by the carriage lamps she
could see his face. He looked grim.

"Why do you say that, sir?" she asked, not at all certain
she wanted to hear the answer.

But he seemed to give himself a little shake, and when he
looked down at her again, his expression had relaxed. "I have
not been a very good husband, sweetheart, and I have not the
least right to blame you for being angry with me, but I'm afraid
I must ask you to keep that Russian fellow at a distance."

"I only met the prince tonight."

"Did you? His attitude indicated a more intimate acquaintance than that."

"Well, he is foreign, you know," she said quickly, anxious to explain the matter to him. "I daresay that is why he is
so particular in his attentions on such short acquaintance. I
am persuaded he can mean nothing untoward."

"Are you?" The question was a pointed one, and Mollie squirmed a little. She had noted this distressing habit of Hawk's on previous occasions, when she had attempted to avoid discussion of an issue by making a glib statement. She hoped the prince meant nothing, and so she made hope into a statement of fact. But Hawk tended to look at matters in more precise shades of black and white. He disliked prevarication. When she did not answer him, his tone altered, becoming a shade sterner. "Do you truly believe that fellow has no motive other than simple friendship? Surely you recognize his type, Mollie."

"I can take care of myself," she muttered. "His attentions do not distress me, sir, whatever he may or may not hope to accomplish." There was another small silence. She looked out of the window, staring at the houses as they passed along Mount Street.

"I forbid you to encourage his attentions," Hawk said flatly.

Mollie stiffened, turning to face him. "Forbid me? You forbid me, sir?"

"I do. I know you do not wish me to interfere with your pleasures, madam, but I do not care to hear your name linked with his by the gossips, if you please."

He had never sounded so stern before, and resentment churned in Mollie's breast. She wanted nothing more than to lash out at him, to tell him he had no right to order her life. But the fact that he did have the right and the fear that he might take her to task over certain other matters stilled her tongue. Instead, she stared out the window again, pointedly ignoring him until they arrived in Grosvenor Square.

It was not particularly late, and she half-expected him to bid her good night before taking himself off again, but he did not. Instead, he ordered brandy sent to her sitting room, then placed an arm around her shoulders and gave her a little hug.

"Shall we go up, sweetheart?"

Both the coaxing note in his voice and the feeling of his arm across her shoulders sent a small thrill up her spine, but she ignored it, sending him a speaking look and saying nothing in response to his question, though she went with him obediently enough. A fire crackled cheerfully in the sitting-room fireplace, and there was a faint odor of wood smoke in the air. Mollie drew a little away from her husband.

"Mathilde will be waiting for me," she said, her tone dismissing him.

"Send her away." It was not a request.

Glancing at him first in defiance and then more uncertainly, she decided the time was not ripe for rebellion. She had no wish to hear him order Mathilde off to bed himself, so she walked quickly to the door to her own bedchamber and opened it. The room was empty.

"It is early yet," Hawk said, close behind her. "Perhaps she did not expect you so soon. I will tell Lofting when he brings our brandy to send her to bed. You will have no further need for her services tonight."

Lofting entered just then, so Mollie had no immediate opportunity to tell Hawk that he was becoming high-handed again, and when the butler had gone and the marquess turned toward her, holding the two brandy glasses in his hands, the words refused to come. He was smiling, but his expression was uncertain, as though he thought she might be about to lose her temper and was wondering how to deal with such an eventuality.

Her anger melted. She took the glass he held out to her. "Shall we sit by the fire, sir?" He agreed, but when she moved toward the smaller armchair, he took her arm and gently drew her with him to the larger one, pulling her down to sit in his lap. He had a comfortable lap, she thought as she snuggled against his chest. "I'll crease your coat," she said.

"No matter. Mawson will press it out again."

She sipped the brandy, enjoying the warmth as it trickled down her throat. They sat quietly, watching the crackling fire.

Finally Hawk said, "I expected you to say more."

"About the prince?"

He nodded.

"You haven't been jealous before, Gavin. Gwen said you would be, after the play at the King's Theater. She expected you to fly up into the boughs because I was flirting so outrageously."

His mouth twisted a little. "I was afraid of having my head handed to me on a platter if I ripped up at you that night."

"What?" She stared at him, then her eyes narrowed as her mind raced back over the evening at the play. They had sat in the Colporter box with the Worthings, Lady Bridget, and

Ramsay. Several people had visited them during the intervals, but no one . . . Her thoughts bumped into one another when she remembered the second interval. "Harriette Wilson! That's it, isn't it? You thought I'd fling it in your teeth that you'd visited her in her box." When he nodded, still watching her warily, she shot him a saucy grin. "Does that mean you will let me do as I please so long as I extend the same courtesy to you, sir?"

He frowned, and for a moment Mollie feared she had gone too far. He certainly seemed to be taking her teasing in a more serious vein than she had intended.

"I don't mean to give you that impression at all," he said carefully. "I cannot explain all my motives to you just now, and for that matter, I cannot even claim that it is anything more than simple jealousy that makes me forbid you to pursue your acquaintance with that Russian fellow. And I certainly cannot expect you to trust me when the Lord knows you've little reason to do so." He paused, sipping his brandy, then said, "I saw you flirting, right enough, and I didn't like it. But I knew your intention was to punish me for not paying sufficient attention to you." Mollie bridled, and Hawk smiled wryly, his free hand drawing idle patterns along the bare skin of her upper arm. "Was that not the case, sweetheart?"

"You warned me that you would be busy," she said, sidestepping the question. But, as usual, he wouldn't allow that.

"Did you not mean to punish me? Or did you wish to discover how far you could go before I would call a halt?"

"I never meant to make you angry," she muttered.

"You still avoid my questions," he said, "but I think you have said something more important than you know. We have each tried to avoid making the other angry. In fact, we have been at pains to keep our relationship a placid one. But neither of us is placid by nature, Mollie. We have been playing games. You have, because you wish to discover what manner of man you are married to. And I have, partly because there are still vestiges of guilt remaining and partly because I have a natural preference for peace over war. But this state of affairs cannot be good for either of us. We must be able to talk honestly with each other."

Silence fell between them again as Mollie digested his words. A log shifted. There were fewer flames and more coals now in the fireplace, but the room was cozy, and Hawk's fingers stroking her arm did nothing to distract her thoughts. She felt relaxed and secure. She remembered his admission that his antipathy to the prince might stem from simple jealousy. The thought lingered. What had he meant, precisely? Was he jealous because he counted his wife as one of his possessions, or did his feelings run deeper than that? She had not thought about his feelings toward her before. Or had thought about them only casually, as when she had realized she still had the power to attract him as a woman attracts a man. She was his wife. And Hawk was a proud man, so he would wish her to reserve her favors for him. But he had certainly never said he loved her. For that matter, even in bed, he was scarcely a demanding husband. He still treated her with the utmost consideration, almost as if he feared he might break her.

Had she been playing games, as he suggested? Perhaps she had. Perhaps he was right and she wanted to test him. Certainly, the moment she feared he might have angered him, she had ceased her foolish flirting and had begun to behave with more restraint. Did that not prove he was right? Or did it simply reflect the fact that she still didn't know him very well, didn't know how angry he might become or what that anger might prompt him to do. Lady Gwendolyn had shown a healthy respect for his displeasure, and she knew better than Mollie what to expect from him. It was all confusing, and she didn't know that she could put her feelings into words even if that was what he was suggesting she should do. At any rate, it didn't matter now, for he had finished his brandy, and his hands had become busier as a result.

His fingers fumbled briefly with the little silk bow at the center of her low-scooped neckline, but a moment later the ribbon was loose, and he held her left breast cupped in his hand. His fingertips brushed across the nipple, and when she gasped a little, Hawk smiled.

"You have such silky skin, sweetheart. I like to touch it."

"Yours is hairy," she replied, pushing her brandy glass into his hand so that he could set it on the table near the chair. Her hand moved to the buttons on his waistcoat. "Moreover, you've got a good many more layers of clothing to protect it. Should we not go to bed, Gavin?"

"No one will disturb us here," he said, shifting her in his

lap to give his hands clearer access to her lovely, firm breasts.

She had the waistcoat open now and was working at his shirt, trying to ignore the feelings that went racing through her body at his lightest touch. Suddenly he placed a hand beneath her knees as if he meant, after all, to carry her to his bedchamber. But he did not stand up. Instead, he merely shifted from the chair to the hearth rug, where he laid her down before him. Mollie looked up at him as he shrugged off his coat.

"I feel like a captive damsel must have felt in medieval days," she said.

Grinning at her, he draped his coat over the chair, an act that would undoubtedly earn him a scold from his valet. The waistcoat followed. Then his shirt.

The dying firelight sent golden highlights dancing in the crisp curly hair on his chest and gave his bronzed skin a glow that made Mollie long to touch him.

"Gavin, come to me," she murmured huskily, reaching her arms up to him. He caught her up, holding her close for a moment. Then his hands were busy with her gown again. It was but a moment's work before it joined his clothing on the chair.

He pressed her back against the hearth rug, but this time he lay beside her, his hands caressing her velvety body while his lips claimed hers in a deep, exploring kiss. Mollie responded instantly, every fiber urging him to greater lengths of passion. Hawk's tongue played games with hers while his teasing hand moved lower, first with the stroking palm flat against her stomach, then lower yet, until his fingers were enmeshed in the soft curls at the juncture of her thighs.

Still he was gentle. Even when his lips left hers and moved to her breasts, when Mollie began to feel as if her entire body were on fire and longed for release, he still seemed to be holding himself back, as though he were afraid to match his passions to hers. It occurred to her then that she was doing little more than wishing he would show more urgency. Perhaps it was up to her to stir him to the heights she inhabited. Her hands had been moving idly before. Now she gave them purpose, using all that he had taught her to awaken him. What had been gentle loveplay soon turned into a struggle between them to see which of them could move the other onto higher planes of passion. Grinning, she pushed him onto his back to prove to him that her lips were as talented as his own, but it was not long before, with a low moan, he toppled her backward again, taking her with all the sense of urgency she could have hoped for. When his body relaxed against hers again, Mollie looked up into his eyes, smiling contentedly. He gazed back at her, his expression intensely speculative.

"You enjoyed that," he said, and the statement had a flavor of accusation.

She cocked her head a little on the hearth rug. "Should I not?"

"I was afraid I might have hurt you."

"You are always afraid you might hurt me," she pointed out. "I am not made of glass, Gavin. I do not break so easily."

"I guess I know that now, but still, you are so small."

"You would prefer an amazon?"

He chuckled, relaxing. "No, sweetheart, I would not prefer an amazon."

"Well, I may not be overtall, sir, but I am not so small as you seem to believe either. I am a woman, Gavin."

There was a brief moment of silence while he regarded her searchingly, perhaps wondering if she was prevaricating once again. But she met his look steadily and his expression warmed. " 'Tis just as well you are not easily broken, for if you meant to stimulate me as you did tonight, you will have to be most resilient, my lady."

"I have learned much from you, sir, about the art of stimulation."

"Aye." He smiled at her, but she was certain she detected a glint of doubt in his eyes before he looked away again. She was tempted, in view of his earlier words on the subject of being honest with each other, to demand that he explain both his reasons for assuming she was so fragile and that look of sudden doubt. But she could not bring herself to do it, for she sensed the topic might be a dangerous one.

The following day he presented her with his guest list for their forthcoming soiree, and she glanced over it curiously. There were one or two names that were barely familiar to her and two that were not familiar at all.

"Who on earth are Germaine and Albertine de Staël?" she asked.

"You will meet them Sunday at Lady Jersey's reception," Hawk said. "Madame de Staël is the daughter of Monsieur Jacques Necker, who was Louis the Sixteenth's Quatorze's Minister of Finance. She is a woman full of great and noble sentiments, who was, like her father, in favor of the French Revolution. They, and others like them, wanted to establish a constitutional monarchy. When things began to get out of hand, Madame de Staël—for she had married Sweden's ambassador to Paris by then—became an ardent supporter of the king and queen. She risked her own life, in fact, to present a petition in favor of Marie Antoinette to the revolutionary tribunal, and at one point she actually arranged a plan of escape for the royal family."

"She sounds like a woman of resolution," Mollie said, "but I collect her plan did not succeed."

"No, but it says much for her resolution, and her intelligence as well, that she managed to remain in France afterward. Under the Directory, her influence brought Talleyrand to power. She has always opposed Napoleon, however, and he exiled her from France eleven years ago."

"Where did she go?"

"Oh, she came here and settled in an émigré colony in Sussex, but she did not remain long. Instead, she went back, and Napoleon tolerated her presence until recently, but her last book was too much for him."

"She writes books?" Mollie asked. She could not decide whether Hawk had an extraordinary interest in the woman or if he was merely intrigued by her history, but she was looking forward to making the acquaintance.

"She does, indeed, and *De l'Allemagne*, her latest, is filled with references to the evils of imperialism. Napoleon was not amused. The book was seized by his police, and Madame has been exiled again."

"So she returns to England and is introduced to the *ton* by Lady Jersey. It seems as if her sponsor here ought more logically to be the Countess de Lieven. She sounds a most political sort of person," Mollie said.

"Ah, but her motive this time is not a political one, I think," Hawk said, chuckling. "You forget Albertine."

"Her daughter?"

"Indeed, and a daughter of marriageable age at that. Madame has a wish to see young Albertine suitably established, and I think her preference is for a wealthy English lord."

"Any lord in particular?"

"No, and I doubt if the title matters a great deal. Money does, however, as it does with most émigré families. I think they will interest you, my dear."

"Well, I shall certainly make it a point to invite them to our soiree. It seems we are to enjoy a variety of company that evening," she said pointedly. But Hawk didn't take the hint, making no effort to explain why he had chosen the names he had for his list. And one of those names stirred Mollie's curiosity more than the others, for by her husband's own command she was expected to invite his highness, Prince Nicolai Stefanovich, to her soiree.

9

On Sunday morning Mollie descended to the breakfast parlor, dressed to attend services at St. George's Chapel near Hanover Square with Lady Bridget. There was no sign of Hawk or Lord Ramsay when she joined the old lady at the table. Mollie knew that Hawk was up and about, but she realized she had scarcely seen Ramsay for several days. She mentioned the fact to Lady Bridget.

"Yes, dear, and he looked rather peaked, I thought, too. I daresay he has been too much occupied with his own affairs to spare us a thought. 'Tis often the case with gentlemen, though Gavin is all that is most considerate. You are fortunate, my dear."

"Oh, fortunate indeed," Mollie replied, chuckling as she spread marmalade lavishly upon a muffin. "Every wife should be fortunate enough to be spared her husband's presence for four years at the outset of their marriage."

"Well, perhaps he ought not to have gone away," Lady Bridget conceded, "but now he is back, no doubt enriched by his many experiences, so we may all be comfortable again."

"Nothing more than a lengthy grand tour, in fact," Mollie said teasingly.

Lady Bridget looked over her spectacles. "He was very young when he went away, my dear. He is a man now. I daresay it has all been for the best."

She looked flustered but determined, and Mollie relented, reaching across the table to pat her hand. "I own, ma'am, that things have been a deal more comfortable with him home."

"You like him, don't you, dear?"

The question caught Mollie as she was taking a bite of her muffin, so she could not answer immediately, which was just as well, since she hadn't actually considered the matter. An

interruption occurred before she was forced to put her tangled
thoughts into words.

"I say, Mollie, have you got a few shillings you might
lend me?" Harry demanded, bounding into the breakfast
parlor without ceremony. "My pockets are all to let, and
Bates says he will take me up to the Tower to see the
animals. I thought we might stop in to see Sir Ashton Lever's
science museum in Leicester Square as well. They've got
drawings of Trevithick's locomotive, you know, and a model
of Puffing Billy. By Jupiter, don't I wish Hedley would bring
the real thing to London! Imagine a locomotive that runs on a
smooth rail instead of cogs! Wouldn't I give anything to see it."

"Your pockets are not the only thing to let, young man,"
Mollie said calmly but with a pointed look. "Your manners
have gone begging as well."

"Sorry," he replied, quickly and without any lessening of
his good humor. "Good morning, Aunt Biddy. Good morning,
Mollie. May I please have six shillings if you've got them to
spare?"

"Six! You must have mistaken me for Golden Ball, sir.
Whatever will you be up to with such a fortune?"

"No one could mistake you for Golden Ball," Harry replied,
twinkling irrepressibly. "I've seen him. However, three shillings will do if you're at low tide. I asked for six because it
has been my experience that if one begins by asking for twice
the sum one wants, one is less likely to be disappointed in the
end."

"Is that a fact? And have you already tried this method on
your brothers, my friend?"

The boy chuckled. "You are the most complete hand,
Mollie. I did ask Ramsay, but he went all grim and testy, so I
daresay it's low water with him as well. And I didn't ask
Hawk because he has already said I must make do from
Monday to Monday. He *says* he makes me an adequate
allowance, but I can tell you, Mollie, though it might be
more than adequate at Hawkstone, here in the city it simply
disappears like so much smoke. And if you are thinking," he
added coaxingly, "that Hawk will not quite like it if you lend
money to me, I can pay you back first thing tomorrow. Only
today is when I need it." He regarded her soulfully, an
urchin with no other means of support who would starve if
she refused to fund his needs.

Mollie laughed, casting a rueful glance at her ladyship. "What do you say, ma'am? Shall I assist this penniless waif?"

"Well, he isn't penniless exactly," observed Lady Bridget, always a stickler for facts. "His mother left him very well to pass and Thurston did not forget him. Moreover, I was unaware that Sir Ashton charged an entrance fee. Perhaps you would prefer, if that is truly the case, Harry, to visit the Academy, where they are exhibiting some very fine pictures by Mr. Joshua Reynolds."

"No, thank you," Harry responded, valiantly attempting to conceal his revulsion. "There is no fee, Mollie, but several of the exhibits can be made to operate by inserting a penny or a sixpence in a slot. A fellow wants to be prepared."

"Very well, scamp. My reticule is there on the chair. Bring it to me and I'll see if I can stand the nonsense and still have something to put in the plate later."

"You're a trump, Mollie," he said as he took the shillings she pressed into his hand. With a grin he dashed off to inform Bates of the success of his mission, and Mollie smiled at Lady Bridget.

"I hope his lordship doesn't disapprove. I daresay he's right when he says we spoil Harry abominably."

"There is no harm in the child," Lady Bridget replied, "and Gavin is not so harsh a guardian as to deny him simple pleasures."

As they prepared to depart for the chapel, Mollie remembered Harry's casual remark about his brother's finances, or lack thereof. She decided to talk to Ramsay, but no opportunity arose to do so before that afternoon, when she was expected to accompany Hawk and Lady Bridget to Lady Jersey's reception for Madame de Staël and her daughter. In the coach, the subject crossed her mind again when Hawk mentioned that he had seen little of Lord Ramsay since the de Lievens' rout.

"I have been taking your advice and giving him a long leash, Mollie, but I cannot help feeling he may be getting into low company as a result. Pierrepont said he saw him with a group of lads at old Seventy-seven last night."

"Old Seventy-seven?"

"A gaming hell in St. James's Street."

"Well, at least he was not down at the docks, sir," Mollie

said with an attempt at levity. She caught a reproachful look
from Lady Bridget for her trouble, but privately she was
beginning to wonder if Ramsay might be under the hatches as
a result of his gaming. She determined to find out before
Hawk did, if that was the case. It was all very well to agree
to submit to her husband's authority, but she was certain he
would come down hard on Ramsay if her suspicions were
correct, and Mollie preferred to avoid that.

There was no time to spend worrying, however, for they
were already nearing Berkeley Square. Mollie's thoughts turned
to Lady Jersey, and some of her feeling must have shown in
her face, for Hawk, seated across from the two ladies, lifted
an eyebrow. "What is it, Mollie?" he asked gently.

Her smile was a little forced. "I always get like this before
meeting Lady Jersey," she confessed. "I never know if she
likes me or not. She is always so theatrical."

"A tragedy queen," he agreed. "It has been said that she
attempts the sublime and only succeeds in making herself
ridiculous." They were approaching the tall, elegant Jersey
town house. Hawk glanced briefly out the window before
continuing calmly, "If she looks down her nose, it is merely
because you outrank her, sweetheart." The coach had come
to a halt, and a flunky approached. "Her ladyship is incon-
ceivably rude and her manner is often ill-bred. One of the few
times I ever found myself in complete agreement with my
father is when he said George Villiers ought to have beaten
her soundly once a week until his lady learned how to behave
as a countess should."

"Gavin!" protested Lady Bridget, scandalized. She glanced
pointedly at the flunky, now opening the door and letting
down the steps. But once safely on the flagway with the boy
giving directions to the coachman, she said in an undertone,
"You should not say such things, my dear. Frances Villiers is
one of the foremost leaders of the *ton*. Moreover, though I
am sure you never knew him, George Villiers was a foppish
macaroni, scarcely the sort of man to beat his wife. And he is
dead," she added, as though that ought to clinch the matter.

Taking her elbow and following Mollie up the wide, steep
steps to the front door, Hawk said, "Lady Jersey fancies
herself a leader only because she thinks her erstwhile relationship with the Regent entitles her to certain privileges."

"Oh, Gavin," said Lady Bridget, diverted, "do you remember what a furor there was— No, of course you don't, for it was years ago. Only think, she insisted upon sitting next to the Princess of Wales instead of opposite her in the royal coach!''

''She lost that round, as I hear the tale. Even Prinny could scarcely insist that his mistress be accorded the same treatment as his wife.''

''I think,'' Mollie put in over her shoulder, ''that it was outside of enough for him to make his mistress Lady of the Bedchamber.''

The front door opened just then. Various minions stood ready to take their wraps and usher them into her ladyship's presence, so their conversation came to an end, but as a result of it, Mollie was able to greet her hostess less apprehensively.

In her sixtieth year Lady Jersey was very well preserved, if a trifle plump. She always dressed according to the height of fashion and received her guests now with her figure stiffly corseted beneath a gown of richly embroidered rose mousseline. Her greeting was cordial, though she did indeed look down her nose at Mollie. The effect was not what she might have hoped for, however. With Hawk's words still echoing in her ears, Mollie smiled and was forced to repress a chuckle. She contrived to retain her poise, however, and politely inquired after the guests of honor.

''Oh, Germaine is conversing with his highness yonder,'' replied Lady Jersey with a casual gesture. ''I declare they have been monopolizing each other for quite three-quarters of an hour.'' She did not seem in the least distressed by the fact. ''And dearest Albertine is there with that Russian prince of Dasha's.''

Mollie glanced in the direction indicated and immediately perceived Prince Nicolai Stefanovich in conversation with a plain but elegantly garbed young woman with about sixteen summers in her dish. The prince looked up just then and, catching her glance, smiled as warmly as though her appearance had made his day complete.

''Who is that rude young man?'' Lady Bridget asked in an undertone. ''He should not look at you so, my dear. Not here, in any case.'' She glanced back at Lady Jersey, still in conversation with Hawk. ''She is not known as Silence because of any ability to keep a still tongue in her head, you know.''

"Why, you sound as if you think I am having an affair with that gentleman," Mollie said teasingly, though she, too, cast a glance over her shoulder to see if by some mischance her husband had caught the prince's look. Hawk showed no interest in anything beyond Lady Jersey's conversation, however, so Mollie was able to reply lightly when Lady Bridget protested a sound belief in her virtue. Nevertheless, the older lady seemed taken aback to learn the prince's identity and even, once she had noted Lady Andrew Colporter among the guests, decidedly uncomfortable.

Hawk touched Mollie's elbow. "His highness is preparing to take his departure. Shall we make ourselves known to Madame de Staël?"

"I declare, Gavin, I shan't know what to say to her," Lady Bridget said, not for the first time that day. "I have been given to understand that she is quite a bluestocking, you know, and although I do read books and quite enjoyed the new one by that young gentlewoman who wrote *Sense and Sensibility* two years ago—such charming stories, both of them—well, I simply do not read such stuff as Madame de Staël writes."

"From what I know of her, Aunt Biddy, you needn't bother your head searching for conversation. She will talk enough for the three of us."

Mollie scarcely heeded his words, for she had been having all she could do not to stare at the woman seated upon a settee that looked too fragile to bear the massive weight of the Prince Regent beside her. Madame was no lightweight herself and was, moreover, quite the ugliest woman Mollie had ever seen. Her face was square and Germanic. Her hair and eyes were black, her mouth wide and disfigured by two very projecting upper teeth, and her complexion was swarthy. But although her figure was broad and heavy-bosomed, Mollie noted as they drew nearer that Madame's arms were very fine beneath the tiny puffed sleeves of her green sarcenet gown. She noted, too, that the black eyes were alight with wit and intelligence. The Regent was lumbering to his feet. He nodded.

"Hawkstone and the beautiful Lady Hawk. Haven't spoken to you, my lady, since the dinner I gave in honor of her majesty. Permit me to introduce Madame de Staël. A fine woman. Most entertaining. A pleasure, ma'am," he added, his Cumberland corsets creaking as he turned back to the dark woman. "Damme if this hasn't been the most pleasant hour of my day."

Madame de Staël had also risen and her smile was ingratiating. "You converse like a sensible man, your Highness. A credit to your education. I have learned many things from you in the course of a fascinating conversation."

The Regent nearly preened himself as he took his departure, and Mollie was hard-pressed again not to smile. She turned her attention firmly back to Madame, who was saying she had found his highness most kind. Since she went right on talking in a nonstop stream, even Lady Bridget was soon able to relax. It was a relief when Lady Sefton and Mrs. Drummond Burrell stepped up to claim Madame de Staël's attention and the Colporters were able to excuse themselves and move away.

Sir James Smithers approached them immediately, grinning. "See you've met the guest of honor. Did she toady to you, my lord?"

Hawk's eyes twinkled. "Since she said I must know more than anyone else in England about Wellington's plans and strategies and was no doubt a hero besides, I'll thank you to cast no aspersions my way when next you speak with her. Don't you like her, Jamie?"

"Not in my style," Smithers replied. "Dashed woman lays herself out for admiration any way she is able, purchasing any quantity of anybody at any price. She traffics in mutual flattery, Hawk. I trust you paid your toll."

"I did. She is recently come from France, Jamie. We cannot afford to snub her."

Sir James' round eyes took on a more intelligent expression than was their wont, and he nodded slowly. "Just so. The lady," he added cryptically, "might well know where a body or two be buried. Well, in that case, you'd best keep an eye on Brummell, Alvanley, and that lot. They're plotting mischief over yonder."

Hawk glanced toward an alcove where the Bow Window set from White's seemed to have taken up residence for the afternoon. Mollie, mystified by most of his conversation with Smithers, paid little heed when Lady Bridget's attention was claimed by their hostess, and followed her husband when he began to move toward the dandies. Brummell, Lord Alvanley, Lord Breckin, Sir Henry Mildmay, Henry Pierrepont, and

Tom Raikes were all seated together at their ease. It was Tom Raikes who greeted them.

"Welcome, Hawk! And welcome to your lady. I see your husband's been making sheep's eyes at Madame Bluestocking, Lady Hawk. Don't fret, though. Alvanley means to cut him out."

"Not so," interjected Mr. Brummell with a lazy smile. "His lordship will be pursued by young Libertine. 'Tis a certainty."

"No such thing," said Breckin in his customary affected tones. "Alvanley prefers a woman with well-developed lungs, and while the younger de Staël is not ripened sufficiently, the old dame has a thoracic development worthy of a wet nurse."

"Sirs," protested Alvanley, lisping as always, "I've little wish to develop an acquaintanth with either one. They are more in his highneth's style than mine."

"You've little choice in the matter, my lord," Brummell said softly."I told that woman you enjoy an income of one hundred thousand pounds a year. And since her response to that bit of fiction was to tell me you've a pretty face, I'll lay any odds you like that she puts young Libertine on to make a dead set at you."

Raikes chuckled, turning to Mollie. "The Beau is getting even, you understand, my lady. Alvanley put him out by pretending to know some fat, perspiring cit at the Opera and introducing Brummell to his notice. Fellow was delighted. 'Brummell? Brummell?' he said. 'Ain't you the fellow as sung such a good song at our club?' Alvanley whispered in the fat man's ear that he must be right, 'cause George certainly *does* sing a good song, though he's too shy to admit it. So the fat man up and invites Brummell to his hunting lodge for Christmas. Promised him as good a bottle of port as any in England. It's a fact. Heard him myself."

The Beau's expression did not change, but Mollie was certain he could not like hearing a tale that made the others laugh at him, so she was glad when Hawk returned to the original subject. "If you're laying odds, George, I might as well take the bet," he said, twinkling. "Seems to me you've lost well nigh every bet you've laid since I came back to England."

Mollie again expected Mr. Brummell to take umbrage, but he did not. The lazy smile reappeared instead. "This is a sure thing, my lord. She won't be able to resist the bait.'' He patted Alvanley's plump shoulder. ''Then, too, my luck is about to change. I'll not deny I've had a run of bad fortune at Macao, but when Breck here and I were walking home from Berkeley Street the other night—''

''At five o'clock Friday morning,'' Lord Breckin corrected, lifting an eyebrow.

Brummell gave a slight shrug. ''In any event, when I saw something glittering in the gutter, I stooped and picked up a crooked sixpence, which anyone knows to be a harbinger of good luck.''

''Previous owner must have thought so,'' drawled Breckin. ''Dashed thing already had a hole in it.''

''Can't have brought him much luck if he tossed it in a gutter,'' Hawk pointed out. The others laughed, and the discussion turned to matters of superstition. After a few moments, seeing that her husband meant to stay a while, Mollie excused herself and wandered off to find Lady Bridget. Before she could do so, however, she was accosted by Lady Andrew Colporter.

''How do you do, Margaret? You are looking well.''

Mollie answered politely, but the look in Lady Andrew's eyes caused her some misgiving, and when her ladyship demanded a private word with her, she followed her reluctantly into a small anteroom.

''I cannot think what you want with me, Beatrix, but Hawk must be nearly ready to depart.''

''Don't take that high-handed tone with me, young lady. I want to know if the news I've heard about you and that Muscovite is true or not!''

''Good gracious, Beatrix, what maggot have you got in your brain now?'' Mollie demanded. ''I collect that you are referring to Prince Nicolai Stefanovich, who is a perfectly respectable member of Monsieur de Lieven's staff, so I cannot conceive—''

''Oh, can you not!'' Her ladyship's high-pitched voice dripped with sarcasm. ''I suppose that next you will deny traipsing all over Dorothea de Lieven's back garden with the man. Shifty, that's what he is. And I'll tell you to your head, Margaret, that he is more than you can handle. I have already told Hawkstone what I think about such a liaison, and

he says there is nothing in it, more fool he. But I know you
for what you are, better than he does.''

She went on in the same vein, but Mollie had ceased to
listen, her heart thudding into her shoes at the thought that
Hawk would now think every gossip in town was linking her
name to Nicolai's. Still, he had said nothing further to her, so
perhaps he had assumed Lady Andrew was exaggerating. As,
indeed, she was. The thought brought anger upon its heels,
and when Lady Andrew took that moment to insist in her
haughtiest tone that Mollie never so much as speak to "that
fellow" again, the sparks leapt to her eyes. Drawing herself
to her full height, Mollie told Lady Andrew to be silent.

"What?"

"You heard me, Beatrix. I have listened to more than I
wish to hear from you on that or any subject. Whether or not
I speak to his highness or walk with him in a garden—hardly
a private walk, at that—it is my business and solely my
business. Neither you nor Hawkstone, for that matter, has the
right to tell me not to speak to the man. I have done nothing
for which I need to feel ashamed. Not now and not during the
four years of my husband's absence, though you choose to
think otherwise. Oh, I know you think you know all about
me, and I freely admit I did some foolish things. But they
were foolish, Beatrix, not scandalous. I should not have gone
to the Bartholomew Fair, but only because it meant hobnob-
bing with rustics and cits, and because of the unfortunate fact
that that particular fair very nearly turned into a riot!"

"I suppose you will next pretend to have been all decorum
at Margate last year as well," Lady Andrew retorted scathingly.

"Lady Bridget was with me." Mollie's tone was snubbing,
but Lady Andrew was made of stern stuff.

"More shame to you that you dragged her there. And
Biddy was *not* with you when you attended that dreadful
masquerade at Dandelion Gardens dressed as a Vestal, of all
things, and accompanied by a knight whose only claim to the
title, as I understand it, was that he was errant!"

"Good gracious!" exclaimed Mollie, hoping she sounded
more astonished than she felt. "Where on earth did you come
by such a tale?"

"Do you dare to deny it?"

"I shouldn't think of dignifying it with a denial," Mollie
retorted. "I have come to know that you derive your greatest

pleasure from believing the worst of me.'' When Lady Andrew looked as if she would speak further, Mollie held up an imperious hand. "I won't hear another word. You have tried to make mischief and you have failed. There is nothing further to be said." With that she turned on her heel and left the room.

Inwardly she was seething, but there was a sense of relief as well. Lady Andrew had censured her behavior at Margate before, but her strictures had always centered upon her belief that Mollie had no business to be in a holiday resort while she was still in mourning. Mollie had not known for certain that Lady Andrew was aware of her attendance at the masqued ball. Since the woman had hitherto made no mention of the subject, it must be that she had heard only rumors and did not know that the story was true. She had not named Mollie's escort, after all, though her description of him was accurate enough, and since Mollie had been masqued and had left the party before midnight, there was no way now for Lady Andrew to make certain of her facts. But if she had heard the rumor, no doubt she had passed it along as fact to Hawk, for it was not in her nature to have done otherwise. And if Hawk had heard about the masquerade, he had heard the worst of his wife's follies.

Oddly, the thought that he must have chosen not to believe the tale, since he had not so much as asked her about it, stirred her old resentments. She had been treading lightly for fear he would cast old accounts in her face, but if he had not seen fit to write her when he first heard about it—as, indeed, he had written to blister Lady Gwendolyn when she had taken up with Lord Featherby—and if he had said nothing to her since then, except to apostrophize his aunt for a long-nose, then she had nothing to fear from him. And since there was nothing to fear, there could be no reason not to go on as she pleased.

She had been making her way through the crowded room, absently searching for Lady Bridget, as these thoughts tumbled through her head. But suddenly a broad, bemedaled chest loomed up before her.

"My lady, I am pleased to see you."

"Your Highness!" She looked up to find him smiling at her. There was no hint of the overbold attitude he had taken with her at Ashburnham House. Instead, his expression reminded her of a puppy uncertain of approval. Her first inclination had been to exchange a polite word or two and then be on her way, but the prince exerted himself to charm her, and his methods were much more to her liking than they had been before. Added to that fact was her lingering resentment at being ordered first by her husband and more recently by his interfering aunt to have nothing to do with Prince Nicolai. Mollie wanted to show them both that she could captivate the prince without being captivated by him. Thus it was that she allowed him to engage her in charming conversation for a full twenty minutes before she saw Lady Bridget signaling to her that it was time to depart. She smiled at the prince.

"I must go, sir, but I hope we will see you at our soiree Thursday evening."

"You will see me, my lady," he assured her. "Nothing could keep me away."

Blushing at his tone, Mollie turned away to join Lady Bridget.

"I cannot like that gentleman," her ladyship said in a worried undertone.

"Oh, he is perfectly harmless, ma'am, I assure you. I cannot think why you have not been presented to him before, but I shall make a point of doing so Thursday, when he attends our soiree."

"Never say you invited him, Mollie. I am certain Gavin will not like it, and for that matter I cannot think why you want a soiree. You never wish to go to them yourself, and though I cannot but know there is some fine talent among our friends and acquaintances, most of them are amateurs compared to what one hears at Covent Garden or the Opera. Lofting tells me you have even arranged for a harp to be brought in."

"Yes," said Mollie, chuckling, "for Hawk particularly wished to hear Miss Aisling play. Just as he wished me to invite Prince Nicolai and Madame de Staël. I think he has some game in mind that he does not choose to share with us, ma'am."

"Oh," said Lady Bridget, her forehead smoothing at once. "If Gavin desires it, then there is no more to be said. I tell you, my dear, it is so comforting to have one's affairs in a gentleman's capable hands again. I know you have managed well enough since Thurston passed on, but you will own that it is never so comfortable when the running of things is left to a mere female. Only think what it must have been like to live in England when a woman was actually governing the entire country! Things must have been always at sixes and sevens. 'Tis no wonder the Spanish thought they could sail over and take the throne.''

Mollie stared at her. Clearly Lady Bridget had little understanding of either history or current politics if she believed the Regent or his mad father more capable of handling the reins of government than Queen Elizabeth had been. Or any other English queen, for that matter. It was all of a piece, though. Trust sweet Lady Bridget to assume that Hawk was better able to guide their affairs than Mollie had been, simply because he was male. Well, she would show them all that she was capable of handling her own affairs, at least, without interference from anyone. She had successfully routed Lady Andrew. Now she would show Hawk that she could choose her friends, run her life—yes, and even deal with Ramsay's problems, whatever they were—without help or hindrance from a mere husband.

10

Mollie went in search of Lord Ramsay as soon as they returned to Grosvenor Square. He was not anywhere to be found, but he had left word with Lofting that he expected to dine at home, so she asked the butler to tell her brother-in-law that she wished to speak with him immediately upon his arrival. Then she joined Lady Bridget in the large drawing room overlooking the rear gardens, where she was discovered some moments later by an enthusiastic Lord Harry.

"By Jove, Mollie, the Tower is something like! They've got all manner of creatures there. I saw a black bear all the way from the colonies and even a tiger from India. Bates says we may go again, and I think you would like it above all things if you was to go with us. You, too, Aunt Biddy," he added kindly to the little lady, who sat in an armchair near the window, plying her needle.

"Dear me," she replied, "but I should be afraid such horrid beasts might attack someone. I wonder that they allow them to be kept in the city."

"Oh, pooh, there's not the least danger," Harry scoffed. "They've got them in cages."

"Did you get to see the displays at Sir Ashton Lever's museum?" Mollie asked.

"Yes, and there was a music box from Germany, Mollie, a huge thing. Filled a whole wall. One puts in a sixpence and it plays like a complete orchestra. The most marvelous thing. I'm not much of a dab for that fellow Haydn, and it played one of his pieces, but it was remarkable all the same. There was a mechanical bird in a golden cage, too. For a penny one might hear it sing. It sounds like a real canary, I promise you."

"In fact, you enjoyed yourself."

"By Jupiter, didn't I! There are so many things to see

here. Gaslights and who knows what all? If only I needn't do lessons all day, I might see a great deal more," he added coaxingly.

Mollie grinned at him. "You won't get 'round me so easily as that, Harry. You know your brother is making arrangements to send you to Eton. You would not wish to be unprepared and have the other boys think you a dunce."

"No, of course not," he agreed, much struck. "And I shall be going on for ten before I even set foot in the place. Ramsay and Hawk both went when they were eight."

"Indeed, so you must apply yourself in order to avoid being sent to the headmaster's study. I understand that can be a most painful experience."

"Oh, I don't worry about that," Harry said scornfully. "I suppose I know better than to ask for trouble."

When he had gone, Mollie turned to Lady Bridget, smiling. "You know, I believe school will be a wonderful experience for him, but I confess I'm not overanxious to see him leave."

"Well, you'll soon have children of your own for us to cosset, my dear," her ladyship replied comfortably, "and a gentleman must always benefit from a good education."

Mollie agreed with that sentiment, but although Lady Bridget seemed disposed to continue the conversation, she soon excused herself to change her clothes for dinner. With the assistance of both Cathe and Mathilde du Bois this task was speedily accomplished, and no sooner had she dismissed them and retired to her sitting room than there was a light tap on the door and Lord Ramsay stepped inside the room.

"Lofting said you wished to speak with me." He looked tired and his tan seemed to have faded. There were lines at the corners of his eyes and dark circles beneath them, both signs that he had been going the pace too hard.

"Come in, Ramsay, and sit down," she said.

"I've got to change for dinner, Mollie."

"I'll order it put back, if necessary. I want to talk to you."

"What's amiss? You in the briars again?"

"No, it's your problem I wish to discuss. Sit down."

Eyeing her warily, he took his seat with an air of forced casualness. "I cannot conceive of what you might want to discuss," he said.

"You are in some kind of trouble, Ramsay. It stands out all over you."

"Fiddlesticks. All your eye and Betty Martin, Moll. What put that maggot in your cockloft?"

"A number of things suggested the possibility, but now that I see you, I know it for a fact. Cut line, Ramsay."

He smiled faintly at the slang expression. "It's nothing. Merely a reverse or two. Nothing I can't sort out in the wink of an eye, and certainly nothing for you to get into a pother about."

"Have you discussed these little reverses—I collect you mean financial reverses—with Hawk?"

The young man shifted uncomfortably in his chair. "No, I haven't wished to bother him. Not that there is a problem, Mollie. You've imagined things," he added lamely.

"How much, Ramsay?"

"I beg your pardon?"

"You needn't, for I mean to get to the bottom of this. How much do you owe?"

He looked as though he would continue in his denials, but Mollie stared at him unwinkingly, and finally, with a dismissing wave of his hand, he said, " 'Tis the merest trifle, Moll. Not a cent above five hundred, I promise you."

"Five hundred *pounds*!"

"Well, guineas, actually, but I'll come about. Even Brummell's luck is said to be on the turn, you know."

"All because of some silly sixpence," she told him. "I heard all about that. But I've yet to hear that he has actually *won* any money. Surely, you cannot mean to go on betting when you're already under by so much."

"Well, I've got to raise the ready, don't I? And I can certainly think of no other way to come by it."

"But if you've got no money, how can you stake yourself?"

"I can go to Jew King in Clarges Street or Hamlet's in Cranbourne Alley if I have to."

"Don't be nonsensical, Ramsay. You are under age and your name is known. They won't touch you, or if they do, they'll go straight to Hawk to get their money, saying they only meant to do you a favor. Then you would be in the suds. I haven't got enough left in my account or I'd lend you the money myself in a twinkling."

"I wouldn't let you, Moll." He sighed. "I got myself into this, so I must get myself out. Luckily, all the money is owed to one fellow, and he knows it's low water with me just now, so I daresay he won't raise a dust. Matter of fact, he offered to lend me a bit to stake if I needed it. I didn't like to do it, but maybe I should let him.''

"No! Who is this generous spirit, anyway?" Mollie demanded.

"A friend of Hardwick's. Name of Gaspard d'Épier. You may meet him anywhere, Mollie. From a distinguished émigré family. But, I can tell you, he knows what it's like to be at low tide financially.''

"One may indeed meet Monsieur d'Épier anywhere," she agreed, favoring him with a long look. "In fact, one may meet him in this very house on Thursday next. Nonetheless, I cannot think him a suitable person to be your friend, Ramsay.''

"Fustian. I collect you refer to the rumors that Gaspard is a spy or some such muck. Lord, Moll, don't be such a nodcock! As if Hawk would have him here if that were true. Fact is, every time a paper or memo goes missing, every stuffy Englishman looks down his nose at the nearest poor émigré, thinking the fellow must be a spy.''

"*Is* there something missing?" Mollie's eyes widened.

"Lord, how should I know? Very likely. Hasn't the *Times* been squawking for weeks about Napoleon's 'uncanny foreknowledge' about Wellington's movements and how shocked the French were at Vitoria? Stands to reason something went missing sometime, don't it? But that don't make Gaspard a spy. Not by a long chalk!''

Mollie looked searchingly at him. She was liking the business less and less with every passing moment, and she could think of only one course of action that made any sense. However, she was certain he would be even more reluctant to follow it than she was to suggest it. "Ramsay," she said gently at last, "I know you will not like it, but I think you must go to Hawk.''

"The devil I will!"

"He won't eat you."

"Won't he just? Well, I won't do it, and I forbid you to do so.'' He leaned forward in his chair. "He as good as told me I wasn't up to snuff, Mollie, and maybe I ain't, but I don't need his help in this, and so I mean to show you both. I'll deal with it myself.'' He regarded her anxiously. "You won't squeak, will you, Moll?"

"No, of course not.'' Then, as he leaned back in his chair

again, relieved, she added, "Not if you promise me you'll do nothing foolish. You must give me your word that you'll not borrow from the moneylenders or from that d'Épier person."

"Then what am I to do? My quarterly allowance ain't due till the first, and even the whole amount won't cover what I owe."

"How came you to bet what you didn't have?"

"I was a trifle bosky, Moll. I'd been winning, you see, and I thought I *did* have enough. But when we counted up the markers, I was five hundred short. Can't think how I came to be so careless, even in my cups."

She frowned. "Could the game have been—"

"No, no, don't even suggest it! I was with friends, I tell you."

Despite the words, she sensed doubt in the very strength of his denial, but she was sensible enough not to press the matter. Instead, she told him she wished to think the whole business over, promising him she would take no action without first consulting with him. He agreed, though he did not seem to be much cheered when he left her.

Mollie had been given a good deal of food for thought, and she heartily wished she had someone she could discuss the matter with. Briefly she considered asking Lady Gwendolyn's advice, but the notion occurred only to be discarded. Lady Gwendolyn might sympathize with her younger brother, but she would no doubt recommend confessing the whole to Hawk and taking the consequences. Lady Bridget would say the same thing. Mollie herself had more than one urge as the week passed to lay the matter before him. Her husband had proved upon several previous occasions to be a fair man, and she did not think he would treat Ramsay harshly. Moreover, there was still doubt in her mind regarding the fairness of the game in which Ramsay had lost such a sum, and Hawk was in a better position than she was to investigate that portion of the mess. On the other hand, if she applied to him, she would incur the wrath of her young brother-in-law, and she would also prove to everyone's satisfaction that a mere woman could not manage successfully without a man's assistance. At the very least, she decided, she ought to give herself time.

Accordingly, she racked her brain for the next four days. She even considered asking Hawk to deposit a further five hundred pounds in her own account, knowing that despite

Ramsay's insistence that he would not take money from her, he would scarcely refuse if she simply handed it to him. But Hawk would demand an explanation, and he would want precise details. He would never be fobbed off with some glib tale or other.

By Thursday Mollie was no nearer an answer. Her only consolation that night as she left the dinner table with the other ladies was that since Ramsay had chosen to dine with young Hardwick and d'Épier was drinking port with Hawk, Lord Bathurst, Monsieur de Lieven, Prince Nicolai, and the other gentlemen in her dining room, the two were not out gaming together. Gathering her wits with an effort and more thankful than ever to have the comfortably placid Lady Bridget to aid her with her numerous guests, she turned her attention to minor last-minute arrangements for the entertainment.

Since Miss Aisling was to play the harp for them later, Mollie sent for a footman to help her set it in position. The piano likewise was opened, and a branch of candles set to light the music. As she turned away from that task, she found young Albertine de Staël waiting to speak with her. Smiling at the child, she thought it really was too bad of Mr. Brummell to insist upon referring to her by such an odious nickname. Albertine had done nothing to merit the rudeness of being called Libertine and was, in fact, a prim and amiable young lady. However, she was her mother's daughter, and the dandy set had no use for literary or political persons. Madame de Staël was both. Moreover, Mollie told herself shrewdly, the woman was an acknowledged genius, something mere men could not be expected to tolerate in a female.

The girl smiled shyly. "Pardon, my Lady Hawkstone, but your dinner was most pleasant."

Mollie replied politely and then expressed the hope that Albertine was enjoying her stay in London.

"Oh, yes." She hesitated, lowering her lashes. "I sat next to Prince Nicolai this evening, you know. He has a pretty face, has he not?"

Mollie chuckled. "He has at that."

"It does not signify in the slightest, however," spoke a faintly guttural voice behind them. "The prince is not for you, *mon petit chou.*" Madame de Staël laid a gentle hand upon her daughter's shoulder. "His title is an empty one and his prospects are questionable," she said. "Go away now, *enfant*, and make your curtsy to Lady Sefton. I wish a word with our so charming hostess.''

Albertine excused herself obediently, and Mollie found herself alone with Madame de Staël. "I hope you do not think I was matchmaking, madame."

"Do not puzzle yourself, my lady," her guest replied graciously. "The child is young. She will allow herself to be guided by her mother. And it will not be into the arms of such as the Russian."

"You say his prospects are unknown, madame? I should think, placed as he is, that he has a brilliant diplomatic career ahead of him."

"He is capable, not brilliant, and though he obtained his position with Monsieur de Lieven through influence, the fact that his mother was French will impede his progress."

"French!"

"Yes, and though the family were royalists, and she is now deceased and the lands confiscated by the Empire, still it is considered wisest to have no feet in the enemy camp, lest a toe or two be trodden upon."

Mollie was not sure she followed Madame de Staël's reasoning, but she could scarcely ask her to explain more fully when other ladies were waiting to claim her attention. Nevertheless, the information cast a different light on his highness. She had assumed before from his numerous medals and his air of consequence that his family was both wealthy and influential. But she could think of no reason for Madame de Staël to say the things she had said if they were not true.

It was a long time before the gentlemen joined them, as Mollie had predicted it would be, and she was beginning to get a headache from all the feminine chatter. But the men came in at last, and Mr. Brummell, invited along with Lord Alvanley and several others among the dandy set to help Mollie make up her numbers, strolled up to her, flicking open his snuffbox with his left thumb and taking a pinch. Closing the box again with his left index finger, he put the pinch of snuff on the back of his left hand, lifted it gracefully to his nostrils, and inhaled delicately, then flicked away imaginary residue from his coat with his handkerchief. Mollie had seen him go through the procedure dozens of times, but the grace and flair with which he accomplished the ordinary move-

ments fascinated her. Brummell moved to restore the snuffbox to his pocket.

Prince Nicolai, suddenly appearing beside them, held out
his hand. "An elegant piece, Mr. Brummell. May I see it?"

"Indeed, Highness," responded the Beau in a bored voice.

"Exquisite, but there appears to be no hinge."

"I thay, Brummell," Lord Alvanley demanded, peering
over the prince's arm, "is that the Lawrence Kirk box you
had from Fribourg and Treyer?"

"It is." Brummell was watching as the prince turned the
box over in his hand. "Even the Regent could not discover
the trick of it, Highness."

"Damned if I can open it," Nicolai said, frowning. "Your
pardon, my lady."

"That's quite all right," Mollie said. "May I try?" Reluctantly he gave it to her, and she examined it. She had seen the
Beau open it, so she knew it could be done, but she could
find no hinge or clasp. When Alvanley demanded a turn, she
gave it to him, watching carefully to see if he would be more
successful.

His lordship, with a small, mischievous grin, reached into
his pocket and extracted a pen knife. When his intention
became clear, Brummell protested vehemently.

"My lord, allow me to observe that's not an oyster but a
snuffbox!"

Hawk approached them as the laughter was fading into
chuckles, and Mollie quickly explained what had happened.
Grinning, Hawk turned to Brummell.

"I understand your lucky sixpence has had its effect,
George."

"Aye, that and changing my game to hazard," the Beau
confirmed. "Fact is, Mildmay, Pierrepont, Alvanley, and I
had a fantastic run at Watier's and we mean to celebrate.
You'll all be receiving proper invitations for a fancy-dress
ball at the Argyle Rooms."

"Oh, Mr. Brummell, we shall be delighted to attend,"
Mollie assured him.

"Inviting Prinny?" Hawk asked, *sotto voce*.

"No, that we will not," replied Brummell, lifting his chin.
"I am out of charity with him at the moment, as you well
know."

"He won't be pleathed," Alvanley put in anxiously.

"Well, he had best not raise a dust over it," Mr. Brummell said severely, "or I shall be forced to bring the old king back into fashion."

Chuckles greeted this sally, and Hawk turned to Alvanley. "How is your courtship proceeding, my lord?" The chubby little man winced expressively.

Sir James Smithers, overhearing the question, clapped Alvanley on the back. "He's a success. Chit follows him everywhere. At Almack's last night she said *his* face was prettier than Jersey's!" There was more laughter at these words, since Lady Jersey's eldest son was considered to be one of the handsomest men in town, while poor Lord Alvanley had little to recommend him other than his title, his charm, and his propensity for living well beyond his means.

"Good Lord, Mollie," Hawk said just then, close to her ear, "what is that Aisling wench about?"

She twinkled up at him. "Did you not request a harpist, my lord?"

"You wretch! You know I did no such thing." But his eyes twinkled back at her. "Getting your own again? I apologize for this," he added, still speaking in a low tone, though the others had moved away to find seats for the forthcoming entertainment, and Mollie was amused to see Madame de Staël maneuvering young Albertine away from Prince Nicolai to a seat beside Alvanley. But Hawk's apology made her look at him sharply.

"Why do you apologize, sir?"

"Because I've put together a pretty rum lot, sweetheart. Good notion of yours to invite the dandies. Adds leavening. Surprises me that Brummell would condescend to grace such an affair, though."

"He has even agreed to read a poem, sir," she informed him saucily. Then she grinned, demanding to know if he doubted her ability to entice anyone she chose to her entertainments.

He put two fingers beneath her chin. "If I had doubts on that score, my girl, I'd have described myself as astonished, not merely surprised."

She wrinkled her nose at him. "I hope your game is a successful one, my lord."

He glanced around the room, his gaze coming to rest upon the slim figure of Gaspard d'Épier, and he made no attempt to deny the charge that he was playing games. "I hope so, too. You've certainly done your part," he added, grimacing as Miss Aisling tilted the harp and strummed the first notes of an étude.

A poetry reading by another young woman followed the harpist, and then Alvanley and Pierrepont agreed to sing a duet if Mollie would play for them. That was followed by Mr. Brummell's poem. Since his unkind allusions to Mrs. Hertford were only too transparent, Mollie hoped news of the event did not soon reach either the Regent's ears or those of his mistress.

Her headache lingered, and the sight of several gentlemen at the rear of the room slipping out, including Monsieur d'Épier, Sir James Smithers, and Lord Breckin, did nothing to reconcile her to her plight. One side of the huge saloon overlooked the rear garden, and Mollie noticed that some thoughtful person had opened one set of French windows near the back of the room. The heavy curtains moved, indicating a breeze. Though the windows gave no egress to the gardens, a full story below, there was a balcony, and it occurred to Mollie that if she could manage to reach it unobtrusively, she might step out there for some fresh air. She was seated near the side of the room, so it was simply a matter of moving slowly enough so that she did not draw every eye toward herself.

Only Lady Bridget paid her any notice as she made her way to the window, but Mollie smiled at her reassuringly and stepped through the curtains, hoping she wouldn't find the balcony already occupied by some gentleman who had chosen to step outside to blow a cloud.

The balcony was empty, however, and the gentle breeze was everything she had hoped for. There was a light fog, making haloes around the lanterns in the gardens below and giving an eerie quality to the view. Though there were no stars to be seen above, the fog did not entirely obliterate the moon, although it did soften the points of the crescent, making it appear almost as if the moon were melting.

Mollie smiled at the thought, taking a deep breath. A voice from behind startled her.

"Are you ill, my lady?" It was Prince Nicolai, and his tone expressed concern.

Mollie turned to him with a smile. "Not ill, Your Highness,

merely indulging myself in a bit of fresh air. It was stuffy inside.''

''Ah.'' He moved closer, his handsome face outlined in the shadowy, silver glow cast by the fog-meshed moon. ''You are certain you are not ill, Mollie?'' His voice was low, and there was a note in it she could not misinterpret.

''Your Highness, I am obliged to you for your concern, but I must return to my guests. I have stayed away too long already.''

''There is no need for hurry,'' he said, effectively blocking her way simply by standing his ground. ''We can hear the music well enough. A Handel concerto, I believe. Rather amateurishly executed. Good technique but no style, no flair. This sort of entertainment is not what one has been led to expect from you, my dear.''

Startled by the endearment, Mollie nearly informed him that Hawk had commanded tonight's performance, but a sixth sense stopped her. She was as certain as she could be that her husband did not want it known that he had orchestrated the entire affair. ''I attempt to provide for all manner of tastes,'' she said simply, taking an assertive step forward and hoping he would move aside. He did not. Instead, his strong hands gripped her shoulders.

''You are a beautiful woman, Mollie.''

''I have not given you leave to use my name, Your Highness, nor have I invited familiarity of any other sort. You will oblige me by ceasing to talk absurdities and by letting me pass.''

''It is never absurd to tell a woman she is beautiful,'' he replied smoothly, still holding her shoulders. ''Nor is it difficult for a man of experience to know when a passionate woman's 'no' means 'yes' instead. I know you want me, Mollie. I'll prove it to you.'' And then, to her astonishment, he pulled her forward, slipping one hand to the small of her back while the other captured her chin, tilting her face up so his lips could find hers. There was nothing seductive about the kiss. Instead, it demanded. Her lips were crushed beneath his, and his tongue immediately sought entrance between her gritted teeth.

When her struggles proved pointless against his superior strength, Mollie drew back one dainty foot, intending to kick him as hard as she could in the shins. Fortunately she recalled in time that her thin satin slippers would afford her little protection and, consequently, altered the position of her leg to bring her heel down upon his instep as hard as she could. He grunted but held on to her, so she lifted her foot again, cursing the pencil-slim skirt that made it impossible to put her knee where she would have liked very much to put it. So intent was she upon her purpose that she was only dimly, peripherally aware of the parting of the heavy curtains behind the prince and the large hand that clamped down upon his shoulder before he suddenly released her and turned abruptly to meet her grim-faced husband.

"The fact that you are a guest in my house," Hawk said evenly, "not to mention a guest in my country, prevents me from tossing you over that balcony, Highness. But it does not prevent me from interrupting this pretty scene to send you about your business. I will have my butler show you out." He stood aside to let the prince pass by, but before he followed, he looked directly at Mollie, and despite the uncertain light, there could be no mistaking the fury in his eyes.

"I suggest you return to your guests at once, madam. You and I will discuss this incident fully at a more appropriate time."

11

It was a few moments before Mollie could gather her wits. Hawk's sudden appearance and patent misunderstanding of the scene had shocked her to the point where she was unable to think clearly, but one thing was certain: she must stifle the emotional upheaval that was threatening to overcome her. There was no time for shock, worry, or anger. She must return to the saloon and she must make it appear as though nothing had occurred to distress her. There would be eyes everywhere, and the scandalmongers would have a field day if they thought Hawk had interrupted a tête-à-tête.

The piano concerto was approaching an end, so the time had come. Taking a deep breath, she stepped through the curtains, smiling as naturally as she could at the first person who chanced to look her way, which happened to be Lord Breckin. Then Lady Bridget came quietly up to her, her brow slightly furrowed.

"Is everything all right, my dear?"

Mollie nodded, feeling as if she had suddenly been split into two persons, one concentrating on what Hawk must be doing and thinking, while the other smiled and chuckled and nodded in response to a number of curious expressions.

"I am fine, ma'am. If anyone should inquire, I had a slight headache and stepped out for some air. His highness popped his head out to ask if I needed assistance, and Hawk came looking for him to discuss some matter of business. Please do not allow anyone to refine too much upon the matter."

She knew that she was babbling and that Lady Bridget probably wasn't swallowing the half of it, but the exchange helped Mollie gather her resources sufficiently to parry the one or two oblique references to the situation that came her way.

Some fifteen minutes after he had left it, Hawk came back

into the room. The servants had begun to serve tea, and a number of people were ready to take their departure. Moving into the hall, Hawk put a casual hand at his wife's waist as they bade their guests farewell, and though Mollie trembled at his touch, she forced herself to smile up at him, knowing that such an open display of affection, rare in their set, would do more to stop any pending rumors than whatever nonsensical tale she or Lady Bridget might put about.

It was some time before they saw the front door shut behind the last guest, but the moment still came too soon to suit Mollie. She wanted nothing more than to link her arm in Lady Bridget's when that gentle dame informed them that they might stay up all night long if they chose, but she, for one, was going to bed. Stifling her more cowardly instincts, Mollie meekly said good night, and a moment later, except for the footman extinguishing candles in the downstairs rooms, she was alone with her husband. She glanced at him hesitantly.

"We will go upstairs," Hawk said, his hand firmly in the small of her back. He did not actually push her, but she knew there would be no point to be made by resisting that pressure. She did attempt to speak, however.

"Gavin, it was not what you think."

"Upstairs, madam. I have no wish to discuss the matter where we shall be overheard."

Swallowing hard, she followed him, and nothing more was said before they reached her bedchamber, where both Cathe and Mathilde du Bois awaited her. Hawk dismissed them without ceremony, and the moment they were gone, he turned to his wife, letting his anger surface at last.

"I told you to have nothing more to do with that fellow."

"And then ordered me to invite him here," Mollie countered, her own temper stirring.

"That has nothing to do with the matter. I didn't bring him here for your entertainment."

Mollie forced herself to speak more calmly. "That business on the balcony was not what you thought," she said. "What you saw did not occur by my choice, sir, but entirely against my will."

"Do you deny you have been flirting with the fellow everywhere you have met him?" Hawk demanded.

"I have not been flirting. I have merely been friendly."

"With a man of his stamp it amounts to the same thing,"

he returned implacably, "and, I confess, the minor differences between your notions of friendship and flirting would be difficult for any ordinary mortal to discern. Moreover, I specifically told you to have nothing to do with him."

"I won't be told who my friends will or will not be," Mollie said bitterly. "You agreed to let me go my own way, my lord, and to discuss matters, not to give arbitrary orders. Yet, in this instance—"

"In this instance I gave orders because it was necessary," he said, interrupting her.

"Why was it necessary?"

He hesitated, but her glare dared him to answer, so finally, goaded, he said, "It was necessary in order to stop the tattlemongers. You have indulged in a good deal of folly over the past four years, my lady, and your reputation is more fragile than you might suspect."

Surprised by the line of his attack, Mollie turned away, biting her lower lip. "You said you didn't believe those tales," she reminded him.

"Are they all untrue?"

She turned back, words of defense springing to her tongue, but when her gaze met his, the most she could manage to say the tales were exaggerated. "I cannot know precisely what was written to you, of course, since you have not told me, but I do know Lady Andrew, sir, and most of your other relatives are cut from the same cloth."

"Other people are not, however. Gwen, for one."

"Good gracious, Gavin. Gwen would never tell tales of me! What are you implying?"

"I merely mentioned Margate to her. I daresay she assumed I knew the whole, for she attempted to defend you, Mollie. Do you intend to dress as a Vestal virgin for Brummell's fancy-dress party as you did for that wretched masquerade?"

Her cheeks flushed with deep color. "That costume was not so bad as you have been led to believe, my lord," she muttered. "It was merely a white gown, bound across the bodice and around the waist with twisted gold cord. Others were amused to designate it a Vestal's gown. I did not."

"No doubt it was vastly becoming to you, my dear, but it was scarcely proper attire for a lady in mourning. My father had not been in his grave for three months."

"And what were you wearing just then, sir? Perhaps you

condescended to wear a black armband while you were out hunting. We've heard grand tales about Wellington's officers' behavior, I can tell you, and masqued balls are but the least of *their* entertainment. Are the Spanish ladies as alluring and generous as one hears?''

"We will leave my behavior out of this discussion, if you please," Hawk said firmly, refusing to be diverted. "What of your escort on that auspicious occasion? A damned loose screw if the tales come anywhere near the mark. Were you having an affair with him?''

It had taken the bulk of her courage simply to reply to his mention of the masquerade, and she quailed at the thought that he had heard about her escort, but she had never expected such an accusation as this from him. Her hands flew to her hips as fury overcame apprehension.

"I never had an affair with him or with anyone else," she snapped. "You are the only man who has ever touched me, sir, and you should think shame to yourself for suspecting otherwise."

"Oh, come now, Mollie, don't expect me to swallow such a rapper as that one." He looked almost amused by her anger. "You enjoy our bedchamber exercises far too much now to plead such innocence to me."

She gasped, "How dare you!"

"Don't poker up, sweetheart," he replied, a weary note entering his voice. "I daresay you are afraid I shall cut up stiff, but I'm not blaming you. I'll even go so far as to thank you for not presenting me with a nameless brat or two. Four years is a long time. I'm willing to put it all in the past, but I am not so willing to put up with a Russian prince now. Nor will I allow you to flaunt your affairs before the eyes of the *beau monde* as you did tonight."

Speechless with indignation, Mollie could only stare at him. It had never occurred to her that he might believe her capable of adultery. Surely Lady Andrew might have suggested the possibility, but there was not a grain of truth in the accusation. She might have flirted. She might even have behaved occasionally in a manner that would have been more loudly condemned in a lady of lesser rank and fortune. But she had never had an affair with anyone! She attempted to tell him so, but he clearly disbelieved her.

"Look here, Mollie, I don't care about the past. You may have had a dozen affairs for all I know, and—"

"As you did yourself?" she cried, snatching up a brocade pillow from the nearest chair and flinging it at him. He glared, and she grabbed for whatever came nearest to hand. "Is that why you're so willing to forgive me, sir?" Her hairbrush missed his shoulder by inches. "Is it? Does it ease *your* conscience to believe such a thing of me?" A hand mirror followed the hairbrush, knocking over a small vase of flowers. "Does it?"

Hawk sidestepped a gold candlestick that crashed into the mantelpiece behind him. Then, his face set with grim purpose, he moved toward her, deflecting a hail of other objects without seeming to take his eyes from her. "Dammit, Mollie," he said furiously, "whatever you may believe of me, I will not allow you to fling the furniture about. Come here."

She dodged out of his way, snatching up a framed miniature of her mother in one hand and the book she had been reading earlier that day in the other. She hefted the book, ready to throw it as Hawk advanced steadily toward her. Neither of them paid the slightest heed to the sudden pounding on the door.

"Give me that book."

"I'll give it to you!" She drew back her arm, her gaze pinned to his.

The door banged back on its hinges. "I say, Mollie—" Ramsay's voice broke off as he stared in astonishment at the scene that greeted his eyes.

Startled, both Mollie and Hawk turned to face him, the book still poised high in Mollie's right hand.

"Get out," Hawk ordered.

"I—I can see I've come at a bad time," Ramsay stammered, eyeing his older brother in dismay. When a sudden glint of humor flickered through Hawk's eyes, he relaxed, though his voice had not gained much strength when he spoke again. "I was looking for you," he said. "Heard a crash and thought perhaps Mollie had done herself an injury or even that there might be housebreakers." His words were met only by silence, and he shook his head as if to clear it. "I'd better go."

"Put the book down, Mollie," Hawk said then, gently.

She looked at it, surprised to find it still in her hand. Then, sheepishly, she dropped it into the chair and turned to Ramsay "Thank you for your concern. Is your business urgent?"

Her husband shot her a speaking look, but Ramsay said gratefully, "By Jove, it is at that, Mollie. You won't believe what happened less than an hour ago."

"I daresay we won't," Hawk said, "but it can wait. I have business now with Mollie."

Ramsay's cheeks reddened with embarrassment, but he stood his ground. "No, it shouldn't wait, sir." He looked at Mollie. "The devil's in it, Mollie, but we've got to tell him the whole."

She stared at him, her consternation plain. "Must we? Can it not wait?"

"The whole of what?" Hawk looked from one to the other.

"It is nothing that she did," Ramsay explained hastily "She merely hoped we could sort it out without confessing my sins to you. But, Mollie, d'Épier means to put the screws to me in a way you'll not believe."

"What?" She set the miniature back on the table. "What do you mean?"

"What have you got to do with d'Épier?" Hawk demanded at the same time. "He's no one you should be associated with."

"Don't I know it!" Ramsay admitted. "But I met him through Hardwick, you know, so I thought he was harmless Only then I lost five hundred guineas to him—"

"You *what?*"

"Gavin," Mollie put in quickly, "I'm certain the outcome of that game was somehow contrived. Ramsay said he was sure he had more markers on the table, enough to cover his wager, in any case. Only when they counted them afterward he was short by five hundred."

"I know I said you were wrong to think that," Ramsay told her, "but now I believe you must have been in the right of it. Hawk, d'Épier offered tonight to forget the debt if could contrive to obtain certain information from you about Wellington's intentions for the late summer and fall."

Mollie stared at him in astonishment, then turned to look at her husband, expecting fireworks. But instead of flying into the boughs as she had thought he would, Hawk gave a small sigh of what could only be described as satisfaction.

"So, we were right. We knew we were on the track after Vitoria, for the French completely misunderstood the military situation there. Until then, Wellington had been having nothing but difficulties. However, that time he sent false information through regular channels, indicating his intent to retreat out of Spain. Only Bathurst and the Regent knew the truth."

"Because you told them," Ramsay guessed, his eyes sparkling.

"Bathurst met us at Hastings," Hawk admitted. "We brought secret dispatches with us, but by the time we got here, word was already spreading about Wellington's weakened troops and the necessity for retreat. It was clear that someone was leaking information, and we decided to do our possible to flush him out. We could discover nothing solid, however, and what with the Season rapidly drawing to a close and the Regent planning to move down to Brighton a day or two after his summer fete, it will become more difficult to contain military information here in London. We had hoped, by bringing a number of possibles together here tonight and giving them plenty of port and a chance to mingle, with an odd hint or two tossed to the wind, to stir something, but I never expected this much. Not that d'Épier can be more than an agent," he added grimly. "We want his contact. But what exactly does he want from you? I hope you did not refuse outright."

"Well, I nearly did," Ramsay confessed, "for I can tell you I was never so astonished. I mean, I thought d'Épier was a right one, and here he was practically ordering me to discover the damnedest things. You can imagine my feelings. But I realized in the nick of time that it wouldn't do to put him off entirely until you could discover what devilry he's up to, so I said I'd do my possible. Was that right?"

"Very right. But tell me exactly what he wants. No, wait, that door is open. We shouldn't be discussing this here, in any case. Come into the sitting room, or, better yet, we'll go down to the bookroom. Go to bed, Mollie. We'll finish our discussion tomorrow."

"We shall not!" She glared at him, outraged. "What I mean is you'll not go off and leave me like this after saying so much. I intend to know what is going on, my lord."

But he would not be gainsaid, and a moment later she found herself alone in her bedchamber, surrounded by the wreckage she herself had created. Her first inclination was to slip downstairs after them and attempt to overhear their conversation, but Hawk had ordered her in no uncertain terms to stay put, and he was already angry enough with her that she dared not try his patience further. Besides, she told herself, he would be certain to satisfy himself that no one was listening, since he had made it clear he wanted the discussion to be a private one.

She did not immediately prepare for bed, however, choosing instead to clear away the mess. The last thing she wanted was to give Cathe any reason for impertinent speculation the following morning when the maidservant brought her chocolate. It took a good deal longer to clean the room than it had to create the mess, but her thoughts were busy while she worked.

It was perfectly clear now that d'Épier was indeed a spy of some sort, and she did not have to tax her brain to recognize his motive. Other members of émigré families, who were too young to remember the terrors of the Revolution and who were dissatisfied with their lot in England, had had occasion before now to throw in their lot with Napoleon in hopes of future favors from the emperor. But what would happen now? She knew that Hawk, in the midst of a challenge that must delight him, could be depended upon to tell her nothing. Her only hope was that she might learn more from Ramsay.

Brummell's invitation to the dandies' fancy-dress ball at the Argyle Rooms arrived as promised the next day, and since the ball was scheduled to take place shortly before the Colporters planned to leave town, Mollie's time was filled with preparations for their departure as well as the choosing of costumes for herself and the others. She decided to attend as Queen Elizabeth, with Hawk as the Earl of Leicester, and Lady Bridget and Lord Ramsay would also wear sixteenth-century attire.

She saw little of Ramsay for several days, and when she did chance to meet him, he always seemed to be in a hurry. Hawk made no further attempt to call her to book over the scene with the prince either. Indeed, he seemed preoccupied. Mollie found both men's behavior frustrating, but though she was tempted more than once to do something to focus Hawk's attention upon herself again, she was not so foolish as to encourage Prince Nicolai to dangle after her when they chanced to meet, as they still did, often, in other people's homes.

What with packing and shopping for things that were needed at Hawkstone, where they would stop briefly on their way to Brighton, plus the necessity for several protracted sessions with her dressmaker, Mollie was too busy to worry about the men and their spy hunt more than once or twice a day. But at last the packing that could be accomplished ahead of time was done, and the costumes were ready the day before the ball, so Mollie was able to spend that afternoon at her leisure. She had no sooner settled upon her favorite settee in her sitting room, however, than Lord Harry bounded in, his face alight with excitement.

"Mollie, Ramsay says he will take me to St. Margaret's Parish to follow the lamplighter on his round. They have the new gaslights there, you know, and I have been forever asking Bates to take me, only he never will, because he says it is too dangerous. But that is stuff, because they hardly ever explode, and this afternoon he has gone to visit an aunt, so I have a holiday, and Ramsay has said he will take me." He caught his breath, then regarded her in the manner of one offering a treat of the highest order. "I came to invite you to go with us. You will like it above all things, Mollie!"

She nearly told him she had already had occasion to see the lights, though she had never been so fortunate as to see one lit by a lamplighter. But then it occurred to her that it would be an excellent opportunity for private speech with Lord Ramsay. While Harry focused his attention upon the lamplighter, she would have Ramsay as a captive audience. If she could not worm the details of his dealings with Hawk out of him under such advantageous circumstances, she did not know her own capabilities. Consequently, she informed Harry that she would gladly accompany them to St. Margaret's. It was Ramsay himself who nearly foiled her plan by informing her, when she and Harry joined him in the hall, that she couldn't go.

"Nonsense," she retorted, "of course I can."

"Not dressed like that, you can't," he told her firmly, gesturing toward her stylish lemon-colored walking dress, broad gypsy bonnet, and tan half-boots. "You'll have all the rustics gaping at you. You just can't go gallivanting after them like the veriest urchin."

"There will be a crowd?"

"Usually is. Certain to be if they see you in that getup. Sorry, Mollie, but there it is."

"No, it isn't," she assured him. "You wait right here, and I'll be ready in a trice. Now, mind," she added, glaring at him, "don't go without me, or you won't believe the dust I'll raise, the both of you."

Ramsay regarded her warily but said nothing, and Harry only grinned, so Mollie flew back upstairs, where she unearthed the gentleman's clothes she had not forgotten to bring with her and flung them on as quickly as she was able. The arrangement of a cravat was beyond her, so she merely flung one around her neck, snatched up her beaver hat and a long cloak, and hurried back downstairs.

"You'll have to help me," she told the astonished Ramsay. "No, don't," she added when he opened his mouth to expostulate with her. "Just fix this stupid neckcloth and let us be off. I've a mind to see the lamplighter, and no mere matter of dress is going to stop me." She tucked her hair firmly under her hat while Ramsay quickly did what he could with the cravat.

The boy chuckled. "By the Lord Harry," he said, "you make a bang-up gentleman, Mollie, but what if Hawk catches you?"

"He won't. He's gone to White's for the afternoon, and we shall be back long before he is. Did Bates know you intended to leave the house, by the bye?"

"Oh, of course," the boy replied carelessly, adding as he moved toward the front door, "I'll just call up a hack. We don't want to make a stir by taking the coach."

"Good Lord, no," his brother agreed. "The coachman would recognize Mollie in a trice."

The oil lamps in the parish of St. Margaret's, in Westminster, had been replaced by gas nearly six months previously, but crowds of the curious, hoping to witness an explosion, still followed the lamplighter on his rounds. The Colporters found a number of such people awaiting the arrival of that worthy when their hackney coach set them down in Margaret Street just across from the New Palace Yard. They discovered that they would have some minutes yet to wait, however, for as one rather ragged, bewhiskered fellow told them, talking around a bite of fish taken from a chunk wrapped in greasy newsprint, "The lamplighter dassn't begin till nigh onto dusk, me young coves."

Harry was fascinated by the myriad of folk gathering for

the event, and Mollie took her opportunity while his attention was diverted to speak to Ramsay. He had clearly been awaiting her questions.

"I can't tell you a thing," he said flatly. "Hawk said we must keep the lid on it."

"But I wouldn't say anything to a soul," she promised him. "You know I wouldn't. Was he angry with you about the money?"

He grimaced but assured her that Hawk had not been nearly so angry as he might otherwise have been.

"Because of what you discovered about d'Épier," she put in shrewdly. "That he is a spy?"

"Now look here, Mollie, you cannot go about saying things like that. This is a public place, after all. The Lord knows who might overhear you."

"Pooh. No one is giving us a second glance. They are all on the watch for Harry's lamplighter. So you might just as well tell me why he wanted you to spy on Hawk?"

"We should never have said so much in front of you," he said distractedly. He gave her a long look. "Very well, Mollie, I'll tell you what I can, but you must say nothing to anyone else until Hawk and Bathurst can get proper evidence to hang the fellows."

She paled. "Hang them?"

"Well, of course. What else does one do to traitors?"

Mollie thought about it and could come up with no satisfactory answer. She stared at Ramsay. "What is your brother mixed up in, exactly?"

He admitted reluctantly that he did not know. "Not exactly, anyway. I have been putting d'Épier off as much as I can get away with it by telling him all the information he wants is in Hawk's and Bathurst's heads, that in order to prevent information from falling into the wrong hands, nothing has been written down. He thinks I have been pumping Hawk over the port after dinner, or some such stuff, when in fact Hawk decides just what I am to tell him. I say, Mollie, you won't tell Hawk I've spilled the gaff, will you? He'll be angry, since he said I was to keep mum."

"You haven't told me anything he would care about," she reassured him. "I'm sure he doesn't want the news bruited about town, but I shan't tell anyone, so you needn't fret. Where has Harry taken himself, I wonder?"

They found him, and the lamplighter came at last, but darkness had fallen and it was much later than they had expected it to be when their hackney coach returned them to Grosvenor Square. It was decided that it would be safer for all concerned if the coachman were to let them off on Upper Brook Street near the mews road, so that they might take advantage of the rear entrance to the house. Realizing that she would have to hurry if she was to be dressed in time for dinner, Mollie hurried on ahead, and while Ramsay was paying off their driver, she slipped through the garden gate and in at the back door. She made it safely to the upstairs hall, but as she hurried across the landing toward her bedchamber, Hawk, elegantly attired in leg-hugging gold tights, a green velvet doublet, and green trunk hose slashed with gold satin, stepped into the hall from her little sitting room. She stopped dead, regarding him in dismay. He lifted his quizzing glass and peered at her, his right eye horribly magnified.

"Where the devil have you been in that rig?" he demanded, both eyes narrowing. "By heaven, Mollie, if I find you've been meeting—"

"I'm sorry to be late, because I know you wish to leave directly after dinner, but truly, we—"

"We? Who, pray tell, is 'we'?" There was a clatter of footsteps on the stairs behind her, and Mollie stepped aside to give him a clear view of his two brothers as their heads cleared the landing. "What the devil?" Hawk repeated, lifting his glass again.

It was Harry who answered him, looking anxiously from Mollie's worried face to his older brother's angry one. "She went with us to watch the lamplighter light the gaslights, sir. We thought you would not mind her going if she took care not to be recognized as a lady."

Hawk's stern gaze turned upon the boy. "I'll deal with you later, young man. Right now you may go up to the schoolroom and explain to Mr. Bates how it comes about that the lessons he assigned for this afternoon have not been attended to. He has been looking for you."

"By God, you rascal," Ramsay exclaimed on a note of exasperation, "you assured me that you had Bates' permission for this outing!"

Harry made no attempt to answer him or to meet Mollie's

reproachful look, but Hawk informed Ramsay that he would have to wait his turn if he wished to scold the boy.

"I'll have a word or two for you as well, sir, on the subject of escorting ladies who dress in male attire," he added sternly, "but for now you may as well go to your rooms and get dressed for the evening."

"Dear me," said Lady Bridget, appearing in the doorway to her bedchamber at the end of the hall, "what is all this row?" Then, as she recognized Mollie, "Good gracious, Mollie, never tell me you have dared to wear those clothes here in town! Whatever will people think? Gavin, you ought never to have allowed such a thing."

"I did not allow it," he replied grimly, turning back to face Mollie. "May I assume from her words, my lady, that you have made it a common habit to don such clothing for occasions other than to practice your archery?"

Much as she would have liked to be able to deny the charge, Mollie didn't dare. "There have been certain other times," she said carefully, meeting his gaze as steadily as she could.

"I cannot think she has been wise to do so, Gavin," Lady Bridget said with unaccustomed firmness, "and so I have told her a number of times. Perhaps you will be able to convince her that the practice is an unwise one."

"Indeed, I shall," he promised her. "Do not wait dinner for us, Aunt Biddy. This may take a while. I shall join you, however, in time to depart for the Argyle Rooms. Mollie, I fear, will not be going with us."

"Not going!" Mollie stared at him. "Of course I shall be going. Do not heed him, ma'am. I shall be down to dine directly."

"Oh, no, you won't," Hawk informed her, taking her arm in a firm grasp. "I have been a deal too easy with you, my girl, but the time has come for a reckoning between us. Your folly seems to know no bounds, but I intend to see an end to it tonight, once and for all."

12

Pulling off her beaver hat as she entered the sitting room, Mollie shook her long hair free and turned to face her husband. Without taking his eyes from her, he shut the door carefully behind him. Mollie tossed the hat into a nearby chair.

"What are you going to do?" she asked.

"We're going to have a talk," he replied, gesturing toward the chair where her hat reposed. "Sit down."

"Very well, sir," she said, obediently moving the hat and taking her seat, "but I warn you, there is nothing you can say that will keep me away from the Argyle Rooms tonight."

"You will remain here," he said flatly, "because I command you to do so. It is time and more that you recognize the fact that I am home to stay, my girl, and that you no longer have the privilege of doing as you please simply because whimsy moves you. I can think of no better way to make your position clear to you. Perhaps the punishment is a trifle severe, even arbitrary, but there are men who would deal even more harshly with you as a result of your little escapade this afternoon."

She knew that was perfectly true, but the knowledge did nothing to reconcile her to her situation. She wondered how far he would go to ensure her obedience. "I will not stay here, sir," she said calmly. "You will have to lock me in my room if you mean to prevent my going."

The expression in his eyes hardened. "I shall do no such thing, Mollie, but I can promise you that you will not like the consequences if you defy me."

She believed him, but she could not submit so easily. "You are not being fair, Gavin. I was wrong to go out dressed like this, but nothing dreadful came of it, and I shan't do it again. You *are* being arbitrary and dictatorial as well, all the things you promised you wouldn't be."

LADY HAWK'S FOLLY   151

"You still don't understand, do you?" he said, frowning.
"I know you are used to going your own way, and I know
you resent the fact that a husband who has neglected his
duties for too long a time still has the legal authority to
interfere with your pleasures. I have done my damnedest to
grant you the freedom you desire. But you have not kept your
part of the bargain. First you allowed your name to be linked
with that damned Russian, and now this. You don't meet me
halfway. You do things without counting the cost. In other
words, madam, you have grown *too* accustomed to going
your own road. Someone needs to call a halt, and it's my
responsibility to do so." He moved a little away from her
then and stood looking out the window into the shadow-filled
square below.

Mollie glared at his back, but deep inside she knew he had
made a valid point. She *had* promised to recognize his authority,
but she knew she had been thinking at the time of his
authority to rule over Hawkstone Towers, over Ramsay, and
over Harry. She had not really accepted his right to command
her obedience. In point of fact, she had fought him every inch
of the way. With a grimace she realized the fault this time
had been entirely hers.

"Very well, sir," she said at last, sighing. "I own that you
have the authority to keep me at home. I shall not defy you.
However, I still think your decision is arbitrary and unfair."
Her glance sharpened. "Moreover, I should like very much
to know what you will tell Mr. Brummell when he asks you
where I am. Will you tell him I am indisposed? I had thought
your passion for truth would make such a response impossible.
Yet, if you tell him you have ordered me to remain at home,
will that not initiate the exact sort of gossip you wish to avoid?"

Hawk shifted his position and turned his head to look at
her. There was a warmer expression in his eyes, and the
stiffness in his countenance had relaxed. "You would remain
here if I ordered you to do so?"

She nodded, wondering at the change in him.

"Come here, Mollie." There could be no mistaking the
look in his eyes now, and the little smile playing about his
lips confused her even more. Mollie sat where she was,
regarding him with a bewildered air. "I said to come here,"
he repeated. "Or is your acceptance of my authority so
short-lived that you would now defy the simplest command?"

Entirely bewildered now, she got slowly to her feet. The cravat around her throat was too tight, and she tugged at it, loosening it. She had no idea what he intended, and though his expression assured her that he meant her no harm, she could not help feeling vulnerable as she approached him. Hawk gave a crooked little smile when she hesitated.

"I won't bite," he said gently. "Come to me." When she stood directly before him, she felt as if he were already touching her, although at first he did not. She looked straight ahead for a moment, her eyes on his broad chest. Then his hand came to her chin, tilting her face up so that she had to look at him. "You are certain you would obey my command without further argument?"

She nodded again. "I have said so."

"Then, you may dress for dinner." There was amusement in his eyes now. His anger had evaporated.

Mollie felt more confused than ever. Would she never understand this man? "And the ball?"

He chuckled. "I certainly don't intend to eat my mutton in this rig unless your gown is equally antiquated, sweetheart."

"Then—" She broke off, staring at him, hoping to read his thoughts in his face. Surely he wasn't satisfied merely to have her verbal submission. Was that all he had looked for? Her thoughts whirled as she tried to figure him out. Then it came to her that she had won a victory, after all, and she could not stop the light of it from leaping into her eyes. "I know what it is," she told him, unaware of the ghost of a smile that teased at her lips. "It is what I said before, is it not, that you would be unable to account for my absence?"

"No, my idiotish child," he replied, his hands moving to her shoulders to give her a firm shake. "I wouldn't hesitate, should Brummell show such uncharacteristic bad manners as to press for an explanation, to tell him we had decided that you would remain at home for an evening of recuperation. The fact of the matter is that I sense a change in your attitude that I have been waiting a long time to see, and since I prefer to attend this ball tonight with my wife rather than without her, you shall go. However, your tone of voice, not to mention that foolish little smirk of triumph, reminds me that you do require punishment for your misbehavior today. I believe I can promise that you will continue to reflect upon your folly throughout the festivities tonight."

Her expression changed to alarm as his hand moved to grip her elbow firmly and he turned her toward her bedchamber. The first thought to cross her mind was that he intended to beat her, but the glint of amusement in his eyes reassured her. Her bedchamber was empty.

"You will first oblige me by removing those disreputable clothes," he said matter-of-factly.

Swallowing hard, but nonetheless reassured by the fact that she could still detect no anger in his countenance, Mollie moved slowly to obey him. Dropping her cloak upon the bed, she soon sent the coat after it, and her hands moved slowly to the buttons of her waistcoat.

He stood patiently, waiting, his hands folded across his chest. At the last button her fingers hesitated. "Take it off, Mollie. Then the shirt. Or do you require my assistance?"

She shook her head, unfastened the last button, and shrugged out of the waistcoat. The cravat was already loosened, so it was a simple matter to pull it off. But she had nothing on under the shirt, and she had no wish to remove it while he stood staring at her. She straightened her shoulders.

"I should prefer to ring for Mathilde to assist me with my costume, sir."

"No doubt. But I do not wish it, and you are learning to submit to your husband, my dear, as a proper wife should. Take off that shirt." When she still hesitated, he gave a little shake of his head as if he had expected no less, and moved to assist her. Mollie backed away, but it was no use. Hawk merely reached out a hand to draw her closer, and the next thing she knew, one of his hands was at the small of her back while the other moved slowly across the shirtfront, teasing her nipples through the thin lawn. Hawk grinned when she gave a little gasp of dismay and tried to pull away from him.

"No, sweetheart," he murmured, continuing to caress her.

As always, her body responded instantly to his touch, and when he pulled the shirt loose at her waist and slipped his hand beneath it to cup her bare breast, Mollie gave a little moan and moved closer, standing on tiptoe to put her arms around his neck, pulling his head down so that she could kiss him.

Hawk gave a little chuckle, deep in his throat, as his lips claimed hers. Both of his hands moved under her shirt and around to her back now, stroking her soft skin, holding her close. Then they moved back to her waist, to the fastenings of her pantaloons. A moment more and the trousers slipped to the floor, baring her hips to his touch. He lifted his head long enough to pull off her shirt, and she stood naked, her eyes alight with passion. Hawk drew her back into his arms, kissing her eyes and the bridge and tip of her nose; then he took her mouth hungrily, his tongue parting first her lips, then her teeth, and then moving on to explore the velvety interior. His hands roamed everywhere now, arousing her until every inch of her skin burned and tingled.

Mollie clutched at him, her fingers moving through his thick hair while her tongue darted and danced with his. His hands were driving her wild, but she wanted more. The stiff cloth of his doublet was irritating. She wanted to feel his skin next to hers. Impatiently, she reached for the lacing, but at the same moment, Hawk scooped her into his arms and moved to sit upon the bed, holding her in his lap. He caught her small hands and held them easily in one of his own behind her back, causing her breasts to thrust themselves forward. Ignoring her protests, he continued to caress her with his free hand while his lips moved teasingly along her jawline and lower to her throat.

She was breathing heavily, her breasts heaving, her body moving against his hand, seemingly of its own accord. He shifted her position slightly, and his lips moved lower to the tips of her breasts. Slowly and deliberately he began to kiss and caress them with his tongue, and his hand moved slowly past her waist to her hips, then back to stroke her stomach before moving lower.

Mollie caught her breath. "Oh, please . . ." The words turned into a little moan as his hand moved between her thighs.

Hawk lifted his head. His eyes were twinkling. "Where is your gown, sweetheart?"

"In the wardrobe," she muttered, straining against him. "Oh, don't stop!"

"But it's time for you to dress," he said, smiling.

"I don't care about that. You can't stop now. Please!"

The smile broadened to a grin. "I must. Any more of this and I should send my good intentions to the devil."

"Good intentions?" Then, as his meaning became clear to her, Mollie gave a little cry. "You beast! You never meant to continue, did you?"

"Oh, we shall continue, sweetheart, but I will choose the time. If you behave yourself tonight, we may even bring this interval to its natural conclusion as soon as we get home. You may reflect upon the possibility while you dance with other men, and perhaps you will thus remember to reserve your warmest smiles for your husband." So saying, he placed her on her feet and turned her around, giving her smack on the backside sound enough to make her yelp. "Get your gown. I shall attempt to help you into it if you like."

Knowing that it was of no use to argue, she marched over to the wardrobe and fairly snatched the heavy gown from its padded hanger, wishing she had the nerve to fling it in his face. But when he grinned at her, the look in his eyes made her skin tingle again as if he had touched her, and in that moment she knew her punishment would be complete.

Half an hour later they found Lady Bridget and Lord Ramsay still in the dining room, and Hawk decided there was plenty of time to enjoy a slight repast before they must depart. Lady Bridget accepted Mollie's appearance with her usual placidity, but Ramsay shot her a quizzical grin. She knew her cheeks were flushed and her whole body still tingled, but she returned a steady look to her young brother-in-law and took her seat, careful at the same time to avoid her husband's twinkling eyes, lest the sight of them put her out of countenance.

A footman appeared at her side with a dish of curried lobster, and she turned gratefully to help herself, glad of an excuse for silence while she helped herself first from one dish and then from another and yet another as if her only interest at the moment were food.

Ramsay turned his attention to his brother, saying with a chuckle, "I say, Hawk, this ought to be famous sport tonight. Is it true what they say? That Prinny forced the dandies to invite him, after all?"

"It is." Hawk shifted his gaze briefly away from his wife to his brother. "Pierrepont said someone told Prinny about Brummell's insistence upon excluding him from the festivities, whereupon his highness simply wrote to Mildmay informing him that he intended to be present. According to Pierrepont there was nothing then to be done except to receive him as politely as possible."

"I heard they even sent him an invitation," Ramsay said.

"So they did. Signed by all four."

"Still, I daresay he's piqued. Prinny's not the man to take lightly to rebuff."

"I fear," observed Lady Bridget gently, "that they have none of them displayed good manners. It was unkind of them to exclude his highness in the first place, when they were inviting all the world, but he should not have forced his presence upon them in such a way."

Mollie was silent throughout the meal, but she was entirely conscious of her husband's eye constantly upon her, and later in the coach, when his foot chanced to move against hers, a series of tremors danced through her body. It was as if they were alone, so conscious of him was she, as if Lady Bridget and Ramsay were miles away instead of sitting right there with them. Mollie could still sense Hawk's touch. Her breasts felt swollen beneath the tight Tudor bodice, and every nerve in her body was alive to his presence. The others chatted casually as the coach passed along Piccadilly, and at last they turned into the Haymarket. There were three or four carriages ahead of the Colporter coach, so there was a slight delay, but at last their coach was at the entrance to the Argyle Rooms, and the steps were let down. They slipped on their loo masks.

"There's Prinny now," Hawk said in an undertone, nodding slightly to direct their attention to the party just ahead of theirs. Mollie had already noted the unmistakable, thin figure of the Regent's aide-de-camp, Colonel Hanger, just behind the much larger bulk of his royal highness. The Colporters followed the royal party up to the entrance, through the foyer, and into the anteroom leading to the main ballroom. It was here that the four hosts lined up at the door, two to each side, to receive their guests.

The Regent bowed to Pierrepont, turned to the other side, saw Mr. Brummell standing there, and at once turned back to Lord Alvanley, standing next to Pierrepont. In the shocked silence that followed this deliberate cut and atrocious piece of ill-manners, Brummell's voice sounded, clear, cool, and penetrating.

"Ah, Alvanley, who is your fat friend?"

It was clear from the chuckles emanating from the group surrounding them that Brummell still could do no wrong, that his query was being regarded as a witty retort to blatant

provocation rather than as an unmannerly insult, but Mollie
had an unobstructed view of the Regent's face. She could see
from his expression that he was cut to the quick by Brummell's
words.

Still visibly shaken, the Regent proceeded into the ballroom,
and the Colporters stepped up to greet their hosts. As Mollie
was speaking to Sir Henry Mildmay, Colonel Hanger appeared in the doorway again, excused himself for interrupting,
and informed Mildmay that the Prince wished to speak to
him.

Mildmay looked down his nose at the wiry little man.
"Surely, sir," he said with an air of weariness, "there must
be some mistake. His royal highness saw me but a moment
ago and took no notice of me whatsoever."

The colonel retreated in good order, and when the Colporters followed soon after, Lord Ramsay observed that he was
glad they were masked. "For I daresay his highness will
remember every face he saw there. Don't you, Hawk?"

"He will not trouble us," his brother said evenly. "Will
you dance, my lady?"

A waltz was in progress, and when Mollie obediently put
out her hand, Hawk drew her into his arms and swung her
expertly into the circle of rapid-paced dancers. She had not
waltzed with him before, but her steps might have been
meant to match with his, because she was unaware of the
movements of her feet. She knew only that she felt like a
feather in his arms. His breath stirred her curls, and her skin
felt alive beneath the warmth of his hand on her waist. She
had not said a word to him since leaving her bedchamber.

"You dance well, sweetheart." His voice was low, with
that caressing note that she had come to listen for, the note
that always sent her blood racing through her veins. Suddenly
the evening spread itself before her in a long, unending
pattern of unknown events to come before they could go
home again. She looked up into his face to find him smiling
at her, then looked away again. "Why so silent, Mollie?"

"I can think of nothing to say," she muttered. "I do not
know you in this mood."

"Do you know me in other moods?" The words were
blatantly provocative.

"I sometimes think I do not know you at all, sir," she
replied to his chest.

"Do you want to know me, Mollie?"

She looked up again, blinking at him, searching his face.

"Do you?" he repeated, looking at her as though there was not another soul in that huge, crowded room. Even if she had wanted to, in that moment she could not have torn her gaze from his if her life had depended upon it.

"Yes," she whispered. "Oh, yes, Gavin, I do."

He nodded, satisfied, and concentrated on the dance with even more enthusiasm than he had shown before. Mollie was breathless and laughing by the time the music stopped.

Her attention was claimed at once by another partner, and she soon lost sight of her husband. But the fact that he was out of sight did nothing to take his presence from her mind. All she could think about was what he had promised for the evening ahead. As time passed, her anticipation grew until she scarcely noted who her partners were. She recognized Prince Nicolai, despite his mask and Cossack costume, but even his blatant compliments failed to elicit more than a vague smile from her. It was not until Lord Ramsay claimed her hand for a Scotch reel that she collected her wits.

"I say, Mollie, I think I'd best take you for some refreshment. They're serving an excellent fruit punch. Not that damned orgeat either. More like ratafia, but it's got a strawberry flavor. I know you'll like it, and you look as if you could do with a breath of air as well. Your cheeks look bright enough to be feverish."

"Do they?" She looked up into his anxious face, grinning at him. "I am fine, Ramsay. Truly. But I'd very much like something to drink. And you're not to leave me sitting in one of those awful little gilt chairs against the wall, either. I shall go with you."

He agreed, and they moved together into a side apartment where a long buffet table had been set up, fairly groaning under the weight of the various delicacies set out to tempt the palates of weary dancers. At the far end a flunky ladled pink liquid into punch glasses.

"They've really put themselves out," Ramsay observed. "This entire spread is from Gunter's. There are even to be cream ices later on, for a shipment of ice arrived last week, and Gunter has kept it stored in his basement in Berkeley Square for just this occasion. That fellow at the punch bowl was telling me about it only a bit ago. Here, Mollie, try one of these excellent lobster patties.''

But Mollie's attention had been diverted. Most of the guests still retained their masks and would do so until the unmasking at midnight, but the Cossack dress made it easy to recognize the Russian prince, and she was certain she also recognized the man with him.

"Look there," she said to Ramsay in an undervoice. "There, by the potted palm in that corner. "Is that not Monsieur d'Épier in the red domino with Prince Nicolai?''

Ramsay glanced in the direction she indicated, a frown gathering on his handsome face. "By Jove, Mollie, I believe it is. What would they be wanting with each other, I wonder?''

The two men were involved in a serious conversation, but suddenly the man in the red domino looked up and saw Ramsay. Hastily excusing himself, he drew away from the prince and hurried back into the ballroom. Mollie thought the prince looked annoyed, and it crossed her mind that, as a member of Monsieur de Lieven's staff, spies were undoubtedly as much to his interest as they were to Lord Bathurst and Hawk. After all, the Russians were as opposed to Bonaparte as the English were, and their recent success in speeding the invader from their land would only increase their interest in seeing that the French stayed where they belonged. No doubt Nicolai was doing a little investigating of his own. She put the incident from her mind and returned to the festivities refreshed by the respite.

Later, in the coach, the four Colporters declared the evening an unqualified success. They chatted comfortably about the various costumes they had seen and conversations they had taken part in, and Lady Bridget announced that she thought the evening had been a good one to mark the end of their London stay.

"I daresay you, Ramsay, might wish to remain for the Regent's summer fete celebrating Lord Wellington's victory, but I for one prefer to miss such a squeeze as that will be.''

Ramsay grinned at her, saying that while it might be fun, such entertainments were too public for his tastes, an opinion that gave his sister-in-law to think he had done some growing up in the past weeks. She smiled at him.

"Do you still intend to accompany us to Brighton?''

"I don't know," he replied, surprising her. "After all the

activity, I daresay it won't take much more than Hawk's little house party before I'm completely burnt to the socket. I haven't actually decided yet, but I might remain at Hawkstone afterward and do a little studying. Believe it or not, I'm growing anxious to return to school.''

Mollie stared at him, then turned to look at her husband, whose face was barely visible in the soft glow cast by the carriage lamps. "House party?"

He nodded. "I invited some friends to enjoy a repairing lease before going on to the dissipations of the seaside. Only a few, at first, but such things have a way of growing," he added ruefully. "I thought I had mentioned it to you.''

"Well, you didn't," Lady Bridget replied before Mollie could speak. "Surely, dearest Mollie would have told me, Gavin, for there are preparations to be made before Hawkstone can be ready to receive guests, you know.''

"Well, I didn't leave all to chance, Aunt Biddy. I sent word to the Bracegirdles nearly a week ago. Are you certain I said nothing to you, sweetheart?''

Mollie shook her head, dimly aware that she was glad he had made all the arrangements and that she would not have to be bothered about them. She smiled at him. "I had thought we were stopping at Hawkstone only for a day or so. How long are we to remain there, sir?"

His grin was unmistakable. "I haven't decided," he replied. "I've told the others they are welcome to stay as long as they like.''

Was there provocation in his tone? She wasn't sure. But it didn't seem to matter. Hawkstone was his home. He could do as he liked. She returned look for look. Ramsay glanced from one to the other, sensing mystery between them, but when Hawk chuckled as though at a private joke, the younger man shook his head and returned the conversation to his reasons for thinking he might remain in Kent instead of traveling with the others to Brighton. Mollie ceased to listen after some moments, when her awareness of her husband's nearness overwhelmed other thoughts. They were in South Audley Street, approaching the square, and it seemed as if the clatter of the horses' hooves on the cobblestones matched the rhythm of her beating heart.

Moments later they were in the front hall, and Hawk turned

to Mollie with a lazy smile. "Go up to Mathilde du Bois, my dear. I've a few matters to attend to in my bookroom."

Her breath caught in her throat. "Will you be long, sir?" she asked, forcing herself to speak calmly.

His eyes were twinkling as if he knew exactly what thoughts were tumbling through her mind. "Just go upstairs, Mollie."

Obediently she turned toward the stairs, but her teeth gritted together beneath her soft lips. How long did he mean to torment her? She had scarcely thought of anything but him since their interval together before dinner. What if he merely went out again and left her to stew longer? Just how much and how long did he mean to punish her?

With these and other thoughts filling her mind, she scarcely paid any attention to Cathe's cheerful questions about the ball and none at all to Mathilde du Bois' careful attention to her preparations for bed. She merely moved as the dresser indicated, letting her remove the Tudor gown and replace it with a soft silken nightdress, obeying her softly spoken commands without a murmur. Only when Mathilde suggested that her nails needed some slight attention did Mollie come to herself again.

"No, no, that will be quite all right," she said a little tartly. "I shan't need anything more tonight. You may both go to bed."

They left, and she turned to stare into the cheerful little fire burning low on the hearth. How long did he mean to keep her waiting? After a few moments she opened the door into her little sitting room. It was dark, but she could see a glimmer of light under the opposite door. With only a moment's hesitation she strode across the sitting room and pushed open the door to her husband's bedchamber.

Wearing a glorious red brocade dressing gown, Hawk sat at his ease before his mirror, rubbing his chin, while his valet finished wiping the soapy residue from a pair of razors. When the door met the wall with a soft thud, Hawk's gaze caught Mollie's in the mirror. His eyes danced.

"Yes, sweetheart?"

Mollie glared at the astonished valet. "Leave us," she ordered brusquely. The man glanced at his master and, upon receiving a nod in reply to his unspoken question, slipped the razors into their leather case and quietly left the room through the door to the hall.

Hawk turned in his chair, raising his eyebrows at the sight

of her in the thin silk nightdress. "Good Lord, Mollie, Mawson will dream of your charms for a week."

"Let him!" she snapped. "Because I care not one whit for his dreams, and I need you right now, for whatever you may think to the contrary, you are the only man I know who can . . . who can . . . Dammit, my lord, do you mean to finish what you began earlier or not?"

He stood up and the dressing gown fell open, revealing that he wore nothing beneath it. His expression softened, and as he moved to take her in his arms, he said gently, "I believe I may have been a fool, sweetheart, to accuse you as I did, and as you can clearly see for yourself, I have as little wish at the moment as you do to prolong the agony."

13

The size of Hawk's house party had indeed grown considerably by the time the Colporters were ready to depart from London. Mollie was well aware that there was more to the matter than a simple wish on the part of her husband to provide a break in the journey to Brighton for his friends. Seeing such names as the de Lievens and Lord Bathurst on the guest list would have told her as much, had her own instincts not warned her. Still, she was amazed to discover, when she sat down with Lady Bridget to add up the numbers, that upward of thirty persons would be joining them—some, though not all, for as long as a week's time.

"And that doesn't include all the servants who will accompany them, ma'am," she said to Lady Bridget, seated across from her in the little sitting room. "I am persuaded the poor Bracegirdles will not know if they are on their heads or on their heels. When Gavin mentioned a house party, I had no notion it would be anything like this, let alone that the Regent himself would choose to honor us with his presence."

"Well, you know, dearest, it is not quite the first time royalty has been entertained at Hawkstone Towers," her ladyship returned calmly.

Mollie chuckled. "I scarcely think the Bracegirdles can be expected to have benefited from that experience, ma'am. It has been quite some time since the Black Prince chose to break his journey into France by spending a week with the Colporters, and that was in the manor house at that."

"But it has not been so long as all that since King George—though to be sure, he was then the Prince of Wales, of course—so honored us," replied Lady Bridget.

Mollie stared at her. "King George?"

"Yes, indeed. Only for the one night, of course, but I can

tell you, everything was at sixes and sevens for a week before the visit. Everyone was in a tizzy."

"Surely not you, ma'am."

"Oh, no, but then I had little to do with anything, for Gavin's mother was still alive then, of course, though I believe she was increasing at the time. Or possibly she had recently suffered a miscarriage. She so often did, you know. She was not very robust, I fear."

"Indeed, I do not know how anyone who seems to have spent her entire adult life in what gentlemen, at least, delight in referring to as an interesting condition can have been expected to be robust. I'm only astonished the poor woman clung to life for as long as she did."

There was a pause. Then Lady Bridget smiled gently. "She was not a happy woman, I fear. She complained a good deal."

"So I should think."

"Yes, dear, but she ought not to have complained so much. She was a charming girl, you know, when Thurston brought her home, but she had been raised to think highly of herself, and not at all of anyone else. She complained to anyone who would listen, you see, including Gavin. And he was quite a little boy at the time."

Mollie took a moment to digest these gentle words before looking more sharply at Lady Bridget. "Are you trying to say something of import, ma'am? Because if you are, I fear your intent has slipped past my understanding. To be sure, it was improper of her to be bewailing her lot to her small son. And no doubt if she had shown the slightest resolution, she might . . ." Her words trailed off when she noted the twinkle lighting Lady Bridget's pale-blue eyes.

"Do you mean to say she ought to have stood against her husband, my dear?"

The vision of the late Lord Hawkstone impressed itself disagreeably upon Mollie's imagination. She frowned, then sighed. "I daresay it would take more than slight resolution for that. No doubt she had cause to complain, but she would have done better to have made her feelings clear to Lord Hawkstone rather than to her son."

"It was not so easy to do, however," replied her ladyship a little sadly. "However, we must not be looking to the past, my dear," she added more briskly. "Do you think we ought to order turtles brought over from the coast for dinner each night while the Regent is at the Towers?''

Mollie was certain she has missed something, but she knew it would do no good to prod Lady Bridget, so she said, "I believe Gavin sent all the necessary orders of that nature to Mrs. Bracegirdle.''

"Ah, yes, of course. He will know what is best to be done, of course. It is so comforting to be able to leave things in the hands of a gentleman again, is it not, my dear?''

Mollie returned a light response and turned Lady Bridget's attention to certain more personal details that must be attended to before the family could leave London for Kent. Though there were times when she actually found herself wishing that she could be as complacent as the old lady was about entrusting every detail of her life to her husband's keeping, and although she found it easier now than before they had come to London to comply with his wishes, Mollie still felt a lingering sense of unease. It was buried deep, but it poked its head up occasionally and thus was still a force to be reckoned with.

The feeling manifested itself from time to time in a recurring dream in which she and Hawk were both struggling to maintain possession of the reins of a team of horses. In earlier days she had dreamed that the two of them sat together on the box, side by side, both holding the reins with their hands placed one atop the other without rhyme or reason as to whose hand was uppermost. More recently in the dream, Hawk had taken all the reins firmly in his hands, but Mollie had not yet settled back inside the coach as he wanted her to do. She still sat beside him and held on to the trailing ends of the traces just in case he might let go. So far he had not done so, but she kept her eyes on the road and her mind alert, so that she might be ready. And whenever a curve came into sight ahead, she tensed, thinking this might be the time that she would have to take over. In those dreams the journeys seemed endless, though she never seemed to have any particular awareness of a destination.

The destination uppermost in her mind during the daylight hours of those last days of July, however, as the summer's heat began to invade the city of London, was the crenellated towers of the lake fortress she had called home for the past four years. Hawk was continually busy, and though she knew he did not spend his days at one or another of his clubs as most men did, she knew just as surely that it would do her no good to pry into his affairs. It did no good to pump her brother-in-law for details, either. Ramsay had indeed grown up a good deal in the past days and weeks, and the new maturity that rested so easily upon his broad shoulders did not come, Mollie knew, merely from a few weeks' worth of town polish.

Only Harry was the same. And just as she had anticipated, Harry was not particularly enthusiastic about returning to Kent.

"But Mollie," he demanded, coming upon her in the midst of her final packing, "what would be amiss with my remaining right here in Grosvenor Square with old Bates? I am persuaded he would like it above all things, for he could visit his aunt whenever the fancy struck him to do so."

"Your thoughtfulness on Mr. Bates' behalf astonishes me," Mollie returned, amused.

"Well, I thought I was being very considerate," he informed her, not in the least abashed by her amusement. "Moreover, there is still a great deal of London that I have not seen, and I am sure it would do my education no end of good if I were allowed to remain here."

"But you know perfectly well that your brother will not allow it, Harry, even if I were so foolish as to propose such a course to him."

"Well, I do not see why I should not stay," the boy insisted. "I am old enough to look after myself, and I shall not learn nearly so much at Hawkstone Towers as I might here."

"But you would learn a good deal in Brighton, however," she pointed out gently.

The boy looked much struck. "By Jupiter, I hadn't thought of that. Everyone has talked of nothing but the house party, you know, and I quite forgot that you mean to go on to Brighton afterward. Of course," he added more gloomily, "no one has actually said that I am to go with you."

"Well, you are."

He eyed her skeptically. "Are you sure, Mollie? You know, Ramsay has said he means to stay at the castle. If he does not go to Brighton, will not Hawk expect me to remain with him? He means to study, you know." The boy's expression plainly mirrored his poor opinion of such a course.

Mollie laughed. "I am sure, dear. You will not need to

study right up until the moment you depart for Eton, you know. No one will object to a holiday for you. You can bathe in the sea, and ride your pony on the Downs, and we will have picnics and go to a grand review or two. There will be all manner of things to entertain us. You shall not miss any of it, I promise you.''

He turned away, satisfied, but it occurred to Mollie that this was the first time she had had to reassure him after she had given her permission for him to do something. And she wasn't at all certain he would really believe he was going with them until Hawk had said so. Truly, her husband had made his authority felt. But when she searched her mind for the old resentment, she could find only amusement that Harry would fear Hawk might deny him pleasure. Certainly, from what she had come to know of him, Hawk would never do so without good reason. And Mollie went on about her chores with contentment in her heart and a little smile playing at her lips.

The day of departure came at last, and what seemed to be a veritable cavalcade appeared outside the doors of Hawkstone House in Grosvenor Square. From one of the tall windows of the saloon, Mollie gazed out in dismay at the group of carriages, luggage, and scurrying minions.

"Goodness, sir," she said, looking up at Hawk, who was standing beside her, "I am certain we did not have so much when we arrived!"

He laughed at her, and she noticed lines of weariness at the corners of his eyes. He was tired, but the laughter was real enough. "You have bought out the city, and now you wonder why it is necessary to hire a wagon or two to fetch and carry the results of your labor?"

She looked back at the activity in the street with rueful eyes. "I had no notion I had purchased so much," she confessed. "The furniture in the rear hall at home is so shabby it really needs refurbishing, and once I began, I seemed to be possessed of a devil. There are the new chairs, of course, though they are small. And the upholstery material for the old sofas. And of course, more material to recover all those cushions. Aunt Biddy insisted upon linen, you know, because she wishes to embroider the lot. I hope you are not vexed, sir.''

"Not in the least," he assured her. "Why should I be?"

"Well, with such an army as this to move, it will take us longer on the road, will it not?" She gazed at him, still watching his expression warily.

Hawk put an arm around her shoulders and gave her a little hug. "It will not," he said firmly. "I have already made arrangements for the wagons and the servants' carriages to follow at their own pace. Lofting is to accompany them. He was forced to leave Kent in some haste, you know, and since he will remain in town, there are things he wishes to attend to there. I have given him enough money to pay for anything he needs on the way, so we shall not have to be burdened with any responsibility for this lot."

"Well, I do wish we might have furbished up the rear hall before you thought to invite the Regent and the Countess de Lieven," she said musingly.

Hawk chuckled. "Now you sound like a proper little housewife, my dear. But if I know you, you will be sending men out to be sure the roads are properly tended and boys to check for produce from the fields and orchards, and all manner of other things before Prinny and the others arrive."

"What? In two days? I am not such a ninny, my lord. If you wish to disgrace us by not seeing to those details yourself, that's your lookout. I shall be too busy seeing to the preparations for the Prince's suite of rooms and accommodations for Lord Bathurst and the de Lievens to worry about anything that you and Troutbeck can see to as well as I can."

Hawk laughed again, then informed her it was time they were off. Less than half an hour later, he bundled her into the first carriage along with Lady Bridget and Harry. Then, mounting his horse, he took his place beside Lord Ramsay, and the cavalcade commenced its journey south. It was not until they had crossed Westminster Bridge, thereby putting the cobblestones of the city streets behind them, that the lead carriages began to draw away from the others.

The day was a bright one and hot, and the interior of the carriage soon began to feel like the inside of a bake oven, but there could be no question of letting down the windows, for the road was so dusty that one could scarcely see the country-side as it was. Even the glass failed to keep the dust out, and by the time the second stage was completed, Harry was utterly bored and uncomfortable, and Mollie could only be thankful when Hawk took the boy to ride behind him for the third stage. She looked after Harry wistfully and with such concentration that she was startled when Ramsay called to her.

"I say, Mollie, would you care to ride old Homer for a while? I should be glad of a chance for some quiet conversation with Aunt Biddy."

She knew perfectly well that the most he could hope for by way of conversation from his aunt by then was a gentle snore or two, but Mollie was not in the least tempted to talk him out of his generous impulse. Without a thought for the fact that her lilac sarcenet frock was scarcely suitable for riding, she allowed him to assist her onto his saddle, balancing herself as best she could while he shortened one stirrup and tied up the other, and wishing in the meantime that she had nerve enough to hoist up her skirts and sit astride.

"By Jupiter, Mollie, you'd best have a care or you'll land in the dirt," Harry warned. "That saddle ain't meant for a lady."

"Don't bother your head about that," she told him. "I'll contrive somehow. I don't want to spend any more time in that hot carriage than you do, young man." Then it occurred to her that her husband had made no comment about the arrangement, and she cast him an anxious look. It was scarcely proper for her to be riding like this, and he might well forbid it. But Hawk only grinned at her and advised her to have a care, before signaling the others to move on.

At first she reveled in the freedom of the saddle. Riding in front of the carriages meant they had fresh air to beathe and little trouble with the dust. The heat was not so oppressive either. However, by the end of the stage, the discomforts of a gentleman's saddle were beginning to make themselves felt. It was not just the saddle but the fact that a good deal more effort was necessary than Mollie had imagined merely to keep her balance. Consequently, when Ramsay asked if she was ready to take her place in the carriage again, she agreed without demur. By then the sun was beginning to settle in the west and the heat was not so bad as before, though the same could not be said for the dust, of course, until they had passed through Cross-in-Hand and actually entered the Bourne Valley, where the dampness from the river kept the road hard-packed in the worst of the summer's heat. By then, Harry, too, was ready to take his place in the carriage again, and at last they were able to let down the windows.

Twilight lingered after the sun had set behind the hills, and it was in that gray light that they finally saw the great castle looming ahead, perched proudly on its island in the middle of the silvery lake. Mollie drew in a long breath. London had been wonderful, but it was lovely to be home again, even if it was only for a short while. Hawk had dropped back to ride beside the carriage, and she looked out the open window to find him watching her.

"Wonderful to be home again, is it not, sweetheart?" he said, speaking just loudly enough for her to hear him over the rumble of the horses' hooves and the carriage wheels.

"Indeed, it is, sir," she replied, returning look for look.

"Are we home?" Harry asked sleepily from the front corner of the carriage, where he had been drowsing away the journey up the valley.

"We are at that, young man. You'll be in your own bed within the hour," Hawk replied with a smile.

"Oh, I'm not sleepy in the least," the boy said, sitting up a little straighter in his seat. "I am hungry, however. I have missed Bracegirdle's ginger biscuits. Perfect doesn't know the way of them, so she could not tell Cook, and Cook never did get them right."

Mollie assured him that if the biscuits were not served as a remove for the second course, she herself would request them for the morrow, and the boy leaned back in his seat again, contented. The carriage clattered across the main causeway and in at the main gate, where the party was met with cheers from servants congregated in the courtyard as well as unadulterated delirium from the shaggy little dog. It was clear to everyone from Mandy's attitude that she had been laboring under a conviction that her entire family had abandoned her forever.

Both Bracegirdles were there to welcome them, and Mrs. Bracegirdle was quick to assure Lord Harry that he needn't wait until the morrow for his ginger biscuits. Indeed, dinner was ready for them the moment they chose to sit down at the table, for she had had men on the lookout for the carriages these last two hours and more. And when did they expect the first arrivals for the house party, if it pleased the master to inform her?

Hawk gave the stout dame a firm hug. "I've not the slightest doubt," he said teasingly, "that if his highness were

o pass through that door just behind us, you would be
perfectly prepared to greet him.''

"Well, and so I should hope,'' she retorted, her fond gaze
belying the sharp tone, "but you never said precisely when
we should expect everyone, and we shall do better, Master
Gavin, if we have proper warning, and so you should know,
sir.''

"I gave you warning,'' he reminded her. "As to when
everyone will arrive, since his fete is Wednesday, I daresay
the Regent will be here on Thursday, but the de Lievens and
Lord Bathurst will arrive the day before. The others will be
arriving as they choose and leaving again in the same fashion.''

Mollie smiled to herself as she watched her housekeeper
accept Hawk's casual confidence in her ability to cope with
such a disorganized party. Truly, Mrs. Bracegirdle seemed to
have the same sort of faith that Lady Bridget had in a gentleman's sense of right. Mollie herself had always made it a point
to make her orders clear and reasonable, but she knew the old
marquess had not been the least inclined to do likewise. She
had an odd notion just now that Mrs. Bracegirdle preferred
the gentleman's way of managing, and she realized that their
casual attitude was by way of being a compliment to the
housekeeper's ability to cope with the most awesome problems.

Dinner was a comfortable meal, made more so by realiza-
tion of the fact that it would most likely be their last opportunity to dine *en famille* for some time. Afterward they adjourned
to the shabby rear hall, where a cheerful fire awaited them,
watched over by the little dog. Conversation, both at the table
and afterward in the hall, focused primarily upon the forthcoming house party, for Lady Bridget had a number of
questions to ask and observations to make, and Harry, who
had been reassured by his eldest brother as to the certainty of
his welcome in Brighton, wished to know how long he must
wait before they would be rid of all their guests and able to
proceed to that famous resort.

"I was mad as fire when Mollie wouldn't let me go with
her to Margate, you know,'' he confided to the room at large,
"but Brighton will be something like, so I don't mind it so
much now.''

Mollie glanced quickly at her husband, wondering how the
boy's casual reference would affect him, and found to her
own discomfort that Hawk was regarding her searchingly.

She remembered then that at least one member of the house
party was going to prove difficult for her to cope with, since
Prince Nicolai would undoubtedly come along with Monsieur
de Lieven. She had said nothing before, and she did not
choose to mention it now, but she knew she could not let
much more time pass by before bringing her worries to
Hawk's attention. Even as she looked away, she realized the
conversation had been brought back from Brighton to the
subject nearer to everyone's thinking. Ramsay was choosing
his words with care.

"I say, Hawk, what if there's a problem? Should we not
discuss the possibilities a bit more?"

"Perhaps tomorrow," his brother replied easily. "I doubt
there is anything to fear, you know. I thought we had gone
over that ground already."

"Well, we have," Ramsay said slowly, piquing Mollie's
curiosity even more, "but I daresay it wouldn't come amiss
to discuss it again. I'm new to this business, you know."

She could scarcely demand an explanation with Harry right
there, but Mollie had been suffering from recurrent bouts of
rampant curiosity ever since Hawk's casual annoucement that
he meant to hold a house party. He had so far returned no
satisfactory answer to any of her questions, and she decided
there and then that before the night was out, she would have
more information from him if she had to tie him to his bed
and torture him to get it. The mental picture created by this
thought brought a smile to her lips, but when she glanced at
her husband, she found him watching her again. Flushing,
she turned pointedly away to stare into the leaping flames in
the great fireplace, and Mandy, mistaking her absent stare for
a wish for attention, stretched languidly and wandered over to
press a cold, wet nose into her hand. Mollie patted the little
dog, then gathered her into her lap to stroke the silky fur.
Perfectly satisfied to oblige her mistress in this fashion, Mandy
curled into a ball in her lap and went to sleep.

Later, in Mollie's bedchamber, while Mathilde du Bois
brushed out her long tresses and plaited them, Mollie considered how best to go about discussing her worries about the
house party with her husband. She knew there was some sort
of intrigue afoot, and she doubted that he meant to take her
into his confidence about the precise nature of that intrigue,
but she hoped he would not be averse to discussing more

personal matters. And perhaps from such a discussion, she might successfully manage to discover more than he meant for her to know.

Finally, Mathilde finished her tasks and departed, wishing her mistress a pleasant good night. Cathe, who had been conscientiously putting Mollie's clothes away, moved now to bank the little fire in the grate before likewise departing. The room seemed cozy and warm, lit only by the branch of candles on the dressing table, now that the flames had ceased their dancing. It was odd, Mollie thought, how a room that ought to feel new and strange, considering that it had been her own for so short a time, could feel right and comfortable.

"Will there be anything more, m'lady?" Cathe asked, straightening.

"No, you may go to bed."

"Good night, ma'am."

Barely waiting for the door to close behind the serving girl, Mollie hurried to the door leading into the sitting room and pulled it open. Hawk stood there in his bright-red dressing gown, his hand poised to turn the latch.

Standing there as he did, with the gloom of the sitting room behind him, he looked larger and more solid than ever, and Mollie found the breath catching in her throat at the sight of him. Would she never, she wondered, be able to look upon this man in a casual way?

"I wondered whether you were ready for bed, sweetheart," he said, smiling down at her.

"I'm sorry to have been so long, sir," she replied, surprised for some odd reason to hear her voice sounding so matter-of-fact. "You must be weary, though. I was not certain you wanted me to come to you."

"Don't be daft, Mollie. Of course, I want you. Your place is with me, sweetheart, not alone in that bed yonder." He took her hand as he spoke and drew her nearer, putting his arms around her and waiting patiently until she tilted her head up. Then, gently, he placed a kiss upon her lips. When he moved as though to draw her toward his own room, she reached up to hold his head where it was, urging him not to stop his kisses so soon. In answer, he scooped her into his arms and carried her to the other bedchamber.

14

Watching Hawk as he draped his dressing gown across the back of a nearby chair and prepared to join her in the huge bed, Mollie remembered the days when she had first met him. His attentions had been flattering, but not so much more flattering than those of the other young men who had constantly surrounded her. Still, there had been something about him that set him apart from the others, something that fascinated her.

It was not so much that he was handsome and dashing, nor that he dressed with a careless air of unstudied grace and elegance. The fascination went deeper than that. Really, she thought now, watching as he strode naked to check the dying embers in the grate, the feeling she had had about him then had more to do with the way he made her feel about herself than with the way she had felt about him. She had liked herself more when she was with Hawk than when she was with other young men. He had made her feel less, somehow, as though she were playing some silly game or other.

She had even thought at one time that she might be more than a mere challenge to him. When her father had informed her that Hawk had actually come to him to ask permission to pay his addresses to her, she had thought he must feel some of the tenderer emotions toward her. That belief, however, had not survived their wedding night, when Hawk had gone rigid the moment she had cried out at his initial penetration. He had withdrawn from her as much in a mental sense then as he had physically. Though he had continued to treat her with his customary gentleness and consideration, things between them had not been easy after that, and he had leapt at the opportunity to join Wellington with much the same attitude that a drowning man might snatch at a straw.

Hawk came toward her through the shadows, and the bed

moved with his weight as he slipped under the quilts and pulled her into the shelter of his arm.

"Shelter," she mused, savoring the feeling.

"What's that, sweetheart?" His breath stirred the wispy tendrils of hair at her temples as he murmured the question.

Mollie hadn't realized she'd spoken aloud, but she turned her head in the hollow of his shoulder and replied easily, "I was thinking about how comfortable we are now."

"Aye, 'tis a good-enough bed," he said drowsily.

She chuckled. "I meant with each other, Gavin."

Hawk pushed himself up a little on the pillows, and his voice was a shade crisper. "Are we, Mollie?" His arm shifted a little beneath her shoulders, and his hand stroked her upper arm. "I had hoped so, but I was not sure."

"Is that why you have invited Prince Nicolai to this house party of yours?" she asked softly. "To test me?"

With a sound perilously akin to a groan he shifted his position again, that he might look at her more directly. The dim glow from the fireplace was enough to define the searching expression in his eyes. "Is that what you think?" he demanded, low.

"I-I wondered," she murmured. "You don't like him, yet you invite him here with the others."

"He comes with de Lieven," Hawk said, as though that explained everything.

"Why?" Mollie asked. "Surely, Monsieur de Lieven does not always travel with his aides. And since you have insisted that our party is to be merely an entertaining interval for your guests, why should the prince come if you do not wish it?"

She had kept her tone carefully offhand, but he was not fooled. "I have little doubt of your intelligence, sweetheart, and I am well aware that you are already in possession of many facts that do not concern you. To tell you more might be to endanger your safety. Don't press me for details I am not at liberty to divulge."

"I daresay it is all to do with spying," she said, sighing expressively. "I know Ramsay must have told you we saw Nicolai with d'Épier at the Argyle Rooms. Is his highness part of the investigation, or is he one of the spies?"

"That's enough, Mollie." His tone was harsh now. "Such questions are naught but foolishness and can do nothing except cause trouble. Don't let me catch you airing those opinions where anyone else can hear you, or it will be the worse for you, my girl.''

A little daunted by his tone, she nevertheless asked, "Is Nicolai a spy, sir?"

His arm twitched under her as if he would give her a shake. "Dammit, Mollie, leave be."

"But I want to know. Perhaps I can help."

At that, he sat up in the bed and yanked her upright, his two hands bruising her shoulders. "You are not to think of such a thing for a moment. Do you hear what I'm saying to you?" A firm shake emphasized his sternly spoken words. "Your task is to see that our guests are comfortable, nothing more. You are to talk to no one about these ridiculous suspicions of yours. Is that perfectly clear, madam?"

"Are they merely suspicions?" she asked evenly, adding more quickly when his grip on her shoulders tightened again, "I have a right to know, sir, if we are harboring spies and traitors beneath our roof."

For a moment it seemed as if he would shake her again, but then his grip relaxed and he gave a little sigh of resignation. "I do not know why I profess to be astonished by your persistence in this matter. Lord knows, you have made it clear enough that you will never be a conformable wife." He chuckled. "I confess, I have already come to the conclusion that I never wanted such a wife, so I cannot think why I make any effort to force you into that mold. Habit, I suppose. And just when I thought I was doing so well, too."

"Sir?" Once again he was confusing her.

He grinned. "I let you make a figure of yourself riding Ramsay's damn horse all the way from East Grinstead to Forest Row, did I not?" When Mollie replied with a gurgle of laughter, he pulled one of her curls, then spoke more seriously. "I do not know all the answers to your questions, sweetheart. I do know that to ask such questions of anyone else might prove dangerous for you."

"Is Nicolai a spy?" she asked again.

"We don't know. He is very smooth and so far has eluded any traps we have set. Moreover, I cannot be absolutely certain that my own prejudices have not influenced my judgment against him. We do know that someone with lofty connections has been providing information to the French. Nicolai's connections are lofty enough, and it is quite possible that the spy is part of the Russian delegation. However, it is equally possible that the man we seek is among the Regent's people or Lord Bathurst's. The information that has gone missing has been available in all three places, but only at the highest levels."

She gave a little shiver. "Is that why you have invited the de Lievens, the Regent, and Lord Bathurst to Hawkstone?"

"Not entirely. The Regent, as you know, has a talent for inviting himself. I had no expectation of entertaining him when I arranged this little party. Bathurst and I had hoped to clear matters up before Prinny left London, simply because the more messages there are to be carried, the more difficult it will be to plug the leak, but he has interested himself in this matter from the outset. So when he discovered our plan and insisted upon being present, we could not be surprised. Indeed, his presence here will actually lend more credence to the rumors we have been so carefully spreading."

"What rumors?"

But that he refused to tell her, further recommending that she keep a still tongue between her teeth when their guests arrived. "I cannot emphasize strongly enough, sweetheart, how dangerous it would be for you to hint at any knowledge of this affair."

"Very well, sir, but I hope you realize that I may have difficulty with Prince Nicolai. I was not prevaricating the night I told you he had forced his attentions upon me. I might have behaved in such a fashion before that as to lead him to believe I would not be averse to receiving such attentions from him. But even if you were right about that part of it, I can still assure you it was never my intention, and I did nothing that night to invite his attentions."

To her surprise Hawk chuckled. "Such exhaustive periods are not necessary to convince me, sweetheart. I have come to believe, regardless of the words I spouted at you out of my jealousy, that you were unaware that you were flirting with him. Well," he amended, "maybe not that, precisely. But I do believe you had no expectation that your smiles and sallies would bring him so quickly to worship at your feet."

"Worship at my feet! Believe me, sir, he had more than worship in mind."

"I do not doubt it. At the risk of repeating myself, I can only say that he had your reputation to encourage him. No,

don't poker up, sweetheart," Hawk said. "You still deserve
to hear a few choice words on that subject. The only reason
you have not heard many is that I, too, have had much to
answer for. Moreover, from what I have been able to observe,
you have not gone much beyond the line since my return."

The conversation was taking a turn Mollie had not anticipated, not to mention one she wished with all her heart to avoid.
Since she knew she could not successfully press for further
details about his plans, she did the only thing she could think
of to stem the lecture she feared might be budding. He still
had his hands on her shoulders, so she leaned heavily against
them, tilting her face up to his.

"Kiss me, sir," she said.

He chuckled. "Would you disarm me, madam?"

"Yes, sir, if it can be done."

"It can be done, sweetheart," he assured her, "by the
lifting of your smallest finger." Within moments it became
clear to her that Hawk had forgotten his weariness entirely,
and it was much later before she was allowed to sleep.

The following day was a busy one, during which, what
with last-minute preparations for all their guests, she and
Lady Bridget seemed not to have a minute to call their own.
But late in the afternoon Mollie managed to escape long
enough to don her breeches and waistcoat and ride to the
south meadow for an hour's practice with her bow and arrows.
To her delight she discovered that the archery butt had been
recovered in her absence with brand-new, freshly painted
canvas. And to her great satisfaction, the only holes in the
new fabric when she left the meadow were to be found in the
two inner rings of color.

As she rode her horse along the rear causeway, she had a
sudden sense of *déjà vu*, for there were horsemen approaching the main entrance of the castle along the other causeway.
For a crazy moment, she half-expected to see the Hawkstone
banner waving above them, but then she saw that there were
only three riders. The rest of the party consisted of a coach
with a crest upon its door. The distance, however, was too
great for her to be able to make out whose it might be. A
moment later, however, a face appeared in the coach window,
and Mollie instantly recognized her sister-in-law. The sight
caused her to give spur to her mount, and seconds later she
clattered through the postern gate into the stableyard.

Her first inclination was to ride straight through to the central courtyard to greet the visitors, but while Lady Gwendolyn would probably not be much shocked by her appearance, Mollie knew perfectly well that the more conservative Worthing would be astounded. And she was nearly as certain that Hawk would not approve of showing herself to his brother-in-law in such garb as she was presently wearing. Lady Bridget, too, would be discomposed if Worthing or the two gentlemen with him, whoever they might be, were to express disapproval to her on the subject. Consequently, Mollie slipped quickly from the saddle, tossed her reins to the waiting Teddy, and hurried into the castle through the rear hall. Taking the stairs two by two, she soon came to the upper landing and was hastening across the worn stone floor when her husband emerged from her own bedchamber.

Hawk grinned at her. "Where are you headed in such haste, my lady? Hoping to avoid a lecture from Aunt Biddy?"

"No, sir, but Lord and Lady Worthing have arrived, and I want to greet them properly and thought I'd best change my clothes before doing so."

He shook his head, laughing, and caught her up in his arms. "Sometimes I think there are two people inhabiting that beautiful body of yours, sweetheart. One is a child constantly on the lookout for adventure, and the other is an elegant lady, at home to a peg in the finest drawing rooms." He set her on her feet again and turned her toward her bedchamber.

Knowing from previous experience what to expect, she skipped hastily forward, thus neatly avoiding a smack on the backside. Tossing him a saucy grin, she pushed open the door and stepped across the threshold.

Hawk laughed again. "Make haste, sweetheart. I shall endeavor to entertain our guests until your arrival. By the bye, did they chance to see you?"

"Yes, no doubt they did as I rode along the postern causeway. However, they will not have recognized me," she added confidently.

"And just how are you so certain of that fact, I wonder?" His eyes narrowed with an arrested look, and profoundly discomposed by that penetrating gaze, Mollie flushed deeply and hastily shut the door behind her. For a moment she waited just inside the door, lest he be tempted to come after her, to pursue that dangerous topic. But though there was a moment's nerve-racking silence, she heard his footsteps at last, moving away toward the main staircase.

Expelling a breath of relief, she rang the bell for Mathilde du Bois. By the time the dresser made her appearance, Mollie's male attire had been safely stowed away, and she was dressed in a chemise, sitting upon the dressing chair, pulling stockings on over her slim legs.

"Mathilde, I must prepare for company," she declared. "Quickly."

Within a few short moments, Mathilde du Bois had slipped a becoming afternoon gown of emerald-green sarcenet, trimmed with gilt lace at the neck and hem, over her head. Clicking her tongue in disapproval, the haughty tirewoman reluctantly agreed to keep her mistress's hairstyle simple, merely neatening the twisted plaits of golden-brown hair and arranging them in a sort of crown at the top of Mollie's dainty head. Not twenty minutes had passed since she had left Hawk standing in the corridor, before she made her way down the main staircase to greet her guests. As the gentlemen rose to their feet, she was somewhat dismayed to see her husband remove his watch from his pocket and cast a glance first at it and then at herself. He said nothing, however, merely flicking the case shut again and returning it to his pocket. Mollie hurried forward to greet Lord and Lady Worthing.

"Gwen, we did not expect you until tomorrow! What a wonderful surprise!"

"Well, we hoped it would be a surprise," Lady Gwendolyn said, laughing. "At least, we knew we would surprise you, and *hoped* the surprise would be a pleasant one. Fact is, there was simply no more bearing that dreadful heat, and when Jamie and Breck"—she indicated the two gentlemen— "decided to accompany us . . . well, that was enough inspiration, believe me. I tell you, Mollie, London fairly reeks in summer. 'Tis the most dreadful thing. One would think the sewers still ran with filth as they did in olden days."

"In some parts of the city, they still do," her spouse informed her gravely.

"Oh, to be sure, but not in Mayfair, sir. There is no explaining it. But I was constantly having the headache, and in my condition, you know, there was simply nothing else to be done. I longed for the cool of Hawkstone Towers, and I was persuaded you would not mind, though we did say we would arrive Wednesday. So, dearest Worthing packed us all up and we are here.''

Mollie had fastened upon only one phrase of the speedy monologue. She stared wide-eyed at her grinning sister-in-law. ''In your condition! Do not tell us, Gwen, that you are increasing again. You've only just escaped confinement.''

''Oh, that was months ago, Mollie. And this time will not be bad at all, you know, for I expect to be confined in January, and there is nothing else of interest to do then, anyway. And by the time next Season begins, I shall be entirely recovered and Baby can be given over to Nanny.''

Conscious of a small pang of envy, Mollie extended her congratulations to the couple, and the conversation turned to other matters. She was glad to see both Lord Breckin and Sir James, for they were always welcome visitors, and it was a cheerful group that sat down to dinner that night. Unsurprisingly, a certain amount of gossip had accrued even in the short time of their absence from the metropolis, and it was with amusement that Mollie learned that Lord Alvanley was no longer being pursued by Madame de Staël's prim daughter.

''Seems the lady discovered Alvanley's penchant for living beyond his means,'' Sir James informed the table at large with an ironic laugh.

''Oddly enough,'' put in Lord Breckin, flicking a crumb from his elegant sleeve, ''that was the thing that served best to lend credence to Brummell's insistence that Alvanley was worth a hundred thousand a year. The man certainly lives up to that reputation.''

''To his creditors' sorrow,'' Hawk said, grinning.

''Well, at least their luck seems to be holding,'' Lady Gwendolyn observed. ''I've heard of nothing but their incredible winnings for a week or more now.''

Lady Bridget said gently, ''Those gentlemen would be well advised to put something by for less prosperous times, would they not?''

''Indeed, ma'am,'' Worthing agreed ponderously, ''but I daresay they will not do so. None of the dandy set is particularly noted for his good sense.''

''Unfair, Worthing,'' Breckin said, shaking his head. ''I have it on excellent authority that Brummell has shown reasonable good sense on at least three occasions, though I confess I cannot call an example to mind on such short notice.''

The others laughed at this sally, and Lord Ramsay requested further information regarding Albertine de Staël. Sir James regarded him with a jaundiced eye.

''Not thinking of making a move in that direction, I hope, dear boy. 'Fraid you won't cut a big-enough dash to suit her mama, don't you know. 'Course, if Hawk here should slip his wind, you'd make a prime target for the woman. Can't deny that.''

''Well, I should say not!'' Ramsay retorted, rising to the bait easily. ''I merely wondered if she had taken an interest in anyone else, that's all. I pity the poor girl, with a mother like that pushing her into matrimony at so tender an age. She is only sixteen, you know. Oughtn't to have been brought out until next year in my opinion.''

''Too true,'' agreed Breckin. ''Such a dab of a creature, too. Not even beauty to recommend her, you know, and always the lurking horror that she might age to look like her mother. Not a pleasant prospect. However, since you take an interest, you will be glad to know that there is a wealthy émigré in the wings, a duke at that, albeit a Frenchie without much claim to the family properties.''

''Like Prince Nicolai,'' observed Mollie, not really thinking about what she was saying. ''It is such a shame that those families lost so much merely by standing up for what they believed. I'm grateful that such things do not happen in England.''

''If you read your history,'' Worthing told her, ''you must know about the injustices of the Cromwell period, when many families lost their property. And later the Jacobites suffered too, you know.''

He would have continued in this pedantic vein had not Hawk interrupted him. Mollie had already noticed that her words had arrested the attention of every gentleman at the table one way or another. Her husband spoke with exaggerated gentleness.

''My lady, what did you mean by your comparison of that Russian prince to Breckin's French duke? I was unaware that the Stefanoviches had lost any property to the czar.''

"Not my duke," Breckin corrected. "Belongs to young Libertine, or will do, if her mama's plans don't go amiss."

No one paid him any heed, however, for the others were all staring at Mollie, who was regarding her husband searchingly. " 'Tis not property in Russia, sir, but in France. Madame de Staël told me that evening she came to supper. The evening of the harpist, sir," she added to clarify matters.

"I remember the evening," he said with a hint of a smile, "but I do not remember the comment."

"You were not there," she explained. " 'Twas before the gentlemen had finished their port. They were an unconscionable time over it, if you recall." Her eyes twinkled, daring him to remember.

"Mmmm," was all he said to that. Then, "But what did she say exactly, Mollie?"

"Well . . ." Mollie searched her brain for Madame de Staël's precise words. "I do not recall everything she said, you know. But it was something about Nicolai's mother being French. She said it didn't matter much, though it might affect his diplomatic career. I couldn't understand how that could be, however, for she said his mother was dead and the family lands had all been confiscated by the Empire, so he can have no connections there now."

A look passed from Hawk to Sir James and then to Lord Breckin before Hawk turned again to Mollie. "That is all? She said nothing more?"

"Nothing more about Prince Nicolai, sir, but you know how she is. She talked a great deal about a great many things. I couldn't hope to remember the half of it. Nevertheless," she added when he continued to look at her, his expression more serious than she was used to seeing it, "I am reasonably certain she said nothing more about his highness."

Sir James sighed. " 'Tis a pity we didn't have this information before we left London," he said dolefully.

"Why?" Lady Gwendolyn inquired. "What possible import can it have to anyone? I, for one, found Madame de Staël's conversation incredibly wearing. I cannot think how one could be expected to remember two words out of ten once one had escaped her company."

Recalled to their senses, the gentlemen at once denied any particular interest in Madame de Staël and pressed her ladyship for further items of gossip that might have come her way. As always, Lady Gwendolyn was delighted to comply, and the subject of Prince Nicolai's antecedents was allowed to take its place in memory.

Though Worthing pleaded fatigue soon after tea was brought into the front hall at ten o'clock and accompanied the ladies upstairs, the other gentlemen remained below, chatting amiably. Mollie would have liked very much to remain with them, but she had a strong notion that Hawk would send her away if she attempted to stay, so she went up to bed with the others. Remembering what he had told her the night before, she left her own bedchamber the moment she was ready to retire, and climbed into bed in his room without the slightest pang of conscience. But try as she would to stay awake until he came upstairs, her eyelids simply would not obey her sternest commands. At last, fearing to set the bed curtains afire if she left the bedside candle to burn any lower, she snuffed it, turned over once, and went to sleep.

When she awoke the next morning, the only evidence she had that Hawk had even come to bed was the fact that the bedclothes were disarranged on his side. When she rang for her chocolate, Cathe informed her that most of the gentlemen has been up for a while and were even now enjoying a large breakfast together in the main dining hall. Mrs. Bracegirdle, the maid confided, had been ordered to see everyone else served in the breakfast parlor.

"Talking gentleman talk, most like," the girl said, tossing her head in a clear opinion of such goings-on. Mollie smiled at her, and thus encouraged, Cathe informed her that gentlemen, to her mind, took themselves much too seriously.

"I am persuaded that you are right, Cathe," Mollie said then. "Ring for Miss du Bois, will you? We've a busy day ahead of us."

The truth of her words was brought home to her even sooner than she expected, for the first of their guests, having chosen to spend the night at Forest Row, arrived well before noon, and others arrived in what seemed like a continual stream until well into the night. Mollie began to feel as if her face were stretched from constant smiling. And after what must have been a thousand words of cheery welcome, she began to long for the chance to snap at someone, anyone. The Countess de Lieven was haughtier than ever away from London, and many of the other women adjusted their own manners accordingly. More than once, Mollie found her sister-in-law's dancing eyes turned in her direction, and that, more than anything, helped her to remain calm and poised.

Of the gentlemen they saw little. Those who were directly involved in whatever plots Hawk was brewing engaged themselves in seemingly innocent pursuits for the larger part of the day, but she knew well that there was another long night session after the others had gone to bed. Prince Nicolai approached her only once, but her reception was so blighting that he made little effort after that to engage her in anything more than polite guest-to-hostess conversation, for which Mollie was profoundly grateful. She had scarcely known where to look when he first approached her, and she was certain that every eye in the room was upon them, speculating. She glanced at her husband, at that moment taking his ease, one foot on the fender of the fireplace, his elbow resting upon the mantelpiece while he chatted with Lord Bathurst. Hawk raised an eyebrow as if he were asking her if she needed his assistance, but he showed no sign of disapproving of her conversation. Encouraged by his trust in her, she soon made her escape from the prince, excusing herself to see to some newly arriving guests.

Only once had there been a moment that stirred her curiosity. Conversation had turned to Wellington's success at Vitoria, and a general discussion had ensued, during the course of which Mollie had surprised an odd look on her husband's face. Someone had clearly said something to pique his interest, but she had been paying little heed to the conversation, so she had no idea what, specifically, had been said. She was certain that the clearest voice just before she had glanced at Hawk had been Prince Nicolai's. However, there was no break in the conversation, nor was there any opportunity for her to ask her husband about the incident.

By the following morning nearly everyone who had been expected had arrived with the exception of the Prince Regent and his party. Mollie was already so tired that she could scarcely enter into Lady Gwendolyn's enthusiasm and found relief, for once, in Lady Bridget's placid acceptance of things.

"I cannot believe this house party of yours," Hawk's sister said soon after they had left the Countess de Lieven and several of her followers in the breakfast parlor. "I had no notion Hawk was on such terms with men like Lord Bathurst or Monsieur de Lieven, let alone the Regent. Why, I'm sure he hadn't so many as two political notions to rub together before he went to the Peninsula.''

"Well, they seem to have become well acquainted over the past weeks,'' Mollie replied noncommittally.

But Lady Gwendolyn had not been acknowledged as one of London's greatest gossips for a number of years by virtue of a dense mind. She regarded her hostess narrowly. "I cannot pretend to know what goes forward here,'' she said almost tartly, "but I know my brother well, Mollie, and there is something stirring beneath the surface that has nothing to do with simple entertainment.''

"Well, don't ask me what it is,'' Mollie replied wearily, "for I cannot tell you. And don't eat me. I am as much aware of the atmosphere as you are, but when I attempted to discover what was going forward, your charming brother nearly snapped my head off.''

"He is charming, isn't he?'' Lady Gwendolyn said, allowing herself to be diverted. "I wasn't by any means certain that the two of you would ever make a match of it, you know, though I hadn't the slightest awareness of his reasons for leaving so precipitately, but I want you to know, Mollie, that no one could be happier than I am to see the two of you constantly looking sheep's eyes at each other.''

Mollie stared at her in astonishment. "I'm sure I've not the slightest notion what you mean, Gwen.''

But the other young woman merely laughed at her, and at that moment Lady Bridget approached them to suggest that someone be posted to look out for the Regent's arrival.

"Like Mrs. Bracegirdle did the other night, you know,'' she explained. "It would give ample warning for a proper welcome, I think.''

"Unnecessary, Aunt Biddy,'' Ramsay said behind her. "Hawk and Lord Breckin have ridden to meet them, and Hawk already gave orders for one of the stableboys to ride up to the ridge to keep a lookout. I think, as a matter of fact, that Harry rode along with him.''

"With Hawkstone?'' Lady Bridget inquired, frowning slightly. "I cannot approve of that,'' she said. "It is not fitting that the Prince Regent should be met by a little boy.''

"No, no, of course not,'' he said, chuckling. "Harry went off with the stableboy, I believe.''

Lady Bridget's face smoothed again at once, but her relief was short-lived, for less than an hour and a half later the Prince Regent and a party of some twenty cavaliers rode into the central courtyard unannounced. There was no sign of Hawk or Lord Breckin.

15

Mollie, Lady Gwendolyn, and Lady Bridget did the honors of the castle, hiding their worry as best they might, their hospitable efforts warmly seconded by the Countess de Lieven and her husband as well as Lord Bathurst. It was the latter who asked what had become of their host.

"Damme if I know," replied the corpulent Prince Regent. "Haven't seen hide nor hair of him, you know. Damme, but I haven't."

"Didn't you say Harry and a stableboy went to keep watch?" Mollie inquired of Lord Ramsay in an undertone.

"That I did. Wonder what became of them. I can tell you, Moll, I don't like this."

Lord Bathurst assumed that Hawk and Breckin had merely taken a different route than that chosen by the royal party and had somehow missed them. But a few judicious questions made it perfectly clear that such was not the case.

"It cannot be," Lord Ramsay stated flatly, "for it will have taken his highness some time to reach the valley from Cross-in-Hand. There is only the one road, and there is no way Hawk could have missed him. Besides the which, we are also missing my younger brother, Harry, who was to have kept watch over the valley road."

The Regent was distressed by what was rapidly being accepted as Hawk's disappearance, and was disposed to discuss at length various possible courses of action to take in the matter. In the meantime Sir James Smithers, acting with uncharacteristic haste, demanded to know who among the men employed at the castle best knew the surrounding countryside and who among them was best at reading sign. Lord Ramsay, responding automatically to the note of authority in Sir James' voice, not only gave him Haycock's name but sent for the gamekeeper and his two sons to attend Sir James a once in the rear hall. He was anxious himself to accompany the search party Sir James meant to form, but Mollie grabbed his arm before he could follow the older man.

"Ramsay, wait. Have you seen Prince Nicolai?"

"A few moments ago in the courtyard," he responded promptly. "He came out with the de Lievens." He looked around. "I don't see him now, however."

"Well, we must find him," Mollie said anxiously.

"What for? He cannot have had anything to do with this. I'll swear he's not left the castle. No one has, or we should have been told."

"He might be in league with someone, with d'Épier, for example."

"For heaven's sake, Mollie, d'Épier is still in London, and we do not know that Hawk's disappearance has anything to do with anything. It might well be that he and Breckin were merely set upon by footpads who took their horses and left them in a ditch somewhere."

She shuddered at the thought but stood her ground. "I don't think so. Anyway, we must find Nicolai. He might slip away in all the excitement."

It was an anticlimax to encounter the Russian prince descending the main stair as they entered the front hall. He nodded at them, volunteering the information that Monsieur de Lieven had sent him upstairs to fetch some important papers he wished to present to the Regent. Mollie looked after him skeptically.

"He was anxious to explain being upstairs, was he not?"

Ramsay shrugged. "I think you are seeing bogies, Moll. I mean to go with Smithers. If Hawk needs assistance, I want to be there."

Filled with misgiving, she followed him to the rear hall. Every feeling told her that Nicolai was somehow involved in Hawk's absence, but she could think of no way to convince her brother-in-law. They found Smithers delivering rapid-fire orders to a sizable group of men, and Mollie was in the process of attempting to convince herself that if Hawk could be found, the search party would find him, when the door from the stableyard crashed back on its hinges. The sound, followed by the clatter of quick footsteps across the anteroom floor, startled them all, and as one, they turned to see Harry charge into the room.

"Mollie, Ramsay, they've abducted Hawk! We saw them!"
The boy's face was flushed, he was breathing heavily, and
his clothing was in disarray.

"Where?" Smithers asked tersely.

"On the upper valley road just below where we were
waiting on the ridge."

"How long ago?"

"More than an hour, I believe," the boy told them. "I
don't know for sure, but it seems ages and ages. There was a
group of them, four or five at least, and they just swooped
out of the woods, taking them quite by surprise, I daresay.
Anyway, it was over in a flash."

"Why did you not tell us immediately?" demanded his
brother.

"They headed down the valley toward Hurst Green, and
we tried to follow them," Harry explained, "but it took us a
while to get down to the road, and by that time they had
taken to the woods again and we couldn't find any sign of
them. We searched for a long time, and when we came back
to the lake road, we learned that the royal party had already
passed by. Since we knew you would want to hear what
happened, we came back."

"Look here, Harry," Smithers said. "You will have to come
with us to show us just where all this business took place. We
should be able to pick up a trail. Never fear, my lady," he
added kindly, speaking to Mollie, "we will get them back."

She nodded, knowing he meant every word he said, but
still unable to rid herself of the notion that his efforts would
be in vain. She touched Ramsay's arm, and he turned to look
at her, worry plain on his face.

"Ramsay, don't go with them. Call it feminine instinct or
whatever you want to call it, but I have the strongest feeling
that Hawk's life is in danger and that the danger comes from
Prince Nicolai. You must know they suspect him of being in
league with the spies, for you know more about that business
than you have told me. Hawk insisted that it would be
dangerous for me to know what was going forward here, but
I'm certain the plotting and planning has much to do with his
disappearance. I remember you said you had been told to
insist to d'Épier that all the information he seeks is in Hawk's
head. What could be more logical than that they have abducted him in order to force him to reveal what he knows?"

Ramsay grimaced. "I didn't realize I'd said so much, but I am certain that one reason Sir James is so distracted is that that same possibility has occurred to him. But whatever Hawk's suspicions regarding the Russian may have been, he's kept them to himself, Mollie. I've no reason to believe Nicolai is any more likely a suspect than anyone else."

"What about that business about his French mother last night at supper, and what about his conversation with d'Épier at the Argyle Rooms?" she demanded.

He thought about her words, as he always did, but finally he shrugged. "I don't know that there is any great importance in his mother's origin, and his conversation with d'Épier might just as well have been innocent as not. I do know that the leak might as easily have come from Carlton House or the War Ministry as from the Russian embassy."

They had drawn away from the others, and at that moment Sir James indicated that he was ready to leave. He called to Ramsay, desiring to know if the young man meant to accompany them. Mollie stared hard at her brother-in-law, willing him to remain.

"Look here, Mollie," he said, biting his lip, "I cannot remain behind. Only think how it would look if I did. I am Hawk's brother, after all."

"But I may need your assistance," she pleaded. "Please, Ramsay."

He paused indecisively, but finally he shook his head. "It would look too odd, Moll. Think about it. If I remain behind, and Prince Nicolai *is* involved in the business, we shall only succeed in putting his guard up. He cannot do anything in broad daylight, after all, and there will be light for some hours yet. You must do your possible to keep your eye on him, just in case. I own, it is odd he has not offered to assist in the search." He thought for a moment, then gave his head another shake. "If he is behind all this business, it stands to reason that the abductors will want to keep Hawk alive until he can speak with him. That much *is* part of the plan."

"I wish you will not be so cryptic," she complained, watching the others begin to file out of the room. "Tell me, Ramsay. You must."

"Only this much then," he replied quickly. "It has been put about that Wellington sent Hawk to help Bathurst and the others firm up plans for a massive offensive strike against

Napoleon's forces, and that that was the chief reason for this house party—so they could meet without putting a lot of other backs up.''

"But how could anyone believe that secret military plans would be discussed in such a situation?" Mollie demanded.

"There's no time for a long explanation," Ramsay told her. "I must go. Just believe me when I say that sufficient foundation was laid to make the spies believe it. That was part and parcel of the information I passed along to d'Épier. Since the victory at Vitoria, they are desperate for whatever information they can get, and are correspondingly, we hope, more gullible.'' He was already crossing the room to follow the others, but he looked back over his shoulder. "I shall send Harry back to you just as soon as he points out the trail. Perhaps he can help you keep watch over your prince.''

. Mollie bit back words of reproach. Clearly he did not put much faith in Prince Nicolai Stefanovich as a villain, no doubt because Hawk had bent over backward to avoid accusing the man just because he feared his suspicions had been prompted by his jealousy. She sighed, turning to go back to the front hall. She was still the hostess of a house party, and the first she had to do was to arrange for the Regent's entertainment. He certainly would not expect his visit to be disarranged by the mere fact of his host's abduction. She found the Countess de Lieven.

"Madame, may I ask a favor of you?"

"But, of course, Mollie dear. I know you must be well nigh distracted, poor child. What is it?"

"Everything has been arranged for the Regent's comfort, of course," Mollie began, "and Lady Bridget will make certain he finds his suite satisfactory. But I would be grateful if you would take it upon yourself to see that he is not bored. I know you are great friends with him, and it would be such a help to know I can depend upon your good offices.''

"You need not bother your head any longer, my dear. Consider the matter attended to. My husband has business with his highness, and so does Lord Bathurst. Among the three of us, I think I can promise he will not be bored.''

"Thank you, madame.''

"Call me Dasha, Mollie. All my friends do so. And do not worry. Your husband has a knack, so I am told, for landing upon his feet. It will be well.''

The slender young countess turned away, and Mollie smiled. She had long thought Madame de Lieven to be the haughtiest lady in London, and she knew the woman had a penchant for mischief and intrigue, but she had never expected such kindness from her.

It was a simple matter for her to watch Prince Nicolai until dinnertime, for he remained in the main hall with most of the other company. Their principal guests had withdrawn together to speak privately in one of the small saloons, but everyone else who had not joined the search party seemed perfectly content to converse or play card games in the hall. Harry returned about an hour after the searchers had departed, saying Ramsay had told him to help her keep an eye on Prince Nicolai. Mollie suspected that Ramsay had meant only to make the boy feel useful, but she quickly accepted his offer of assistance, telling him that she wanted to know the moment Prince Nicolai even looked like he might be leaving the castle.

Half of the search party returned with Lord Ramsay shortly after the guests in the castle had risen from the dinner table. Ramsay reported that Sir James had sent them back to eat and rest, having decided that since Hawk had not been found immediately, it would be best to work in shifts.

"We found a trail, all right," Ramsay said, "but the devil's in it, because it looks as if they expected us to follow and meant to confuse us. We followed it for miles through the woods, but we never saw so much as a horse, let alone the abductors, and eventually we ended up near where we had first found the trail. That was when Sir James split us up and sent my lot back here to get something to eat."

"Well, I am very glad to see you," Mollie told him. "Do you remain long?"

"We are to meet the others at midnight. There should be a full moon by then, which will be a help, but I sent two of the lads back to Sir James with torches. I only hope they don't set the woods afire. I'm going to bed just as soon as I get a bite to eat. My man will wake me in time to join the others."

Mollie nodded, making no attempt this time to talk him into staying behind. Most of the guests would retire soon after the tea tray was brought in at ten o'clock. If Prince Nicolai meant to stir from the castle that would be his best time. And if he tried to leave, she would have no difficulty persuading Ramsay to follow him. If he did not leave until the others had gone, she would follow him herself.

The party became gayer after dinner, when the Regent condescended to tell several of his favorite anecdotes. Several guests offered to sing or play the pianoforte, and the time passed swiftly for most, until tea was brought in. Mollie had sent Harry up to eat his dinner in the schoolroom with Mr. Bates and had told him he might as well go to bed afterward, but he had informed her indignantly that he had no intention of sleeping until he could be perfectly sure the prince would not leave the castle.

"But you cannot stay up until he goes to bed, Harry. He might very well stay up past midnight."

"Pooh," scoffed the boy. "I daresay he will begin yawning about nine and then make a thing about retiring as early as he can without drawing attention to the matter. That is what I should do if I meant to creep out of the castle."

"How will he get a horse?"

"Nothing simpler. The lads in the stable all go to bed early, because they must be up betimes."

"But the search party will be leaving at midnight. The grooms who attend those gentlemen will have been told to stay up."

Her words brought a frown to Harry's face. But even as he pondered, Mollie realized what Nicolai's best course would be.

"Harry, he will let the grooms think he means to go with the search party. It will be a simple matter then for him to lose himself in the woods. He could not have done so in daylight, of course, and he could not have known that some of the gentlemen would return." Mollie paused, looking at him. "What do you think?"

Harry drew himself up to a greater height, so gratified was he to have his opinion sought in the matter. He did not speak hastily, but weighed his thoughts. Then, finally, he said, "I say, Mollie, what shall we do?"

"Well, you've got to look as if you're going up to bed. Even with Hawk missing, it would be taken as an odd thing if I were to allow you to stay up so late. However, you may do as you think best about keeping an eye on Prince Nicolai. He certainly won't wish to ride out in the clothes he wears to dinner. But don't let him catch you watching him. It would be as well, I think, if he doesn't see you at all. I believe he is a very dangerous man, Harry, and your brothers wouldn't thank me if I let anything happen to you. One thing you can do," she added, thinking aloud, "is to go out to the stables and warn Teddy to have my horse saddled and ready to go with the others. Tell him also to put my bow and quiver close by. I wish to be well prepared."

"The men will never allow you to go with them, Mollie," Harry warned.

"They will not know about it," she assured him. "I've no intention of letting the prince get away while I stand arguing about whether he is the master spy or not."

"Oh, famous!" Harry said approvingly. "Shall you tell Ramsay?"

She thought about it. "I don't think I shall say anything until we know for certain that the prince is our man. If he says straight out that he means to join the search, I shall begin to have my doubts, for the others would miss his presence rather quickly. But if he means only to use the activity that must attend their departure as a cover for his own business, then he will say nothing. When you speak to Teddy, ask him to watch out for the prince's man. If he saddles his horse, and the prince says nothing about joining the others, we shall have our answer."

"I want to go, too," Harry said, his eyes alight.

"Well, you cannot. And don't argue the point, young man. Your brothers would both have my head if I were to allow such a thing. Ramsay would only send you back again, and that might well warn someone that something unusual is afoot. We cannot know that there is only the one spy in our midst, after all. Perhaps there are henchmen right here within the castle walls. Surely the prince's man, at least, must be party to his master's plots, if indeed the prince is our man."

Harry agreed to do as she suggested, and Mollie was able to rejoin her company, feeling that she had done all she could do for the moment. The rest of the evening passed quickly enough, and she was almost amused to see Prince Nicolai cover a yawn once or twice before the tea tray was brought in. The Regent made it plain that he, for one, had no intention of retiring at such an unseasonable hour and was much gratified when Lord Bathurst, Monsieur de Lieven, and Lord Worthing agreed to engage him in a game of whist. These four gentlemen adjourned to a smaller saloon, and the rest of

the party began to drift off to their bedchambers. Prince
Nicolai was indeed one of the first to go up.

Lady Bridget confessed that she was exhausted. "All this
chatter, my dear, gives me the headache. No doubt that is
because we are all worried about Gavin, of course. I cannot
conceive of what may have befallen the dear boy."

Lady Gwendolyn came up in time to hear her last words.
She shot Mollie a speaking look. "Have you any notion,
Mollie, of what goes forward? Is Gavin truly in danger or not?"

"I don't know, Gwen, but I fear he may be. The fact that
Sir James and the others have not been able to find him, and
Lord Breckin leads me to fear that there is more at hand than
a mere attack by footpads."

"They say he was abducted," Lady Gwendolyn reminded
her.

"I know. At first I hoped that was merely Harry's imagination gone mad. But I'm afraid he may have seen exactly what
he says he did."

They chatted for some moments more, and then Mollie
suggested that their best course was to retire with the others.

Lady Gwendolyn chuckled. "I believe I might just as well.
Worthing will be playing at whist into the small hours. And
for pound points, no doubt. It makes me almost long for the
next time he chooses to read me a scold for outrunning the
constable."

Mollie shook her head, grinning. "You know perfectly
well that gentlemen never remember their own peccadilloes
when they choose to discuss ours."

"I see you have experience in the matter," Lady Gwendolyn said. Then, as Mollie's expression changed sharply, she
put a quick hand to her shoulder. "I apologize for that," she
said quietly. "I should not tease you when I know you must
be alarmed for his safety. In point of fact, I am certain he will
be all right. I just cannot make myself believe anything
dreadful might happen to him. He is so . . . so capable. You
know what I am saying, Mollie."

Mollie nodded, but her thoughts would not be silenced,
and as she went slowly up to her bedchamber, the situation
seemed to impress itself more solidly upon her mind than it
had done before now. Cathe and Mathilde du Bois were both
waiting to attend to her, but she sent them away and sat down
at her dressing table, staring at her reflection in the glass,

while she attempted to arrange her thoughts in some sort of order.

What if they could not find Hawk? What if he were already dead? From what Ramsay had told her, that did not seem likely. Surely, if they thought he had secret information that could be readily gained from no other source, they would at least keep him alive until he had told them whatever it was they wished to know. And surely, they would not begin questioning him until their principal arrived. But what if Prince Nicolai was not the principal? What if she had made his participation in the plot up out of whole cloth? After all, the only evidence she had against him was based upon intuition and a couple of odd occurrences. Perhaps there was no legitimate reason to doubt his integrity.

She remembered Hawk's attention stirring when she had mentioned Madame de Staël's comments about Prince Nicolai's French heritage, but she could not imagine how that could have anything to do with the matter at hand. Madame had not even mentioned that he still had relatives in France. Surely they had either emigrated or been killed. So what possible connection could there be? Nevertheless, Hawk had clearly seen one. And there had also been the odd look she had seen on her husband's face the previous evening when everyone had been discussing Wellington. And the person speaking loudest just before that moment had been Prince Nicolai. Surely he must have said something he ought not to have said. The more she thought, the more she came to believe she had not been imagining things. Prince Nicolai was involved, and he was not simply investigating matters on his own, as she had once thought possible. It stood to reason that he was the most likely person to be the principal. Surely he would lead them to Hawk.

It occurred to her for the first time then that she had not once spared a thought for Lord Breckin's safety, only for her husband's. But is that so unusual? she asked her reflection. To worry most about the man one loves? What if he never comes home to me? But suddenly she could not face that possibility. Hawk would come home. She would see to it. She had never told him she loved him. She had never really thought about it, and at the moment she could not think when it was that she had first recognized the fact. It was not a thing one thought about, after all. Love was not what one looked for in one's marriage. Other things were supposed to be more important, and love, after all, was most unfashionable. Peasants indulged, of course. And married persons, though not, of course, with their respective spouses. But no one else had ever stirred her like Hawk could merely by speaking to her. And his touch—well, one need not think about that right now.

Indeed, just the thought of him sent shivers up and down her spine. Her skin seemed to quiver all over as though he had run his hands up and down her sides, and even her breasts swelled. Only from the thought of him. It was unthinkable that he might not return to her. On that thought she jumped up and hurried to the wardrobe, flinging things from the drawer at the bottom as she searched out her breeches, shirt, waistcoat, and boots. Then, from the top shelf, she dragged down the long cloak she had worn in London. It would conceal her figure, just in case anyone should take more than a casual glance in her direction. Her hair was more of a problem. The beaver hat was not to be thought of. No one would wear such a thing riding out in the night. But at last she unearthed an old knitted cap. It took some doing, but she managed to push her hair up into it, and when she was finished, she was fairly certain it would take more than ordinary attention to detail before her disguise would be penetrated. Most of the men in the stableyard would be bleary-eyed from their short naps, and hopefully Prince Nicolai wouldn't even see her.

Ready at last, she began to fidget, waiting and wondering if perhaps Harry had fallen asleep. The hands of the little jeweled clock on her dressing table approached midnight and passed it. Five minutes slipped slowly by, then ten. Suddenly, there was a light scratching at her door. Then it opened and Harry slipped inside.

"He's going, Mollie. The others have already gone down, and I thought for certain you were wrong, and he meant simply to go to bed, but then he opened his door and looked out into the corridor. I can tell you, Mollie, I nearly suffered an apoplexy, thinking he had seen me. But he didn't, for he shut the door again. But I saw at once that he was dressed for riding. He means to go. Why hasn't he gone down already?"

"He may have done so," she replied, thinking quickly. "No doubt he means only those who might wonder about his horse being readied to think he has gone with the searchers.

He can move out onto the causeway with them and be thought by the gentlemen to be one of the servants and by the servants to be one of the gentlemen, so long as he takes care to let no one see him too closely. That should not be too difficult at this time of night. Indeed, I am hoping the same thing for myself, am I not?''

Harry looked her over from tip to toe. "You'll do, I think. No one who does not know you well would think for a moment that you are the Marchioness of Hawkstone. That is a certainty. But Ramsay will know you, and so will some of our men if they see you. By the bye, Mollie, Teddy said he will be ready for you. He will have Baron standing just inside the stable in the shadows, he said.''

Taking time after that only to extract his promise that he would go to his bedchamber if not to bed, Mollie left Harry and hurried down the back stairs to the rear hall and out into the stableyard, taking care to take long strides and to move as if she knew exactly where she was going. No one seemed to take any heed of her, and most of the men in the yard were already mounted. Teddy awaited her just inside the stable.

"Thank you, Teddy. Where is his highness?''

" 'Is man be 'olding 'is nag yonder, Miss Mollie,'' the man said quietly, giving a slight nod of his head in the direction of the archway leading into the central courtyard. " 'Aven't seen 'is 'ighness yet. Wait now, there 'e be. Just slipping through the archway. Musta come through the court, 'e must.''

"Good," Mollie said, enormously satisfied to have her suspicions confirmed. "Now, where is Lord Ramsay?''

"Ahead o' this lot, I'm thinkin'.''

Of course, he would be in the lead, Mollie thought ruefully. "Look here, Teddy,'' she said aloud, "you've got to get him. Tell him that what I suspected before has come to pass and that he must make some excuse for falling behind. I want him with me when things begin happening out there.''

"I'll tell 'im, Miss Mollie. 'E won't like it much, I'm thinkin'.''

No, he wouldn't, Mollie told herself. She wondered if Ramsay would give her away. There was a good deal of activity in the stableyard now, for upward of twenty men, counting their own people, had joined in the search. They seemed nearly ready to depart, and Mollie swung onto her own saddle and took her quiver and bow from Teddy's hand, slinging them across her back without so much as taking her eyes from the milling group of horsemen, now beginning to move toward the postern gate. Suddenly, one of the throng separated himself from the others and moved directly toward her. Mollie held her breath for a moment, then recognized her brother-in-law.

He rode up beside her. "What is the meaning of this, Mollie? You cannot for a moment think I mean to let you accompany us."

"You cannot stop me," she replied firmly. "I am not your only new recruit either. His highness is there in the archway, and I'm thinking he has no intention of calling attention to that fact. He is merely using your departure as cover for his own. We've got to discover his destination, Ramsay, and we dare not tell the others. Two of us might succeed in following him. Twenty men certainly could not do so."

He let out a long breath. "By Jove, Moll, I believe you've had his measure straight along. But there is still no reason for you to go. In fact, it would be downright foolish. I can take one of the other men with me."

"Who?" she countered. "Who among them all is completely worthy of our trust? Even one of our own men might well have been suborned, and you dare not take the chance. Moreover, if you send me back inside, you will draw attention to me," she added, remembering the argument she had used to convince Harry. "You cannot take that chance either, lest you put him on his guard."

Lord Ramsay was silent for a moment. Then he sighed. "Have it your own way, then. I daresay you would only follow behind if I were to forbid you to come with us."

Mollie nodded, grinning at him.

Sparing only a moment to warn her that the occasion was not one for levity, Ramsay then turned his mount away and rode toward the head of the group. Moments later, there was only the echo of their horses clattering hooves in the stableyard, but moonlight glinted on harness and spurs and reflected their shadows on the water as the party made its way across the rear causeway toward the woods lining the lakeshore.

16

Mollie watched from the shadows of the stable until the shapes she knew to be Prince Nicolai and his man had detached themselves from the blackness of the archway, falling in behind the main party as they headed out across the causeway. Before following, she leaned down from the saddle to speak to her groom.

"Teddy," she said quietly, "I depend upon you to see that no one else leaves after I do. There can be no way of knowing whether there are other untrustworthy persons about or not. Use force only if necessary, but do not allow anyone else to cross over to the shore from the castle tonight."

"Aye, Miss Mollie. There be still enough o' the lads left t' see to that. Ye'll not wish to 'ave t' guard yer back. Not wi' that vermin ahead o' ye, 'n all. I'll just see them gates shut for a bit after ye're gone."

She nodded, but then, remembering Sir James Smithers, she reminded Teddy to be on the lookout for those members of the other half of the search party who might be returning to catch a few hours of sleep. He assured her that he would keep watch himself. Satisfied, Mollie guided her horse out into the stableyard as far as the postern gate. She had a clear view of the horsemen on the causeway, the last few of whom were just approaching the lakeshore. Giving them time to enter the woods, she followed, knowing her figure to be as clearly lit by the great white moon above as those ahead of her had been. She had no great fear of being seen, however, for the woods were thick, and the chances of anyone looking back now were slim. Nevertheless, the sound of her horse's hooves on the hard cobblestones of the causeway sounded unnaturally loud to her ears, and although she knew no one up ahead would hear the sound over that of the men's voices added to the jingle of the horses' harness and the thud of hoofbeats, her nerves were on end until she, too, had ridden through the long grass waving gently in the soft breeze blowing across the lake, and into the concealment of the woods.

Moonlight trickled through the trees as the search party followed in reverse much the same route that she and Lord Ramsay had taken over the ridge the day they had returned from the boxing match in Gill's Green. She wondered whether Prince Nicolai and his man would stay with the main party as far as the valley road. Surely it would be easier for them to separate from the group while they still had the thick cover of the trees to protect them. Accordingly, she allowed her mount to draw a little nearer, straining her eyes to make out the two figures at the rear. Even so, she could not be absolutely certain that the two riders she sought had not separated from the others immediately upon entering the woods, so when two horsemen suddenly came toward her out of the dense shrubbery, she nearly cried out in alarm before she recognized Lord Ramsay and his groom.

"Kept Bill with me in case we need him," he said quietly after he had greeted her. "I sent one of Haycock's lads with Bathurst's aide to take the men on to meet Smithers and tell him what we suspect. If your precious prince is no longer with the group at that time, Sir James will take one group of the men to Salehurst to await word from us and send another to Cross-in-Hand. That way, we won't have to search far for help if we find Hawk."

"I am not even sure Nicolai is still with us now," Mollie confessed as the groom fell in behind them. "There was no way by which I could keep him in sight at first without letting myself be seen, but no one has separated since I caught up with the group."

"Never fear. That's his highness just ahead. Got a good look at his face when he rode by us just now. He doesn't know these woods very well, remember. I daresay he will stay close to the others until he can see the valley road before cutting away."

"Where can he be going?" Mollie asked. "If he does not know the countryside, he must be meeting the others somewhere that can be easily described to him."

"Not necessarily," the young man told her. "Hawk suggested that they might have a regular haunt hereabouts. After all, we are located directly between two main ports, and there are highroads both to the east and west of us leading to the coast. All the sign seems to indicate they are heading toward the Hastings Road, but that may be by way of drawing us away from Eastbourne. We should have a better notion of how things stand after keeping an eye on your prince for a bit.''

"He is *not* my prince!" Mollie muttered in low but none-theless angry tones. "And if your idiotish brother had believed that from the outset and put his mind to discovering just what sort of man Nicolai is, instead of wasting time indulging in foolish bursts of temperament—''

"Was it so foolish, Moll?'' Ramsay interrupted without a thought for the curious groom riding behind them. "Seems to me you gave him good reason for his jealousy.''

She eyed him obliquely. "He really was jealous, wasn't he? I thought at first he was merely asserting his authority, you know.''

Ramsay chuckled. "The night you were throwing things?''

She gave a small affirmative sound.

"I'd say,'' he told her with a touch of laughter still in his voice, "that you may safely depend upon the fact that he was not merely coming the stern husband over you. He was still smoldering when we reached the bookroom, so I'd not be far off to say you were lucky I appeared on the scene. Else you might not have gotten out of that business with a whole skin, my girl. Took him a moment or two even after we'd arrived downstairs to put his mind to my little problem, I can tell you.''

She started to explain to him just what had happened to put Hawk in such a state that night, but she had scarcely begun when Ramsay suddenly touched her arm in warning, and she realized that their quarry had slowed their pace. A moment later, she clearly saw the two horsemen at the rear of the search party turn aside onto a barely existent path. No one ahead of the pair seemed to realize that their number had been reduced by two, but Mollie and her two companions were easily able to follow them as they wound their way further into the trees, away from the other riders.

When they came to the edge of a small clearing, it was not the valley road they saw below them, but the Bourne, looking much like a path of glittering silver slicing through the black-ness of the valley. They decided, without speaking, not to follow the others through that clearing, because it was more dangerous now than ever to let themselves be seen. Instead, they circled through the trees. Guided by the sound of the horses ahead, it was not long before they caught sight of the two men again.

It was no longer safe to speak to each other, for they could not be certain that the others might not hear them. The sound of the three horses, so long as the other pair kept moving, would be mistaken for an echo of their own two, but voices would not. Consequently, Mollie found herself alone with her thoughts, and the great fear that she had scarcely dared to recognize before now threatened to overcome her.

There were still so many things she wanted to discuss with Hawk, and once this business was done—and it would be done satisfactorily, she told herself firmly—she and her husband would talk. They had skimmed over a number of important issues, but she had known since the moment she realized he was capable of jealousy that he cared about her, that his behavior was not due to mere possessiveness or a wish to assert his authority over her. So it was just possible she had been right about his feelings all those years ago. If that was true, then why had he gone and why had he stayed away? Truly, it was time to clarify certain matters between them.

If he lived . . . The thought came unbidden and she refused to let it linger. He was alive. She would know if he were not. And he would remain alive. She would see to it. By whatever means were necessary. She glanced at Ramsay and saw that his jaw was set with the same determination she felt within herself. The two of them would carry it off. While other searchers rode in circles trying to make head or tail of false trails by torchlight and moonlight, she and her brother-in-law would find Hawk and Lord Breckin. She smiled as she remembered that his lordship was also a prisoner. She had not spared him much anxiety. He, like her husband, seemed very much the sort of man who would land on his feet, if for no other reason than she could not imagine the gentle fop with a hair of his head out of place.

It seemed that they had ridden for hours along an unseen track that paralleled the river below, but at last they came to the outskirts of a village, and the two men ahead of them slowed their pace from a trot to a walk. They clearly had no wish to pass through the village and seemed to be arguing about their best course, but finally they turned south, keeping near enough to use the village as a landmark but far enough away not to be observed by a wakeful villager. Some moments later, Mollie realized they were nearing the Hastings highroad.

Again, the pair ahead seemed to wish to keep clear of a route that might be inhabited, but after keeping watch for some moments, they rode up onto the road itself and urged their mounts to a canter. Mollie and Ramsay, reining in, glanced at each other in dismay.

"What do we do now?" Mollie asked. "We can scarcely follow them along the highroad in such moonlight as this. They will be certain to see us. And we cannot maintain that pace if we do not. They will outstrip us in no time."

Ramsay frowned, considering her words, but at the same time Bill spoke up quickly, gesturing in the direction taken by the other two. "They be a-turnin' off, m'lord!"

"Ah," Ramsay observed with satisfaction, "they merely wished to cross the road. Come, we'll catch them quickly enough now."

Instead of following along the highroad, however they crossed directly over, slipping at once in the woods on the other side of the road. But it was not long before they came upon a path that looked to be in the right place to have been the turning taken by Nicolai and his man. They turned along it, listening for sounds from ahead that would tell them they were on the right track. It was not sound that stopped them, however, but the sight of a campfire glowing dimly through the trees ahead. Drawing in again, Ramsay leaned close to Mollie.

"I think we'd best pull back into the woods and dismount, Moll. No telling but what whoever lies ahead might not have a lookout or two posted to catch the unwary. We'd be better off creeping on foot through the trees than approaching along the trail like this."

Obediently she turned her mount after his, with Bill following her, and when they were sufficiently distant from the trail, she dismounted and followed the two men, both of whom now has pistols drawn, through the trees to the edge of a clearing. The glow from the fire dimmed as they approached, and she could hear a low voice speaking in a tone of reproach. Creeping up behind Ramsay, who stood close to the large trunk of an ancient oak tree, Mollie peered into the moonlit clearing to see a burly figure scraping dirt over the fire. There appeared to be some sort of low-voiced argument, and she could see the tall, broad-chested figure of Prince Nicolai. There were others as well, perhaps as many as five or six. Mollie shivered. She had not thought there would be so many. Suddenly she wished they had brought other men with them. Then she heard Nicolai's voice clearly above the others.

"Bring them here."

"We'll slip 'round to the other side, Moll," Ramsay whispered quickly in her ear. She nodded, unable to take her eyes from the scene in the clearing.

Two figures detached themselves from the small group and hauled two others to their feet. Even without the light from the moon, Mollie knew she would have recognized the larger of the two being dragged forward as Hawk. Then there was a glitter at Nicolai's side, and she realized he held a pistol.

"My lord," he said sarcastically, "we have a trifling bit of business to conduct. I have not got a great deal of time, however, so I beg you to forgive my rough-and-ready methods. My ship sails with the morning tide. I believe you know what I require from you, but d'Épier here tells me you prefer to be difficult." Mollie realized with a gasp that the man holding her husband was indeed the Frenchman, who was supposed to be safely in London. She strained her ears to hear what Hawk would reply.

"I certainly have no intention of telling you anything," he said evenly. "You'll have to kill me, damn you."

"No, if you refuse to cooperate, I shall have to kill Lord Breckin," Nicolai replied, speaking in a more sardonic tone. "You see, do you not, that he is of no importance to me. However, I believe you have more feeling for the worth of his neck than I do. We shall see. I shall not kill him immediately, of course. I shall simply cause it to happen bit by bit. Put a gag on his lordship," he added to the man holding Breckin.

Hawk struggled in d'Épier's grip, but he could not break loose, and Mollie saw then that his hands had been tied behind him.

"You won't risk pistol shots here," Hawk said angrily. "I know damn well there must be men searching for us by now. They'll be all over this countryside by morning."

"Your dagger, Igor," said the prince to his manservant. "Do you know how long it will take your friend to bleed to death, Hawkstone? There will be time for him to suffer a good deal before he lapses into unconsciousness. Even then, there are means by which to revive him so that he will enjoy full benefit of the pain you will be inflicting upon him. All you need do to stop it, however, is to tell me what I wish to know."

Moving back behind the tree, Mollie slipped the quiver and bow carefully from across her back and set them upon the ground while she removed her cloak. Then, quickly replacing her riding gloves with the thin kid ones from the quiver, she unsnapped the bow and strapped the quiver across her back again. Stringing the bow, she reached for an arrow and moved back to where she could see what was going on in the clearing. Just as the scene came into view, she heard Lord Breckin give a low cry of pain and saw her husband struggle once again in the arms of his captors.

"Well, Hawkstone?" It was the prince, but he was not watching Hawk. He had his eyes on his own man and Breckin.

Mollie wondered where Ramsay and Bill were. She wondered as well whether their aim would be true enough in the uncertain light to do any good. The element of surprise would certainly be lost once they let loose. The manservant glanced at Prince Nicolai, who nodded. The knife moved closer to Breckin's throat. Quickly, knowing every eye to be pinned on the action of that knife, Mollie brought up the bow, nocked an arrow, drew the bowstring to her cheek, and let fly. The man with the knife screamed, dropped his weapon, and clutched at the back of his right shoulder in an attempt to remove the arrow that was lodged there. Before anyone realized what had happened, Mollie had drawn again. The second arrow took Nicolai in the chest. His pistol fell to the ground, and even as his men seemed torn between panic and a wish to rush to their principal's assistance, Hawk jammed an elbow into d'Épier's stomach, doubling him up, and Ramsay's voice sounded clear and stern from the opposite side of the clearing.

"We have you surrounded. Do not move if you wish to see another sunrise." Every man froze where he stood, not so much as daring to look from side to side. Ramsay's voice sounded again. "Release Lords Hawkstone and Breckin at once. If you do not, you will be shot down where you stand."

A man standing near Breckin turned quickly to obey the order, but d'Épier, with a sly look toward Mollie's side of the clearing, began to reach toward his coat pocket. A shot rang out, stopping his hand in midaction.

"I said not to move," Ramsay repeated coldly. "The next time I shall not aim to miss."

Mollie found herself grinning as she wondered whether he had actually meant to miss that time. But then she saw d'Épier move again and quickly nocked another arrow, drawing, then relaxing when she realized the man merely meant to release Hawk.

Within moments Hawk had scooped up the prince's pistol; then he and Breckin, the latter holding an arm tightly against his side, had disarmed the other men and herded them into a small circle near the dying embers of the campfire. It was not until then that Ramsay and Bill showed themselves.

"Good lads," Hawk said when he saw them. "Keep watch over this lot while I have a look at Breck's wound." He waited until Ramsay had moved to a better vantage point, then glanced toward the tree where Mollie stood. "Where's Haycock? Gone for help?"

"Haycock?" Ramsay sounded puzzled.

"Well, I know of no other man capable of handling a bow—" Hawk broke off, regarding his brother more narrowly. He open his mouth as if he meant to question him further, but then, with a sweeping glance at the ragtag bunch of men huddled together like a flock of distraught sheep, he evidently thought better of it, and when Ramsay nodded to Bill, who disappeared into the trees again, Hawk turned his attention to Breck.

"It's not so bad," his lordship muttered. "Damned well ruined this coat, however. I'd like to have the schooling of that lout for a few moments when I'm mended. Teach him to mess about with a gentleman."

"Hush your row," Hawk said gently, pulling his handkerchief out of his coat pocket and making it into a pad, which he then pressed inside Lord Breckin's shirt before fastening his waistcoat again. "Good thing you have your waistcoats cut like a second skin, laddie. Wouldn't want you to bleed to death while you're in my care."

Breckin made a rude sound. "Merest scratch, dear boy. Give you my word, I'd not wish to cause you embarrassment."

Mollie decided before much more time had passed that they meant to wait for Bill to bring Sir James Smithers and the others before returning to Hawkstone. She was certain Hawk had realized she was there, and she began to wish herself elsewhere as the minutes marched steadily by. She could scarcely show herself, for if the ruffians did not pass along the fact of her presence, surely Lord Breckin would think it a very good joke, and word would quickly spread throughout the *beau monde*, thus causing just the sort of scandal Hawk would most deplore. The more she considered the matter, the less she wanted to be present when the others arrived. The thought of returning on her own to the castle was a daunting one, but she decided the experience would be preferable to being subjected to the stares of the men who would come with Sir James. There wouldn't be the slightest hope then of retaining the protection of her disguise. One look at her face would tell most of them who she was. If Hawk knew she was here now, he would be further angered, no doubt, to discover that she had returned alone. But she would much rather face him alone after the fact than have to ride tamely at his side with the others all staring and speculating as to her fate.

As these thoughts tumbled through her mind, Mollie was already unstringing her bow and snapping it to her quiver. Then, snatching up her cloak from the ground, she flung it over her shoulders, picked up quiver and bow, and began making her way back to where she had left Baron. She moved as quickly as she dared, knowing the longer she took, the more likely the chance of encountering Sir James and his men before she was safely across the highroad. A low neigh sounded just as she was beginning to fear she had mistaken her direction, and she altered her course slightly, coming upon Baron and Ramsay's horse almost immediately thereafter. Speaking in a low voice so as not to startle either one, she moved up to Baron and untied his reins from a low branch, then stepped quickly back to stand beside the stirrup while she slung the quiver across her back again. She had just grasped the saddle at both ends when a muscular arm slipped around her waist just beneath her breasts. Before she could cry out, however, a large hand clamped itself across her mouth, and a low-pitched but nonetheless harsh voice sounded near her ear.

"Not a sound, madam. I've no wish to advertise your presence."

Mollie's original terror subsided immediately, but her knees were still weak, so she was glad of the firm hold Hawk retained around her waist. She let herself relax against him, and when he removed his hand from her mouth, she drew in a long breath and straightened a little in his grasp. He released her, and she turned to him, throwing her arms around him and holding him close. He returned the hug, but too soon his hands found her shoulders, and he held her away from him in a firm grip. She could sense his anger.

"I'd tell you what I think of this little escapade of yours here and now," he said grimly, "but we haven't time for it. Up you go." And with that, he spun her around, grabbed her at the waist, and heaved her into her saddle before she had time to do more than gasp her indignation.

"I saved your life," she snapped, having all she could do not to shout the words at him.

"Keep silent," Hawk ordered as he swung up into Ramsay's saddle. "At least until we're well clear of this lot. Follow me."

He dug his heels into the horse's flanks, urging him to a fast trot as soon as they were on the narrow path again, and Mollie did the same, gritting her teeth to keep from hurling angry words at him. How dared he! Where did he think he and Lord Breckin would be now if she hadn't had the good sense to follow Prince Nicolai. Prince Nicolai! She hadn't given him a thought since she had seen him fall. The arrow had gone left of her point of aim, for she had meant only to strike his shoulder so he would drop the pistol. But she had seen the arrow enter his chest. What if he were dead?

They had reached the highroad, and Hawk turned north, giving spur to his horse, urging him to a distance-eating canter. Mollie followed suit, wishing she could shout at him to stop, to tell her about Nicolai, to let her explain that she had done the only thing she could possibly do. She wanted to tell him that she loved him, that she had not wanted to face the possibility of having to live without him ever again. But as her horse drew alongside his and she glanced over at his stern, unyielding face, she swallowed the words in her throat. He was too angry.

They had ridden for some fifteen minutes before they saw

the glow of torches on the road ahead of them. Hawk swerved his mount to the left, and Mollie followed, quickly drawing off the highroad and into the woods alongside. Several moments later a group of horsemen thundered past them on the road. Hawk waited until they were well past before he led the way back onto the road.

"That was Sir James?" Mollie was surprised to note that her voice was perfectly steady.

"It was. Come. I want you safely back before dawn, and we've only a couple of hours."

"Is it so late?"

"It is." His voice was still grim, so she attempted no further conversation until they has passed through Salehurst to the valley road. At last Hawk slowed his pace to a walk to rest the horses.

Mollie took her courage in hand. "No one would listen to me, sir, when I said the prince was responsible for your disappearance. It wasn't until Ramsay saw him in the courtyard, keeping out of sight of the others, that he realized I was right."

"You might have put one of the others on to follow him, or let Ramsay and Bill handle it, instead of placing yourself in jeopardy," Hawk pointed out.

She was silent for a moment, thinking about his words. No doubt he was right. That would have been the most logical course for her to follow. But even thinking about what might have happened had she not been on the scene in that little clearing made her stomach clench. "I could not do that," she said almost fiercely. "I could not bear the thought that you might leave me again."

"Leave you?" He sounded astonished. "I had no intention of leaving you, Mollie."

She hunched one shoulder in a small, defensive gesture. "You might have been killed," she said, nearly choking on the words. "In fact, you very well would have been if I had not—" She broke off with a little gasp. "Is he dead, Gavin? Prince Nicolai?"

"No, sweetheart." His voice had gentled considerably. "He will live long enough for his majesty's loyal hangman to attend to the matter. You did not kill him."

She sighed in relief. "I'm glad. I think my hands must ave been shaking. My first shot was true, but I was so afraid

he would shoot you before I could wing him. The knife . . .
Is Lord Breckin going to be all right?"

"Right as rain. You must have heard him. He's a good
deal more offended by the fact that the fellow ruined his coat
than by anything else. I left him and Ramsay watching that
lot till Jamie gets to them." He said nothing for a moment.
Then, "You very likely saved our lives, Mollie, but you still
had no business to be there."

"I could not leave it to others, sir," she said quietly.

"Do you care so much, then?"

"You must know I do. How would you have felt if our
positions had been reversed?"

"That is a different matter altogether."

"Only in that you are a man, sir. I think the feelings are
the same." She turned toward him, staring hard at that stern
profile outlined in silver by the moon still hovering over the
trees to her right. When he did not reply immediately, she
added softly, "Or am I mistaken in believing that you love
me as fiercely as I love you?"

17

Mollie found that her breath had caught in her throat as she waited for a response from him. Would he deny it? Or would he admit that he loved her, admit that he would have moved heaven and earth to save her if she had been Prince Nicolai's victim?

She had not taken her eyes from his face, and when Hawk turned his head to look at her, she could see, even in the moonlight, the depth of his feelings for her reflected in his expression.

"Of course I love you," he said simply. "I believed it four years ago and knew it for a fact the moment I saw you coming down the grand staircase the day of my homecoming, looking so soft and sweet and beautiful."

"You never said so," she pointed out, muttering.

"Neither did you, come to that. Not till now." He smiled, and there was a rueful note in his voice when next he spoke. "We were not raised to give voice to such emotions. Shows a shocking want of breeding in both of us that we have succumbed to such lower-class stuff, does it not?"

He was not making a joke. Indeed, he sounded bitter, Mollie thought, but she had her own feelings to contend with, and there was a spurt of resentment deep within her that was struggling to make itself felt. "If you loved me four years ago," she said slowly, wishing she were strong enough not to need an answer to the question, "why did you leave?"

"I told you before. I was young," he said quickly, glibly. "Too young, I suppose, for the responsibility of a wife. I sought adventure, sweetheart. Adventure and challenge. And," he added on a sour but, to her ears, more believable note, "I hated my father and wanted to put as much distance as possible between us. I knew he'd never stomach letting me set up a household of my own away from his watchful eye.

That's why I moved so quickly. Had I given him time, he'd have thought of a way to stop me from going."

He shot her a quick look, and Mollie was sure that he was measuring her reaction to his words. More than ever she knew that although his dislike of the old marquess might be part of the answer, it was not the whole of it. She wanted to tell him in words of one syllable precisely what she had thought of him for leaving her in the care of a man he detested, but even more than that did she wish to get to the heart of the reason for his leaving. Nevertheless, she could not think how to begin, so they rode for some time in silence before she gathered her courage and put the matter in the simplest terms.

"I thought I could accept those reasons," she said quietly, "but there must be more to it, or you would have come back when your father died."

"Life was pretty hectic over there."

Suddenly, it was too much. Mollie gripped her lower lip between her teeth, biting hard to stop the tears from coming, but the stress of the past twenty-four hours, added to the anger and resentment swelling within her, was more than she could stand. The tears spilled over and a sob was wrenched from her despite her efforts to stop it.

"My God, Mollie! I'm sorry I went and sorrier that I stayed so long. You must know that!"

"Damn you!" Ignoring the tears spilling down her cheeks, she flung the words at him, then spurred her horse to a gallop as anger outweighed every other emotion warring in her breast.

Hawk followed immediately but made no attempt to stop her until they had reached the road leading up to the lake. Then, riding up beside her, he reached out to grab Baron's bridle.

Mollie waited until the horses had slowed to a walk again before she turned on him. "How dare you continue to play this game with me?" she demanded, swallowing her tears. "Am I supposed to accept your glib words because you are a man and my lord? How can I know what I did to send you away if you will not tell me, if you persist in ridiculous excuses? How can I be certain I will not do something to make you leave me again if I do not know why you left in the first place? And why do you, who have such a regard for the truth that you condemn half-truths in others ... why do you persist in offering half-truths to me in such a case as this? It is not fair, Gavin. It is damnably *unfair*!"

"Oh, Mollie." The words were barely intelligible. He said nothing further until they emerged from the woods and the great castle loomed ahead of them, a dense shadow now, for the moon had set. But the stars were reflected in the lake, making it look like a glittering carpet surrounding the huge bulk in the center. Hawk reined in and reached for her horse's bridle at the same time. "If Prinny is not waiting for me in there, Bathurst will be," he said. "But this is a great deal more important to me right now." He slid from the saddle and lifted her down, his arms going around her in a tight hug. "I'd no idea you blamed yourself," he said quietly.

"What else was I to think?" she asked, her words muffled against his chest. "I thought I'd failed you as a wife. Most likely," she added bitterly, "in bed."

Instead of denying it, he let out a long breath, guiding her gently toward the low wall of the main causeway. "Sit down, sweetheart. It was not you who failed me, but rather the reverse, I fear."

Obeying the pressure of his hand on her shoulder, Mollie sat down, feeling the chill of the stone wall even through the thickness of her cloak and breeches. Hawk sat beside her, drawing her into the shelter of his arm. As he talked, his voice began to take on the caressing tone that was so dear to her, and she snuggled against him.

"You fascinated me from the outset, you know," he said.

"I was a challenge to you."

"True. So many men wanted you. But I meant to have you for my own. I was very young, Mollie. That much of what I said before was true. In fact, all of what I said before was true. But only a half-truth, as you said. I didn't think I could make you understand the whole. In fact, until a short time ago, I didn't understand it myself. But since I'm going to tell you the whole now, I may as well begin by telling you that you owe some of my understanding to Harriette."

"Harriette Wilson!" She stiffened against him but relaxed again when he chuckled.

"It's so easy to get a rise from you, sweetheart."

"Then it is not true?"

"Oh, it's true enough, but it's not what you think. I'd best begin with my homecoming. I told you the truth about that, or as much of it as I was able to tell you. Wellington sent me, but he sent me because Prinny demanded that he send someone who could help flush out the spy who had been making mischief with the British plans of attack. Wellington was only too happy to do so, because the French had been playing us for fools for months, and it was only too clear to him that somehow word was getting to them of his plans. Since all communication between the Peninsula and London is conducted through the dispatches, which never leave the courier's hands, it was fairly clear that the leak had to be in London, and that meant someone in the upper echelons of either Bathurst's staff or one of our ally's. So Wellington chose me, because I had the entrée to such circles socially as well as because of my military experience. Also, he informed me in no uncertain terms that it was time and more I was returning to take up my family duties.''

"Tell me about Harriette Wilson,'' Mollie demanded, not caring a straw for the political details.

"Patience, sweetheart. Let me tell this in the order it happened or I'll get tangled, and you won't understand her part in it. I brought the true plans for Vitoria with me, and Bathurst himself met me at Hastings when we landed. He kept all the information under his hat, not even telling Prinny. The victory told us all we needed to know. Then Bathurst let the word get about that I had brought more information, including Wellington's specific plans for the summer and fall campaigns. We hoped to stir some action that way, but I can promise you I never expected or wanted Ramsay to become involved. I'd no notion he even knew that rascal d'Épier.''

"He told me you gave him information to pass along to d'Épier.''

"Indeed. They hoped at first that I'd have something in the house, copies of maps or even copies of the plans themselves. Failing in that, they wanted Ramsay to pump me for information. We played a few games with them, in that I gave the lad certain bits to pass along, hoping we might flush out something in that fashion. And we did.''

"Whatever it was that Prince Nicolai said last night,'' Mollie put in excitedly.

"Yes,'' he agreed. "That, added to your information about

his French mother. His motive in all this has no doubt been to retrieve the family estate in France.''

"So that was why you found that information so interesting!"

He nodded. "Unfortunately for myself and for Breck, neither a French mother nor the slip Nicolai made last night was sufficient evidence to confront the man or even to suggest his complicity to de Lieven, who was bound to support his own man against anything but unarguable fact. Breck, Jamie, and I didn't even have a good opportunity to discuss the matter. We meant to have it out as soon as Prinny arrived, but d'Épier and his men were waiting for us when we left to meet him.''

"But no one left the castle," Mollie objected. "That was why Ramsay wouldn't believe Nicolai was involved.''

"Jamie probably followed the same reasoning," Hawk replied. "We thought d'Épier was being watched in London, but he must have given them the slip. I think our capture—or mine, at any rate—was intended from the moment they knew we were coming down here. It would give them a chance to discover not only what information I had brought back but what instructions were being relayed to Wellington.''

"But surely they must have known the plans would be changed once you were captured?"

"Why? As far as they knew no one suspected who the spy was, and my disappearance might just as well be attributed to footpads as to any other cause. I daresay after a decent period of time, Breck's body and mine would simply have been discovered in the woods near the valley road where we were taken.''

Mollie shuddered. But when he remained silent for a moment longer, she remembered Harriette Wilson. "And?" she prompted. "Where does Miss Wilson enter into all this, my lord, and how is it that I am in her debt?"

He chuckled again. "I spent my time in London talking to anyone and everyone who might point us in the right direction, and Harriette Wilson has more connections in the *beau monde* than anyone, sweetheart. She was one of the first people I went to in my search for the most likely person to be our quarry. I confess I met her during my first Season and even went to a few parties at her house. We became friends of a sort, but because I knew perfectly well that she was also friendly with my father, the connection never became an intimate one. Nonetheless, during one of our meetings last month, she asked me how my marriage was faring after so long a separation. What with one thing and another, we got to discussing certain matters, and she made me see one or two things more clearly.''

Resentment struggled with curiosity, and curiosity won. ''How so?''

''Do you remember our wedding night, sweetheart?''

Mollie nodded, biting her lip. His hand moved idly up and down her upper arm. ''I was terrified,'' she said. ''Fascinated, but terrified. It was wonderful at first, and I thought everything would be fine, but then something happened, and suddenly it wasn't fine. I thought I must have done something wrong.''

''You cried out because I hurt you,'' he said. ''I thought . . . God help me, I thought you hated it as much as my mother did. You were so small, and I'd hurt you, and I was certain I would always hurt you.''

''But it only hurt the one time,'' she told him earnestly. ''It never hurt again.''

''I know that now. But I had heard for years all about the pain and the indignity of such things, you see, and I had had little experience myself, and only with women of a lower order, the sort my mother had insisted were made for such primitive business. I told you once before that I had feared I might be like my father. But that was only one side of the coin. Far more than that did I fear that you were like my mother.''

''But I'm not!''

''No, I know that now. I had never been the first with any woman before, you see, and no one had ever told me what it was like. I was very young, and my father certainly never talked to me as a young man's father ought to talk to him. Nor did Uncle Andrew, of course. Or anyone else. And while it's very true that we discussed sex to the exclusion of a good many more academic subjects at Eton and Oxford, we never somehow got around to discussing the fact that the first time for any woman is painful. Boys know a good deal more sometimes than the adults around them think they know, but when you get down to it, they only know bits and pieces of the whole. Rarely is there one among them who knows it all.

t was only a small bit of information, but it was a crucial bit
n my case.''

"But surely, you must have learned about such stuff
eventually, sir.''

"Do you take me for a skirt-chaser, sweetheart? I assure you
never was one. I had been raised to feel sorry for my
mother. I knew next to nothing about the facts of life other
han that gently nurtured ladies detested being with their
ausbands in the bedchamber. And when I discovered that I
could scarcely keep my hands off you, it scared me silly to
think I might put you through the same hell my mother had
been put through all those years. That was only a part of the
whole picture, of course, but at the time it made it easier to
leave than to stay.''

"Your nobility was misplaced, sir,'' Mollie told him,
wrinkling her nose. "I welcomed your touch. Always.'' She
turned toward him, lifting her face, inviting him to kiss her.

Before he did, he said, "I think I began to realize that from
your response to me when I came home.''

"Only you attributed that to the fact that I'd had a dozen
affairs,'' she reminded him tartly.

He looked rueful. "That was also Harriette's doing, I'm
afraid. Her suggestion, plus things I began hearing once we
reached London. It didn't take long to realize they were
wrong.''

Mollie's lips twisted into a crooked grin. She peered into
his eyes. "Did you actually discuss me with that woman?''

"That was not my specific intention,'' he said, "though I
asked questions about young women in general that I'd never
asked anyone else. And she no doubt guessed how matters
stood,'' he added honestly, "for she told me some home
truths about my mother, which she had gleaned after some
years of acquaintance with my father.''

"Surely, she never took everything he said for truth,''
Mollie said indignantly.

"No, of course not. But Harriette has a good deal of
experience in such matters, you know.''

"I daresay,'' Mollie said sardonically. "Kiss me, sir, before I favor you with my candid opinion of your behavior.''

He obliged her at last, drawing her more firmly into his
arms and kissing her thoroughly. Mollie strained against him,
returning his kisses passionately and thrilling to his touch

when he impatiently pushed her cloak aside and began to unbutton her waistcoat. Within moments his hand was stroking her breast beneath the shirt, and she gasped as his fingers brushed against her taut nipples. For a moment she indulged herself in a mental vision of what it would be like to be taken by him right there in the middle of the main causeway. But it had also occurred to her husband that their activities might well lead to just such a scene, and reluctantly he straightened, pulling the panels of her shirt back together, and fumbling for the lacing.

"No," she murmured in protest.

"Yes," he replied, making her sit upright again while he buttoned her waistcoat. "This is scarcely the time or the place. Prinny and Bathurst will be in a pother to hear what has been going forward these past hours, and much as I should like to keep them waiting, it will not do for you to be seen like this, or for either of us to be found here in the midst of what we should be found in the midst of, if you take my meaning."

Mollie chuckled. "At least you know now that I should not dislike it, sir."

"Unprincipled baggage," he teased, buttoning the last button and pulling her to her feet to stand between his knees just in front of him. His expression altered slightly as he looked at her, and there was a touch of sternness in his tone when he spoke again. "We have not finished with the other matter, you know."

She groaned. "Gavin, we have already plucked that crow. Surely you do not mean to scold me further for following the prince."

"I don't know that I would call it scolding," he said quietly, "but I certainly mean to assure myself that you'll never do anything so cock-brained again. I shall also have a word or two to say to my idiotish brother on the subject, I assure you. It is bad enough that he should have taken you to a boxing match . . . oh, yes," he added when she gasped, "I figured that out long since. That was foolish, but this was a good deal worse."

"But I have told you it was necessary," she protested. She stroked his face, feeling the slight prickle of his rising beard. "What we did was follow the most sensible course, my lord," she murmured more huskily, leaning forward to kiss him.

"Do not hope to muddle my senses again, sweetheart," he warned her, capturing her hand in one of his own and giving it a squeeze as he pushed her away. "I have been learning to let you be yourself and not to try to force you into any established mold, but you deserve that I should be very angry with you for putting your sweet life in danger as you did. If I were to use you as a properly autocratic husband would, you would find yourself across my knee right now, receiving severe punishment for your foolhardiness."

"Oh!" She took a little step backward at the thought that he might yet do such a thing, but her temper stirred, too. "That is a fine attitude," she told him roundly, "considering that you already admitted owing your life to my actions."

He sighed. "Your capability with a bow no doubt helped at the time, sweetheart, but I assure you there was not the slightest necessity for your interference in the matter. Breck and I are well able to take care of ourselves, and even if we had not managed to secure our freedom before morning, Jamie or Ramsay must have found us by then. The fact is, my love, that such affairs are always better handled by men. You might just as likely have made a mull of it, you know, for that is what usually happens when women meddle in things that do not concern them. But we will not discuss the matter further tonight, my . . . Mollie!" His last word came in a shout of dismay as he tumbled backward, assisted by a mighty shove from his diminutive wife. She had a fine view of his upturned rump and thrashing legs before he disappeared with a satisfying splash beneath the dark waters of the starlit lake.

She did not wait to see his head break the surface again before snatching up the reins of both horses and springing to her saddle. As she dug her spurs into Baron's sides, she heard Hawk bellowing after her, but she did not dare to look back. Instead, tugging on his horse's reins, she forced the animal to a trot behind her and rode on through the central courtyard to the stableyard. Sliding to the ground, she flung the reins at the sleepy groom who came to meet her, mumbled something to the effect that his lordship was just coming, and ran into the rear hall and up the stairs. The hall itself was empty, but she had no doubt that if Bathurst was not waiting up in the great hall to greet whoever came to bring word of Hawk and Breckin, one of his minions would be keeping a lookout to warn him if anyone came back to the castle. No doubt, even now, word would be reaching him of their return. Nevertheless, Mollie was perfectly certain that her husband would not allow himself to be detained for long before he came in search of her.

Rushing into her bedchamber, she began hastily to pull off her clothes, flinging them wherever they might fall. Naked, she pulled the knitted cap from her head, letting her hair fall free again. Then she hurried to the wardrobe to find her laciest nightdress. Once this article had been slipped over her head, she felt less vulnerable and better prepared to greet him when he came to her, as she knew he would. He was not a man to take a drenching without doing something about it. With any luck he would finish what he had begun on the causeway before he left her again. She grinned at her reflection in the dressing-table glass as she sat down and picked up her hairbrush.

She had taken fewer than ten strokes through her tangled tresses before she heard his boots on the stones of the corridor just outside her door. Almost at the same time the door opened, and she turned to see her dripping husband filling the doorway.

"Madam wife, you will pay for your impertinence," he announced, but to her astonishment there was a grin on his face and his eyes were twinkling.

"You cannot deny the provocation, sir," she retorted warily. "You talked a deal of nonsense."

"Granted," he replied, moving toward her and kicking the door shut behind him. "I apologize for suggesting that you are not the most capable of creatures. Nonetheless, I hope you do not think to get away with such tactics unscathed."

Mollie leaned away when he reached for her. "The Regent," she reminded him anxiously. "Lord Bathurst. Really, sir, you must—"

But it was no use. Grasping her arm firmly, he pulled her to her feet and into his arms. "I've sent them both to the devil, sweetheart, so that I may attend to my naughty wife." He hugged her, lowering his head to nuzzle his face against her soft curls.

"Gavin!" she shrieked as his dampness promptly made itself felt up and down her body through her thin nightdress.

For heaven's sake, take off those wet clothes first, my
rd.''

"In time," he retorted, chuckling with delight as his large
nds moved tantalizingly down her back to cup her hips,
lling her more tightly against him. "In due time, my
veet, incorrigible love.''

About the Author

A fourth-generation Californian, Amanda Scott was
born and raised in Salinas and graduated with a
degree in history from Mills College in Oakland. She
did graduate work at the University of North Caro-
lina at Chapel Hill, specializing in British history,
before obtaining her MA from San Jose State
University. She lives with her husband and young
son in Sacramento. Her hobbies include camping,
backpacking, and gourmet cooking.

JOIN THE *REGENCY ROMANCE* READERS' PANEL

Help us bring you more of the books you like by filling out this survey and mailing it in today.

1. Book Title: _____

   Book #: _____

2. Using the scale below, how would you rate this book on the following features? Please write in one rating from 0-10 for each feature in the spaces provided.

POOR		NOT SO GOOD			O.K.			GOOD		EXCEL-LENT
0	1	2	3	4	5	6	7	8	9	10

RATING

Overall opinion of book .... _____
Plot/Story .... _____
Setting/Location .... _____
Writing Style .... _____
Character Development .... _____
Conclusion/Ending .... _____
Scene on Front Cover .... _____

3. About how many romance books do you buy for yourself each month? _____

4. How would you classify yourself as a reader of Regency romances?
   I am a ( ) light ( ) medium ( ) heavy reader.

5. What is your education?
   ( ) High School (or less) ( ) 4 yrs. college
   ( ) 2 yrs. college   ( ) Post Graduate

6. Age _____   7. Sex: ( ) Male ( ) Female

Please Print Name_____

Address_____

City _____ State _____ Zip _____

Phone # ( )_____

Thank you. Please send to New American Library, Research Dept., 1633 Broadway, New York, NY 10019.